But This Is Different

A Novel

Mary Walker Baron

Steel Cut Press
GLENDALE, CALIFORNIA

This is a work of fiction. Names, characters, places, and incidents either are the products of the author's imagination or are used fictitiously.

BUT THIS IS DIFFERENT

ISBN: 978-1936380008
LCCN: 2010933108

Copyright © 2011 by Mary Walker Baron

All rights reserved, including the right to reproduce this book, or portions thereof, in any form.

Cover concept and photography by Jesse Leffler.

Book design by Paul K. Austad (p.k.austad@gmail.com)

Interior text was set in Electra lt, titles in Orator std

Printed in the United States of America

Steel Cut Press
www.steelcutpress.com
P. O. Box 1497
Glendale CA 91209
ph | 818.801.0353

"Our only deadlines are those we impose on ourselves."

Other works:

Contrary Creek by Tom Walker and Mary Walker
   [www.contrarycreeknovel.com]

To Carole—

Remember that time we went bowling in Canada?

With all my being I thank—

Seth Chazanoff for designing a boat from parts never intended to float.

Alan Levine for careful reading and precise suggestions.

Jim Rudolph for the transformative wager.

Paul K. Austad for designing with heart.

Tom Walker for life long mentoring, editing, and support.

Leslie Bergson for three pages at a time over and over again.

Jesse Leffler for believing in dreams and miracles and me.

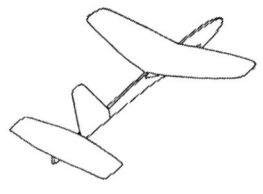

Chapter One

The engine wouldn't start. They knew it wouldn't start and yet they kept trying to coax even a sputter of life from it. For almost two hours the men had labored, pausing only for furtive glances toward the mountain and the hut, almost but not quite hidden by lush foliage, where they knew she sat waiting for the engine's roar. Tension mapped the morning on the faces of the five men. The sun's skyward climb reminded them that time was running out.

The tank was full of precious fuel. The spark plugs were new. Scattered tools littered the dock's rough, wood planks. Their limited knowledge of the internal combustion engine was exhausted and their physical strength long spent. Defeated, the men sat on the small dock and stared out to sea.

"Perhaps it will start soon," Kahil said as he pulled his T-shirt off over his head and tossed it onto the planks.

The men stared at the garment, damp with sweat, as though from it they could divine a solution to the riddle of this miscreant piece of machinery called Pratt & Whitney.

When divination did not appear to be forthcoming, Afi said, "It will not start at all so it cannot start soon."

"Perhaps it will," Kahil, still staring at his shirt, replied.

Kahil, whose name meant "young" despite his years, had been the last to bare his chest to the sun's glare. His back's scars told the tale of long-ago adventures and almost fatal wounds. Kahil did not easily share those tales even though they were stories known to all. Staring at his shirt on the dock, he – not for the first time – marveled at the words his chest proclaimed each time he wore it: *Make love not war.* The words still puzzled him even though their meaning had been explained time and time again. A man of few words, Kahil never wasted them to state what was so obviously true. Nevertheless, he frequently wore the shirt. He liked the feel of the worn cotton on his back's ragged, black skin.

"This engine was never intended for a boat," Rua said as he wiped sweat from his head's tight coils of hair. "The sun is passing. This day we will not make the trip."

Kahil stared at him but did not speak. In his heart he feared the words of Rua were true. Rua, whose name meant "water," knew the seas.

"The engine was not intended for a boat and still it has been on this boat all of my life. How do I know it was not intended to be there?" Peta, whose name meant "rock," forever saw life's possibilities and never seemed to feel the weight of his name.

"You know because I tell the truth," Rua looked out to sea and not at Peta as he spoke.

"We have to make the trip. The engine will start. It has to start." Afi's words were spoken quickly and sharply because his name meant "fire."

"It does not have to start."

"It is machinery not man."

"It will not start."

"We have to tell her."

The men spoke faster and their voices began to hold hints of panic.

"We cannot tell her. She will feel too sad," Orado, whose name meant "power," finally spoke.

No longer a boy, he was the youngest of the men. He had been given the name of power because he had none. He was frail of body and of mind. His spirit, though, was precious. Orado was given always places of honor. His words were valued if not heeded.

Their conversation became animated with gestures and movements and emotions. One stood. Two stood. All stood. One sat down then stood again. They paced the planks. They stood motionless. Their voices grew louder with the increasing intensity of their situation.

"And if we do not tell her?" Kahil questioned the heavens and all five faces turned toward the sun as though it might give them an answer instead of unremitting, glaring heat.

They did not see her coming until she stood among them.

"And if you do not tell me what?" she asked.

She was fit and thin. Her straight, short-cropped hair was completely white. She wore patched khaki pants, which had been cut into knee length shorts, and a loose fitting, faded, short sleeved, crew necked shirt. Like the men, she was barefoot. The muscles in her legs and arms were firm with clear evidence of years of rigorous physical activity. Her tan skin had never glistened like the skin of those with whom she lived. She was not native to the island. Silenced by her arrival, the men looked at each other. They did not meet her gaze.

"It will not start," Kahil finally said softly. "We are ashamed of our failure."

During that moment of shame, Kahil forgot the meaning of his name and feared the weight of his years might crush him. On this island where names gave power and obligation and direction, Kahil marveled that this woman seemed to never lose sight of herself.

The woman looked at the face of each man until each man in turn lifted his face to her gaze. Looking into her eyes, Kahil felt youth's energy return and himself again whole.

Finally she spoke.

"It has to start," she said.

Her simple statement seemed to give the men permission to reclaim their animation. They stood and gathered around her. They spoke as one.

"We know. We know it has to start. But we checked everything and we cannot locate the problem. Perhaps it does not want to cross the water today."

"It has to cross the water today and it will cross the water. Today of all days."

"But the sun has risen too far in the sky," the men chorused again. "Even if it does start, there is not sufficient sun for our return journey."

Again her voice silenced them.

"Tomorrow is the last day of the year. You will make the journey and you will bring back her gifts. The engine will start."

With those words she approached the massive engine in silent study. She of all people knew the engine had never been intended to power a boat and the boat did not resemble anything ever intended for water. Nothing of the grace and sleekness of the island's rectangular-sailed canoes touched this craft designed for speed and capacity. The ancient R-1340-49, nine-cylinder, air-cooled, 600 horsepower Pratt & Whitney rode atop the ungainly craft like a precarious monument to either gravity's or its own defeat. Pulleys and reduction gears and chains and drive belts and drive shafts forced the engine to push the box-like boat through the water. The boat's crew and passengers and fuel tanks and water barrels and rocks and cargo were all below the water level to counterbalance the weight of the engine. In the center of this cargo-passenger-rock-fuel-water space a rudder guided the boat with pulleys and pieces of pipe.

Light reflecting from the boat's keel through water so clear it seemed invisible danced on the woman's sweat-streaked face. She looked back into the water to what was never supposed to be part of a boat but was now a keel and tried to remember two letters and five numbers once so essential. Unable to recall them, she forced her attention back to the problem.

After a moment, she turned to the tools, made her selection, and returned to the engine. She worked in silence. The men did not offer to help. She strained against stubborn bolts. She wiped sweat from her face. Her hands quickly became greasy and she wiped the grease on her shorts. When she ran her fingers through her hair, the white became streaked with black. She balanced on the rails of the cargo hold. She stepped over cables. She braced herself against the mesh safety screen. She removed engine parts and carefully placed them on the wood. She cleaned parts with a handkerchief pulled from her pocket. She left once and returned with a banana leaf, which she carefully cut into rings. The sun rose higher in the sky and the men looked from the engine to the sea and back again to the engine.

Only when the engine had been completely reassembled did she speak.

"Try it."

Kahil stepped into the boat and assumed his place next to her. He looked at the men still on the dock. He looked at the woman. He looked at the heavens. Finally he looked at the instrument panel bolted to boards near the rudder. He took a deep breath and wished he had not left his shirt on the dock. The unintelligible words *Make Love Not War* could perhaps protect him from defeat's painful burn.

He gave the engine fuel as he turned the switch. Black smoke spewed from the back of the boat as the engine coughed and hesitated and coughed again and then roared to life. The woman gently touched Kahil's bare back before stepping away from the engine, jumping onto the dock, and facing the smiling men.

"The only mistake you made was not coming to get me. You men always think you can do things better than a woman. Well, some things you can and some things you can't. One intake valve wasn't sealing right. That caused it to leak during compression so it wouldn't start. I fixed it with the banana leaf. It should hold for a long time. Now get going. It's a big ocean."

The men moved quickly to gather their shirts and their caps. Afi tossed *Make Love Not War* to Kahil who pulled it over his head with one hand while holding fast to the throttle with the other. The woman embraced each man before he climbed into the boat to join Kahil. When all were aboard, she untied the mooring rope, tossed it into the boat, and watched the ungainly craft gain speed and distance until her eyes could no longer track its movement across the water.

Only then did Mere, whose name meant *The Star of the Sea*, allow herself to slump onto the dock with the weight of her eighty years. For several moments she sat rocking back and forth, her head in her hands.

These moments of vulnerability to time and pain vanished as quickly as they arrived and she stood, squared her shoulders, turned her back to the sea, and strode toward the mountains.

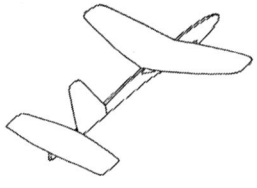

CHAPTER TWO

The Pacific Ocean contains between 20,000 and 30,000 islands all south of the Tropic of Cancer. The Melanesia cluster includes the Fiji Islands, most of New Guinea, and the Solomon Islands. The Micronesia cluster is made up of hundreds of small islands. Notable islands in this cluster include Guam, Wake Island, and the Marshall Islands. The Polynesian cluster of over one thousand identified islands scatters the central and southern Pacific Ocean. Islands in this cluster include American Samoa, the Cook Islands, Easter Island, the Hawaiian Islands, Howland, Baker, Phoenix, and New Zealand.

Some islands are large in land and dense in population. Others, islets, are so small they may as well be invisible. Some islands have never been inhabited by outsiders. Some are privately owned. Some, it is rumored, were hidden by various governments during World War II and remain hidden. Some will be discovered one day. Other islands will remain concealed from public knowledge and view forever.

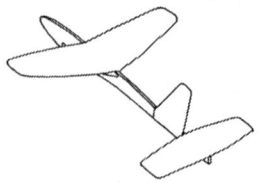

Chapter Three

The islanders called her Mere – The Star of the Sea – because forty years ago she came to their tiny, isolated island from the sea and became almost immediately a bright star in their universe. From the very beginning she worked beside them repairing homes and building new ones, harvesting fruits and vegetables, catching and cooking fish. She aided women in childbirth and provided comfort in death. She shielded children from storms and watched with pride as they became adults. She spoke the language of the island as though she had been born there. She became an integral part of the island life and the island became her life. As requested, the islanders assumed responsibility for keeping her presence hidden from the world beyond Nani, the name given to their home by the woman who came before and before and many times before in preparation. Later their Star of the Sea would agree that Nani, which meant beautiful, was the perfect name.

"How could such a tiny place have so much," she would marvel. "How could everything a person could ever desire be in one place?" she would ask of no one in particular.

As the years passed, though, Mere would resign herself to the reality that Nani could not provide everything she desired. In the early, hopeful times, however, she climbed the mountains and stood on rainy beaches and lay under vegetation lush and damp never doubting the wisdom of their decision planned in almost perfect detail years before her fall from the sky onto Nani's shores.

The days of her life and of her years on the island grew in number and still every year on the day before the last day of the year, the boat left and returned with the gifts.

She forced herself to believe that on this day, even though the departure had been delayed, the boat would return with the crate. As she walked from the beach's heat into the mountain's shade her heart beat faster not from exertion but from anticipation.

The gifts were individual miracles shared by all: Simple, basic clothing of all sizes. Souvenir T-shirts. Hats. Boxes of raisins because Mere believed they possessed curative powers. Basic hand tools. Other tools sufficiently sophisticated to repair pulleys and chains and drive belts and gears. Knives. Scissors. First Aid supplies. An occasional case of motor oil. Miscellaneous engine parts. Tools with which to build the island's huts. The islanders had no real need for many of the gifts but treasured them and utilized them – if not in the intended manner – at least in some way. Other items in the crate served specific and essential purposes, which the islanders had well learned. Then there was always the last box in the crate. That specially wrapped box was for her. As each consecutive year ended, Mere sat in the hut that was her home and alone opened her gift and listened to the laughter and the shouts of the islanders on the beach below and marveled that she had yet to succumb to the sharp stabs of solitude. Alone in her hut she studied each item carefully taken from her box: A magazine. Handkerchiefs. Nose drops. Medications for her frequent and severe headaches. Sometimes photographs. A bound volume of blank pages. Pens. Pencils. Selected newspaper clippings. Sometimes a novel popular during the previous year. Banjo strings. An almanac. A calendar for the upcoming year. And always the long and wonderful and heart-filling and heartbreaking letter.

On this day her almost constant headache extended to her entire face. She had spent years learning to ignore this pain. Today ignoring it seemed impossible. The moment she entered the shaded foliage she leaned her back against the trunk of a fu'u tree and stared skyward at the tree's flowers. The white petals still reflected the morning's rain.

"If I were constipated," she thought, "I could make tea from this bark and cure myself almost immediately."

She smiled to herself and felt the tree's energy flow throughout the length of her spine. Refreshed and strengthened, she resumed her striding walk up the mountain toward her hut.

Kaula, as always, watched Mere navigate the trail. In places the dirt path was red clay and slippery. In other places tree roots crossed it and branches hung low into it. Kaula worried that the once athletic Star of the Sea would one day slip or fall. Injuries to bones becoming brittle with age worried Kaula far less than the injuries inflicted to Mere's spirit should she ever need assistance during the climb. Kaula, whose name meant "prophet," saw that day approaching and dreaded its arrival.

Kaula's mother had welcomed Mere to the island and had, always from a distance and following very specific directions, watched over her. With her mother's death the honor had fallen to her oldest daughter. Kaula had no other obligations.

Near the entrance to her hut, Mere stopped to examine the papaya hanging at eye level. Soon it would be ripe. She gently touched the fruit, backed away from the tree, and bowed to the tree. Then she returned to the tree, touched the fruit, backed away from the tree, bowed to the tree, and returned to the tree until she had repeated the routine five times. She liked the number five. It gave her comfort. Satisfied with the ritual, she entered her hut.

Crudely and ruggedly constructed, the home of the Star of the Sea had withstood storm after storm with little damage. The roof was never quite waterproof and pots and bowls were always ready for the next round of leaks. The inside of the hut was as rich with tropical foliage as was the outside. Mere explained to the islanders that plants inside the home enriched the air with oxygen and moisture. Innate courtesy prevented them from remarking that all island air was rich with oxygen and moisture. They indulged this need as they indulged all of her needs.

The sparseness of the hut did not hide her personality. An airplane made of balsa wood hung by a cord from the ceiling. Breezes blowing through the hut propelled the plane into a circular flight pattern. During severe storms the plane frequently broke free of its cord to fly unfettered before crashing into the walls or the floor or the roof or, once, into a tree outside the hut. So frequent were these storms that the plane was in constant repair and renovation. Whatever its original model, all resemblance had long ago been lost. A bookcase held whatever novels had arrived in the gift boxes throughout the years along with the magazines and the journals. A chipped cup contained pens and pencils and scissors. A weathered and aged frame with a photograph of two young women leaned against the books. The items on the bookshelf were arranged with precision. A trunk held clothing and a sewing kit and medical supplies. Mere's banjo, its case wrapped in plastic, lay on top of the trunk safe from falling or rising water. A battered suitcase stood upright against the wall. An open book lay on it. A forked chief's stick leaned against the wall and next to it hung a wide brimmed, straw hat. A calendar hung next to the hat and indicated that the year was 1977 and the month was December. The first twenty-nine days were crossed off. A padded wicker chair completed the furnishings. Mere owned few possessions but all necessities.

Chapter Four

She slumped into her chair and closed her eyes. Her vision had blurred during the climb to her hut and she sat for several moments with her eyes closed. She felt restless, though, and soon she paced back and forth.

The same questions kept nagging at her. "What if I didn't fix the engine properly? What if it dies? What if they can't get back before dark? What if they die?"

The "what ifs" became relentless. To try to stop them she took her banjo case from its plastic and her banjo from the case. She sat on the floor and played the old Harmony tenor. She picked a melody on the four strings before strumming – pick held between thumb and index finger – snatches of songs and favorite chord runs. Whatever entered her soul, she played. Music echoed through the trees to the heart of the village. The islanders loved hearing her music and many paused in their daily activities to listen. Others moved to the music and still others danced. Her playing continued until her fingers ached and still her restlessness persisted. The banjo wiped down, returned to its case and its protective plastic, Mere left the hut under the watchful eye of Kaula.

She almost passed the papaya then caught herself to repeat her previous ritual. The five cycles completed, she took another trail. Almost immediately she began a steep ascent toward the top of the mountain. Kaula quietly followed her.

The top of the hill was the burial ground and the islanders could not remember any time when their dead had not been carried to that sacred place. It was to this place that Mere climbed. By the time she sat on the ground next to an ancient tree, either the climb's exertion or the tranquility of the cemetery had calmed her. She sat erect and stared at the mounds of dirt. Some mounds were so flattened with age and overgrown with plants they were barely noticeable. Others were so new she believed she could still see the faces and hear the laughter of the deceased. She felt the spirits of all who had made their final journeys to the top of this hill surround her as one energy. When Mere spoke she did not speak the language of the island.

"I so wanted the engine to work. I believed I could fix it. What if I couldn't? What if I have sent those men to their deaths? What if I kill them, too?"

Kaula did not understand the words but knew their tone. Her heart ached for Mere because she heard and saw the pain and the fear.

Mere continued. "And where are you? You have not been here for over two years. Two years! And before that four years. And before that three years. And then, yes, you will remind me of those other four glorious years of your companionship. Four years but not without interruptions which you would argue were unavoidable. And before those four years ten years. And before the ten years there were fourteen. Endless, endless years of waiting for you. I mark the days and weeks and months and, yes, the years. You give me the calendars. I mark the passage of time and I wait for you. Too much time. Too many years. That wasn't our agreement. That was not our agreement."

Her voice became louder and her words faster as Mere stood and walked in circles. She shook her hands into the air. She stomped her feet in the grassy dirt. Her mind raced so fast her voice could hardly keep the pace.

"That was not the agreement at all. You send gifts. Yes. You always send the gifts. And the most consistent gift – the most dependable gift – that I receive from you is your absence. Nicely boxed and wrapped disappointment. So many boxes filled with absence. Those are not the gifts for which I hope. You are the only gift for which my soul yearns. Books and letters are not enough. You know that. You have to know that. You told me. You promised me. You promised me then that you would stay. You would never leave. And then you left for one more necessary interruption but you said you would be back and then you would never leave. These interruptions were not the agreement. When you return, how can I trust that you will stay? That was not the agreement. The agreement. What agreement? Our agreement! And now I have killed those good men. I have sent them out to sea to bring back your gifts because that's all I have. And that isn't enough. I would love to hate you but I can't hate you."

Tears streamed down her face. Her throat felt raw from her own shouting. Her words echoed throughout the island. When their echoing returned them to her wet face she felt covered and smothered by pain. Birds flew from trees. Rocks shuddered. The seas wept. The islanders winced from such desolation.

She shouted and paced and gestured until her energy was spent and she again sat next to the tree. Again she held her head in her hands and again she rocked back and forth. Finally she stood, walked directly to a grave on the perimeter of the mounds, bent down and patted the ground.

"Perhaps I've done it again. All because of that woman. That woman who haunts me and fills my soul with sorrow and joy and rage and calm. She stops my heart with pain and races it with delight. She and I have grown old certainly but not together. Now it appears that, unless she suddenly changes all that is she, we will also die half a world apart. Perhaps I will learn, from this moment forward, to limit the casualties to just us. I had no right to include you. It doesn't matter that you wanted to participate. You laughed and said you would be the king of an island and what man could want more. I should have made you stay behind. You were a fool and I exploited your foolishness. It would have been no deceit to say that you were too drunk to find the charts much less read them. I'm sorry. Forgive me. There's not much I would do differently except, perhaps, this. And now I fear I've sent five men out to sea to drown. Again all because of her."

She began pounding her fists onto the mound of dirt until it seemed as though the earth might open to consume her. It did not, though, and soon she sat so still Kaula wondered if she had turned to stone.

Mere spent a moment longer at the grave then stiffly stood, brushed dirt off her legs and the seat of her shorts, turned, and slowly walked back down the trail. At her home she stopped in front of the papaya tree to repeat her ritual of five and then continued down the mountain to the beach. Kaula maintained her watchful distance.

Mere stepped onto the dock. She stood and looked out to sea.

"Another year has grown old," she said softly to herself. "So have I."

The sun began its descent into the sea. Mere watched it and a pain almost unbearable shook her. She had been standing immobile so long her legs ached. She carefully sat on the rough wood. Her gaze never left the horizon. The sea blackened. Day was done. The men had not returned.

The evening's chill settled onto the island and into the bones of the woman sitting alone in misery on the wooden planks of the pier. Finally the islanders could no longer stay away from their beloved Star of the Sea.

From the village, lit by torches and fires, Oroiti said more to himself than to the others, "I am going to her."

No one responded because all knew it was time to offer comfort for her body and comfort for her soul. Oroiti had not waited for a response. He did not need endorsement for his actions. The islanders believed that Oroiti possessed healing powers. When the rocks fell on him and destroyed his leg, he held the knife in his hand and cut away the mangled muscle and crushed bone.

"I own my fate. This choice is mine," he had told the islanders and they knew he did not want any of them to feel responsible for the pain he was about to endure.

So he had cut off his own leg and changed his name from Ariki meaning "The Chief" to Oroiti meaning "The Slow Footed One." Changing his name did not remove his status of chief, however. The islanders would not allow him to cut that away. While their chief slept after performing surgery on himself, the islanders buried his leg on the mountaintop and made him a crutch. Throughout his recovery, Mere stayed by him. She used medications from her trunk and made bandages from clothing. It was then that the islanders taught her the healing powers of leaf and bark and fruit. She learned well enough to create new remedies and become a healer herself. The wound healed without incident and Oroiti learned to walk with one leg and a crutch. Life on the island resumed its normal pace. Years passed and now both Oroiti and Mere were old.

They sat together on the dock. They studied the dark waters. They studied the sky so full of blazing stars. An old and well-used blanket lay across Mere's shoulders, placed there by Oroiti. Chilled from the night and her memories and her fears, she wrapped it around her.

"Thank you, Ariki."

"You know that I am Oroiti."

"You gave yourself that silly name. That's your second name. The gods gave you your first name. You are a chief. To this island and to me."

She leaned against him and wept. He did not embrace her. He did not pat her shoulder in comfort or sympathy. With a back as straight as his crutch, he supported her weight and made space within his being for her sorrow. Her tears shed and her energy spent, she slept and still he did not move. Eventually, though, he, too, dozed still sitting and supporting her weight. The islanders gathered on the beach to keep watch over their elders asleep on the dock and to maintain the vigil for those still at sea.

The sound of a distant engine woke both Mere and Oroiti as though in their sleep they had still listened for just that sound. The islanders heard it, too, and rushed onto the dock. Oroiti stood and helped Mere to her feet. She handed him his crutch. Only then did they embrace. As their tears fell onto the wood of the dock they formed single drops.

The engine cut off to allow the boat to glide to the dock. Mere caught the mooring rope thrown from the boat. The weary men climbed onto the rough planks. In the middle of the hold, the crate was secured with knotted rope. Mere hugged and kissed each man. Women and children hugged each other and each man. Laughter and joyful shouts echoed throughout the island.

Finally there was silence. The men looked at Mere.

"Forgive us. We are late," Kahil finally said, his voice raspy with fatigue. "We have caused you concern."

"I caused myself concern. Were there problems with the engine?"

"No, the engine is perfect. There were problems with the stars."

Mere did not require further explanation.

Men unloaded the boat. First the drum of fuel for the next trip into the sea. Small boxes. Cloth sacks. Supplies necessary and not available on Nani. Then more men carefully lifted the crate from the boat onto the dock. Other men lifted it to their shoulders, carried it to the village center and placed it on a raised platform built every year for this purpose. Once emptied, the men covered the boat with bamboo and branches. Within seconds it was invisible to all save the eyes of Nani.

When she felt certain the crate was secure and the boat empty and hidden, Mere, exhausted, climbed the path to her hut slowly and cautiously. This night the hill seemed especially steep and the trail unusually slippery. Even though she wanted to walk past the papaya tree, Mere was unable to do so. Summoning what energy the day had left her, she performed her ritual of five. As she finally entered her dark hut, she felt more alone than at any other time in her life. Once inside, she walked without hesitation to the calendar and, using moonlight for vision, drew an 'X' through the date. Only then could she sleep, satisfied that this day had finally ended.

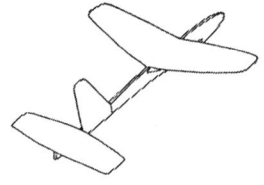

CHAPTER FIVE

Dawn did not awaken the islanders. The warmth of the midmorning sun finally stirred them and they slowly began their preparations for the festival. Mere, however, had risen with the sun. She had completed her morning rituals. She had lifted the basket of rocks fifty times to her chest and twenty-five times above her head. She had done seventy-five sit ups and had used the worn tree branch to chin herself twenty times.

Kaula wondered on this morning if the old woman would ever begin to tire. Her mother had warned her about Mere's behavior, instructing Kaula that even though it seemed she was in pain, the pain was apparently part of this sacred morning ritual. The mother of Kaula had come upon this information in a most unfortunate manner the day Mere released her grip on the branch, fell to the ground, and lay on her back groaning. When Kaula's mother rushed to offer assistance, Mere leapt to her feet and rushed into her hut. No questions were asked and no explanations were given. The next morning Mere again performed the ritual which so clearly caused physical pain. However, Kaula's mother remained in the shadows perplexed but satisfied that their Star of the Sea would survive the experience. The mother's wisdom handed down to the daughter, Kaula watched without interference.

Her rituals complete, Mere returned to her hut to await the awakening of the islanders. Kaula remained in the shaded shadows. From inside the hut she heard Mere softly play her banjo. The music seemed to be of longing and sadness. When she tired of the banjo, Mere returned it to its case and plastic and sat in her chair. She stared out the door to the ocean. She picked up her book. Lately her vision seemed at times blurred and reading was not always pleasurable.

"As long as I can see the sky," Mere softly said, "I will be fine. And your face when you return. The sky and your face. Should you not return, I will see your face always in my soul. But you will return. That is our arrangement. Forgive me my anger and my frustration and my impatience. You must admit, however, that this is not quite the arrangement upon which we agreed."

Mere did not allow herself to continue thinking in that manner. Many times she had traveled that path and found despair. She returned the book to the side of the upended suitcase and sat with her eyes closed. She dozed in her chair until sounds of the village awakened her. Mere waited until she knew that the islanders were ready to begin the preparations. Then she left the hut and walked down the mountain to join them.

This day belonged to her. This approaching night belonged to her. This day and this night and the next day. Two days and one night each year she claimed for her own celebration. The islanders – at first reluctant participants – had years ago internalized the celebration into their own myth and culture. While initially they prepared special foods for Mere alone and watched politely as she ate her holiday meals and opened gifts for them, the entire island now turned itself over to celebrating. She taught them *Auld Lang Syne* and when the stars were positioned just so in the sky, she led them in singing this song. She could not translate it into their language so they sang it in hers not caring about the meaning of the words.

After the singing, Mere always shouted, "Happy New Year!"

The islanders always shouted in return, "Happy New Year!"

The islanders had no paradigm for the greeting they so enthusiastically shouted. For them years did not end and begin. Time traveled a circular path and along that path they walked their lives until their journeys took them to a path unseen by most except those who were already there. That path, too, was circular. It interlocked with their present circular journeys and on those paths lives began and ended and began again farther into eternity than the most remote star.

Always the next day, the first day of Mere's new year, she and the islanders opened their gifts. The gifts arrived even when the two women were together on the island.

"How do you do that?" Mere once long ago asked.

"Do what?" the other woman asked and impishly removed her glasses to clean them.

"The crate. How do you get it here when you're already here?"

Mere truly wanted to understand.

Her attention seemingly consumed with wiping the thick lenses of her glasses, the other woman answered as though speaking to herself.

"Planning and attention to detail. That's what keeps life's trains running on time."

The glasses once again in place on her face, the woman smiled and Mere knew the conversation had ended.

During those infrequent times when they were together on the island, the two women celebrated with the islanders before going into the hut on the hill. Always when they were together, the face of the Star of the Sea shone brightly with a thrill never seen except when the other woman who came before returned to the island she named Nani.

This day just beginning required much preparation. Already women pounded bark into grain. Children gathered seaweed. Men waded into the waters to throw nets into the sea. Other men arranged drums around what would become as darkness fell the bonfire whose sparks would fill the sky making it difficult to distinguish lights made by the gods from lights made by the islanders. Ornate head dresses and masks leaned against the drums. Ceremonial shell necklaces and shark tooth armbands used only for the most powerful of moments would be worn on this night. Mere, herself, would wear a tribal headdress once reserved for queens. The men would paint their faces and the women would decorate their teeth. All of that, though, was for the evening. Until then, each islander owned a task and each islander performed the task without instruction or complaint.

While women sliced fruit into fanciful shapes, Mere walked back up the mountain to the papaya tree outside her hut. She felt the fruit. It was ready. She repeated her ritual of five five times before entering her hut. She returned with a scarf and a knife.

She first kissed the tree and then the papaya.

"I love you. If I do not cut you, you will fall to the ground. You are ready for the separation. You are ready to become part of me and part of the others. You are ready to grow with us and nourish us. We can never become part of that which is bigger than each of us if we do not endure the moment of separation. You are brave. You will nourish us well and we will become a part of you."

As she cut the stem connecting the fruit to the tree, Mere wept. Kaula saw and wondered and remained silent.

The fruit severed, Mere gently wrapped it in the scarf. Holding it to her breast, she returned the knife to the hut and then made her way down the mountain. A light rain had begun to fall and the clay path was slippery. Mere slipped but held tightly to the gift she brought to the feast. Kaula's heart raced but she made no move toward rescue. She knew none was needed today on this trail.

Mere presented her papaya to the women who stopped their work to admire the beautiful, perfectly ripened fruit.

"This will be in the center," they assured her.

She watched with pride and pain as they cut open the papaya. Its seeds seemed as big as marbles or possibly as big as the ball bearings of an engine. The fruit's dark orange meat made a beautiful contrast to the seeds. The islanders would agree that it was the largest papaya any could remember. They would comment that its size and beauty were doubtless the products of loving attention given it by the Star of the Sea. Mere accepted their praise and knew, as did the islanders, that most of the fruit on the island was large and perfect and delicious. She had learned to indulge flattery.

By the time they had cleaned the day's catches of fish, the bonfire was dying into white coals which they moved aside to replenish the fire with wood dried for ceremonial occasions. They placed fish, wrapped in leaves soaked with seawater, on the white coals. Soon the smell wafted throughout the village. The feast was ready. The celebration began. Women bared their breasts. Men oiled their chests.

Into the night the drumbeat continued. Babies in baskets suspended from tree branches slept peacefully. Women and children and men spun around the fire. Feathers and leaves and skirts and robes and headdresses twirled around their otherwise naked bodies. At times Mere thought she saw the men and women become airborne and fly above the village. That night smelled of sweat and smoke and ancient magic. Mere and Oroiti sat side by side in the chairs of the elders. Flames reflected on their faces danced between them and bound their souls each to the other.

As though of one mind, they both looked to the stars and stood. Drums fell immediately silent. Dancers stood still. Mere and Oroiti slowly walked to the center of the ceremonial ring. In the silence they faced each other and each placed hands on the shoulder of the other. Oroiti's crutch fell to the ground as he and Mere began to slowly sway back and forth until their bodies kept time to the song sung by Mere. Her voice was soft. She sang the song slowly. Its words seemed to conjure strength and sadness.

"Every time it rains it rains pennies from heaven. Don't you know each cloud contains pennies from heaven? You'll find your fortune falling all over town. Be sure that your umbrella is upside down. Trade them for a package of sunshine and flowers. If you want the things you love, you must have showers. So when you hear it thunder, don't run under a tree. There'll be pennies from heaven for you and me."

The islanders had heard Mere sing many songs as she played her banjo and as she worked beside them. They knew the words but not the meanings to most of them. They recognized the melodies. This song they heard only once a year as the fire began to die and the stars reached their appointed positions in the sky. Mere always sang the song either in the arms of Oroiti or of the woman who had come before her. The islanders sang softly with her and along the edges of the ceremonial ring swayed to the song's slow rhythm.

A few older islanders remembered a time before this yearly ritual. Most of the islanders, however, had no memories of a time when this song and dance had not taken place. However, all knew that the highlight of the evening had yet to occur and all felt its time approaching.

The song ended. The two tribal elders – the Star of the Sea and the Slow Footed One – ended their dance. They looked each into the eyes of the other for a moment longer as though each feared an end to fires and dances and songs. Then, her body still facing Oroiti, Mere extended both arms and her face toward the sky. She stood motionless. Oroiti turned to stand beside her. He, too, studied the stars. The villagers remained on the perimeter of the ceremonial ring. Their faces were turned not to the heavens but to the woman unbent with age.

She stood immobile for so long that some women wondered if she could continue holding her arms up to the heavens. Men wondered if the stars would align themselves correctly this year. Then it happened. Mere swung her arms from the heavens to the earth in one quick, forceful motion. The drummers resumed their fastest and loudest beat until their hands and sticks blurred. Other islanders danced around Mere and Oroiti and the blazing fire. Masks reflected the fire's flames and light. The ground shook under drumming hands and dancing feet. Babies in their baskets continued their uninterrupted sleep.

As suddenly as the drumming and the dancing had resumed, both stopped. Mere threw her arms around Oroiti and sang.

"*Should auld acquaintance be forgot and never brought to mind? Should auld acquaintance be forgot, and days of auld lang syne? And days of auld lang syne, my dear, and days of auld lang syne. We'll take a cup of kindness yet, for days of auld lang syne.*"

The islanders loved this song. For them it was not the sole domain of this celebration. They sang it throughout the year as they threw nets into the sea, climbed trees to cut the highest fruit, and comforted distraught children.

During their interrupted-by-years-apart times together on the island, the two women often discussed at length the impact of the song on the islanders. Mere had years ago stopped attempting to fathom the connection this song had for them but nevertheless participated in the discussions if for no other reason than to hear the voice of the other woman. Her last explanation was that they sang it to please her because it was the final song of the celebration and, they assumed, must have special meaning and power. The other woman, however, refused to accept such an uncluttered explanation and promised to study the phenomenon at length when she established permanent residence on the island.

"And while you pursue those studies," Mere would comment, "I will be tying pigs to trees."

The other woman would then regard Mere through the thick lenses of her glasses.

Finally she might say, "The implication of your statement is that gravity's forces on this island do not apply to pigs. That possibly explains our dearth of pigs."

"That's doubtless what I meant," Mere would reply. "Surely I would never imply that pigs will fly when you finally make this island your home."

"Of course not," the other woman would say. "Such a statement is far beneath you. Besides, my home is with you. Here you are so here is my home."

The two women would then hold each other feeling frailty in their souls' resolve. Finally they would pull apart to stare deeply into eyes filled with tears.

"So much love," they would each say to the other and smile while their hearts danced.

"Nevertheless," the other would end the moment by adding, "It would make a fascinating study."

Then they would laugh and lose themselves to the night.

The song finished, Mere shouted, "Happy New Year!"

The islanders shouted, "Happy New Year!"

The night's celebration ended. Some remained basking by the fire's warmth. Others tidied the gathering area. Some walked slowly to huts and sleep. Babies in their baskets were carried from the trees to the huts. Mere no longer participated in the tidying up activities and she felt too stiff to remain by the fire. She and Oroiti bade each other peace throughout the night and walked their separate paths, Oroiti into his thatched hut in the village and Mere up the trail on the hill. Kaula followed. When Mere reached the papaya tree she paused to honor the fruit no longer hanging from the branch. She kissed the stem from which she had cut the fruit and then she performed her ritual of five. Only then did she enter her hut to cross yet another day off of the calendar and fall exhausted on her bed and immediately to sleep. When she was certain of the soundness of Mere's sleep, Kaula entered the hut to place a quilt on the woman for whom she kept her hidden vigil.

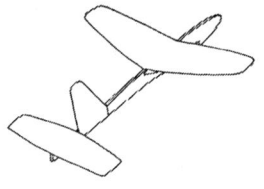

Chapter Six

The island awoke quietly the next morning. Birds had sung all their songs before the first child ventured out into the daylight. Always the children began this day before the adults. They knew that when the sun moved from the middle of the sky to begin its westward descent into the waters the crate would be opened and gifts distributed. Gradually the villagers – adults and children – gathered around it. None moved closer until Mere's arrival.

Always Mere without the presence of the woman who had come before her approached the crate and its contents with dreaded excitement. The gifts thrilled the islanders and delighted and fascinated and amused them. To Mere the gifts spoke of worlds lost and joys interrupted. Then there was always the letter. Even when they were together, she read the letter in the bottom of the box last.

Mere listened to the villagers as they gathered around the crate. She felt their excitement build until finally she forced herself to leave her hut to walk down the path. She passed the papaya tree without pausing. Halfway down the trail she remembered and stopped. She turned back toward the tree.

"You don't need to do this," she said aloud to herself. "It's gone. There is no need."

She turned from the tree to the trail and resumed her descent. Within a dozen steps she stopped again and turned to the tree.

"Don't do it," she said and, with clenched fist, hit her leg.

She turned away from the tree and back toward it. She kept turning away from and back toward the tree until it seemed to Kaula she was spinning in place. When Mere stopped, both women felt dizzy.

"Okay. Go back. Do it. Go back. Do it."

Mere climbed the trail back to the tree. She gently touched the stem from which the fruit had been cut, backed away from the tree, and bowed to the tree. Then she returned to the tree, touched the stem, backed away from the tree, bowed to the tree, and returned to the tree until she had repeated the routine five times. Then she turned toward the trail.

Mere and Oroiti sat in their chairs near the crate. Flames from the recently fueled fire leapt into the air. At Mere's signal Orado severed the crate's bindings and removed the lid. One item at a time he distributed the gifts. With little awareness of the original purpose of each gift, the recipient seldom matched the gift. An infant received a hand drill. A toothless man received a bag of hard candy. The distribution of gifts mattered not at all to the islanders, who had no sense of ownership. A gift opened by one was a gift for all. Mere delighted in witnessing the surprise and joy and often confusion as each villager examined every gift. The process usually lasted well into the night. This year's gift ritual seemed no different from those of all previous years. Mere sometimes offered suggestions regarding the use of items. More often than not, however, she simply observed the islanders' interpretations. Over the years Mere found herself increasingly at a loss to explain some of the gifts.

When a child opened a package of sponges, Mere suggested that he dip one in water. The entire village watched as the sponge expanded and held onto the water and laughed when the child squeezed the sponge and the water fell onto his feet. Certainly natural sponges were not a mystery to the islanders. Blue, square sponges were, however, unique. Everyone took a turn filling the sponge with water and squeezing the water out. A woman opened a box of pin striped bandanas and t-shirts. She gave one to each islander and still several remained in the box.

Oroiti held the shirt in front of him. Mere read aloud, "Yankees v. Dodgers – 1977 World Series."

"Turn it around," she instructed Oroiti.

She read the other side of the shirt. "Yankees World Champs!"

When she looked away from the shirt she saw that all the villagers were wearing baseball caps bearing the insignia of the New York Yankees. She laughed longer and harder than anyone on the island had ever seen. She laughed until tears ran down her face. She laughed until Oroiti laughed with her and finally all of the villagers laughed with her. She laughed until she felt weak, completely spent, and totally peaceful.

Finally Oroiti leaned to her and said, "These gifts bring you joy."

Mere looked at him and smiled. She leaned her head on his shoulder.

When she looked at him again, she said, "No. I always root for Brooklyn. She roots for the Yankees. She is telling us that she won. Yes. They bring me joy."

"What conflict has she won?" Oroiti asked.

"Her team won the World Series."

"A team?"

Mere, throughout the years, had rarely spoken of her world left behind, a world so completely disconnected from life on this island that she lacked sufficient language to make even casual reference to it. An entire village wearing World Series memorabilia spoke more of the gulf than anything Mere could ever have said. As she watched the villagers wrap bandanas around their heads and their arms and their legs, she knew throughout her being that, even without the other, she was home.

"It is of no importance," she answered Oroiti's question and he was satisfied.

When an islander opened a bag of marshmallows Mere walked to a tree and picked up a long, slender branch torn away by strong winds. She took a marshmallow from the islander and pierced it with the stick, walked to the fire, and held the skewered marshmallow into the flames. Just as it was about to catch fire, she withdrew the stick, pulled the marshmallow off, and ate it. The villagers looked at her first with concern and then with wonder. At her signal, the islanders gathered more sticks and took turns roasting their marshmallows. With melted sugar coating their faces, they did not stop until all of the marshmallows were roasted and eaten. Then there were the bags of M&M candies, which the islander adults returned to the box with the announcement that they would be eaten some other time. They knew well the power of candy. The year's gifts always contained candy. No one complained when this year's candies were returned to the crate. The villagers spent a considerable amount of time with the Lincoln Logs and the blank paper and crayons. Oroiti's snoring awoke Mere who only then realized that she, too, had been dozing. They looked at each other and smiled. Mere looked away from Oroiti's face to the other islanders. Several were examining marked papers taken from a book. Curious, Mere stood and went to them.

She held the book at arm's length and read, "How To Fly Paper Airplanes."

She looked from the book to the villagers who clearly did not understand.

"If you fold these papers in a certain way, you make an airplane."

She sat cross-legged in the sand and began folding the paper along indicated lines. When she finished she held the paper airplane in front of her. She looked from it back to Oroiti. His expression was as childlike as that of the other islanders sitting in the sand with her.

"You know," she said more to herself than to the others, "I don't think this will go very far. The stabilizer isn't long enough."

She stood stiffly to her feet.

"We'll give it a try, though."

With a gentle and quick movement of her arm, she sent the paper airplane into the air. It remained airborne for no more than two seconds before it fell nose first into the sand. Mere and the islanders stared at it. The islanders looked up at Mere.

"I told you the stabilizer was too short. I know a thing or two about stabilizers."

She sat back down and began refolding the paper. The islanders sitting in the sand around her watched intently. Other islanders joined them.

'Generally speaking," Mere said to them in a language they did not understand, "a design is no more than a suggestion. Experience is the true judge of engineering. You must believe me when I say that I have great experience in matters such as this."

Again she stood. She held the paper airplane out in front of her. It barely resembled its predecessor. She drew her arm back and released the plane in an upward motion. The plane faltered briefly, caught a gentle, slight thermal and sailed toward the ocean. The islanders jumped to their feet and ran toward the water in pursuit of the plane. They were no more than ten feet out into the water when the wind changed. The plane, too, changed its direction back toward the beach, then changed direction again to return to its point of origin. It circled Mere, lost altitude, and landed at her feet. The islanders cheered and clapped their hands and danced in place. Mere bent down and picked up the paper airplane.

"Welcome to the world of perfect landings," she said, kissing the plane. She handed it to the youngest child in the growing crowd of islanders.

"Use this as the model and all of your airplanes will fly," she said to the child's father in a language understood by all.

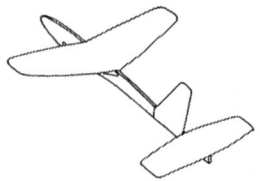

CHAPTER SEVEN

Mere stepped toward the crate. She knew without looking that it contained one last gift. That box was for her. She reached into the crate and lifted it out. She stared at it before turning away from the crate to Oroiti. He stood. They looked each into the eyes of the other. Then Oroiti nodded and Mere turned toward the trail. Kaula, wearing her Yankees' hat pulled down low on her head and her bandana tied around her ankle, followed at her usual distance.

Several times Mere paused on the trail. Kaula did not know whether she paused to rest or to delay her arrival to her hut. Mere's intense and conflicting feelings regarding her gifts were not hidden from the islanders. Once inside her hut, Mere pulled her chair to the doorway to both see and breathe easier. She held the box in her lap and rocked back and forth. Then she opened the box. From her distance, Kaula could not identify the objects as Mere took them from the box and held them in front of her. From her distance, though, Kaula could hear the changes in the breathing and mark the changes in the expressions of this woman who had grown old among them. She could hear Mere's words but could understand nothing. Void of meaning, the words spoken by Mere seemed to Kaula to be sobs for wounds once again opened.

"What is going on here?" Mere seemed to ask the walls.

She held something blue up to the light.

"United States of America Passport," Mere read. "What on earth?"

She held up an envelope and read, "Pan American World Airways – Pan Am."

She opened another envelope and held up green pieces of paper. Then she counted the pieces of paper. They were in a variety of denominations.

"One thousand two hundred fifty dollars? What are you doing?"

Again Mere reached into the box to hold at arm's length slacks and a plaid, button down Oxford shirt.

"Have you gone mad?" she seemed to ask the shirt.

She dropped the slacks and the shirt onto the floor and again reached into the box.

Kaula watched Mere shake her head as she held a pair of leather shoes at arms' length.

"Penny loafers! I haven't worn shoes since – since we – since I – Where's the penny? What is happening?"

When she turned the shoes upside down to examine the soles, a pair of socks fell out of each loafer. Mere watched the socks fall to the floor. She studied her gifts then rubbed her forehead. Finally, she returned the items to the box. She closed her eyes and sat motionless for so long Kaula believed she had fallen asleep. Then Mere opened her eyes and looked into the box.

"Well, let's see how you explain all of this. Frankly, I would have worn a Yankees cap, you know. And you give me these other things, which have neither purpose nor value for me. Where is my calendar? Today is the first day of the New Year and I have no calendar. How will I mark the days? You force me to make my own calendar, which I can do. You know I can do that. And where is my book? Where is my magazine? And my logbook? And my drops? How could you forget those? Let's see how you explain this."

A gentle breeze carried sounds of the islanders below to her hut on the mountain. Their laughter and their shouts of joy nourished her soul. Even when they shouted their name for this woman who had come to the island before her, their voices gave her strength.

"Pilapan. Pilapan."

For a moment it seemed that repeating her name would conjure her presence. Only, though, for a moment. When the moment passed, Mere accepted once again the emptiness of her absence.

Pressing two fingers against her forehead to ease the pain, Mere sat absolutely still. In her mind, she saw the islanders wearing masks and beads and baseball caps and bandanas. She saw them dance around leaping flames and heard the drums sound celebratory and joyful rhythms.

Pilapan, in their language, meant "Mother Chief." It was, Mere acknowledged, a fitting name. Pilapan, whose arrival to the island had preceded Mere's by many, many months, had become a mother and a chief to the people. Shorter in height than most of the islanders, Pilapan seemed to all larger than life itself. Children followed her wherever she went on the island. When she sat, they sat around her and on her. She seemed to never tire of their company. With each successive visit, her lap grew larger for the sole purpose, it seemed, of accommodating more children. She laughed with them and played games with them and told them stories later repeated throughout the island's generations. Adults sat at her feet as they sought her council.

During these visits – some much longer than others – the Star of the Sea did not sit in the chair next to Oroiti nor did she expect to. When the Mother Chief was present, she became the central star in the island's universe.

With a bare foot Mere shoved the gift box across the floor. She stared at it for several long moments. Finally with her ears and heart full of the sounds below her, Mere opened the letter.

November 1, 1977
My Dearest Mere – My Darling Star of the Sea –
As you read this 1977 will have ended and 1978 will have begun. We have not been in each other's company for two years. I picture you during that time active, strong and so full of life. I picture you standing and sitting at the side of Oroiti and, yes, I envy him. I write this letter to you watching winter's first gentle snow and wishing for the warmth of your arms around me.

The years have not passed as we originally pictured and I know you blame me. We've talked and talked about all of this. I wish I could blame you, too, but of course that would be absurd. I don't apologize for my decisions and my actions. You well know I believe that the greater good must always be served and that this often takes place at the expense of individual pursuits. In youth it's easy to believe that a limitless supply of years has been granted us. As the years pass we develop a sense of urgency that time may not be sufficient for the tasks ordained. Always the demands of the whole outweigh the desires of the individual.

At this point who did what to whom can surely no longer matter. Please don't be angry with me any more. Right now, I don't think I could survive your rage. Or perhaps it's my own rage I feel crushing me. I so miss you.

There's no easy way to say what I must now tell you so I'll just jump into it and hope words on paper suffice.

For the past several months I have experienced considerable abdominal discomfort. I've lost quite a bit of weight and, at this rate, I shall soon be thin again. People tell me to either take in my clothes or buy new ones but if I did either I think I'd feel defeated. So I hope to – like a child with hand me downs – grow back into my wardrobe.

The medical community, of which I am inherently skeptical, calls my condition diverticulitis. Doctors suggest a change in diet, more rest, and a less active schedule. The diet I have changed. A less active schedule is out of the question and therefore more rest must follow suit. Still the pain continues. I've always believed that my body would last much longer than current circumstances indicate. I feel betrayed.

I do not intend to bore you with pain narratives nor am I asking for sympathetic quacking. I do need, however, to tell you this. Despite the assurances from all of the doctors that diverticulitis is a temporary condition easily remedied, I hold a different truth in my soul. It is that truth you must know.

I am dying.

This truth has been told to no one except you – the one person from whom I keep no secrets.

I am dying and I need you by my side. That is my truth and that is my request. I don't want to die so far away from you. I want – no I need – you here with me.

Throughout my professional career I have insisted that death is a natural part of life to be celebrated as joyfully as birth and coming of age. I have urged families to allow children to participate in all life offers. How easy it has been to compel my wisdom onto others. That wisdom seems not connected to my present reality. The world – when it learns of my situation – might well smile and say that because of her we know death is a cherished part of life.

But this is different.

I am dying.

I know you expected my usual gifts of calendar and books and magazines and I do apologize for again disappointing you. Again and again and again. The gifts I send you are of a far more practical nature than those for which you doubtless hoped. I send you an open plane ticket and extra funds with which to get to the main island's airport. I also send you a passport not, I'm sorry to say, in your birth name but in a name designed to attract far less attention. Hopefully the clothes I have chosen please you. When you feel them on your skin, please feel also my touch. Please. Please. Please.

I'm also enclosing a list of herbs, which I ask you to bring me.

I also ask you to return to me that which I have hidden.

While I am not yet counting my days and while I continue to actively pursue my teachings and writings, I do sense their finite number.

Even as I contemplate my own death I hope for a cure.

I am, as always, confident that you know I hold you in my heart.

God speed.

M.

P.S. – Oh how I wish I could reach across the miles and hold you as you read these words.

Again, my love. My life.

M.

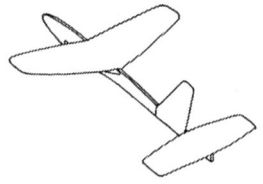

CHAPTER EIGHT

With so much to feel and think, Mere sat in her chair feeling and thinking nothing until the nothings filled her being beyond the point of containment. Her scream ripped through the evening satiated with celebration. Still sitting in her chair, she screamed again. And again. And again. Her final scream ended in a sob so wrenching the entire island for a moment choked. Finally, gasping for breath, she staggered across the room and stood over the gift box. She released the letter from her hand and watched its descent.

When she turned toward the door, she saw Kaula and Oroiti standing just outside her entrance. The moon's light showed their faces outlined in fear. Mere crossed the room and fell back into her chair.

"I don't even know who I am," she said.

Neither islander answered. They maintained their respectful distance and silence.

"What madness possessed us?" Mere asked looking at the photograph of the two young women.

Then she closed her eyes. It seemed as though she slept. Oroiti sent Kaula to rest. Daring to disobey her chief, she continued her vigil hidden by night. Oroiti stood outside the hut until his leg trembled. Only then did he enter the hut to sit on the floor at the feet of the woman with whom he shared his soul. Finally she opened her eyes.

"I am Amelia," she said.

"I know. I remember."

"I don't want to be Amelia. I didn't then and I don't now."

She leaned forward and kissed him on the top of his head.

"In our lives," the old man said, "we wear many faces and many names."

She laid her head on his and asked, "Do we have choices?"

"Yes," he said without moving his head from hers. "No."

She leaned back in her chair and drew him to rest against her legs. Her hands remained on his shoulders. Silhouetted in the moonlight, their image seemed to Kaula one etched forever into eternity by years of closeness. They touched each other with assurance and comfort and certainty. He turned to rest his head in her lap. Comforted by their image, Kaula left the night to finally rest in her own bed.

"She has summoned me."

"So it seems."

"She believes she is dying."

"She knows that dying is another form of living. There is no end."

"She believes that this is different."

"She is mistaken. It is not different."

Mere stroked his head. He placed a hand on her knee not for support but because his hands knew her body and sought favorite places of rest and comfort. The moon made its path through the sky toward morning and still the two sat in silence. With the sun's arrival, she again spoke.

"I will not go."

He lifted his head and turned to see her face.

"Let us greet the day together," he said.

Together they struggled to their feet, made their way slowly and painfully to the doorway, and stepped out into a new day.

Without his crutch, his hand remained on her shoulder. In the shadows he saw Kaula.

"Doesn't she ever sleep?" Mere whispered to Oroiti without looking toward Kaula.

"I sent her away during the night," he softly answered as together they looked through the trees to the ocean.

"Why must she do this?" Mere motioning toward Kaula asked still whispering.

"It is the wish of Pilapan," came the whispered response of Oroiti.

"And her wish is your decree. Our decree. Have I been held hostage here all of these years?" Her voice grew louder.

"You arrived here by your own design. Your leaving, should that be your choice, will also be of your own design." Oroiti continued speaking softly.

"I'm not leaving. This is my home."

With the hand of Oroiti on her shoulder for support, Mere remained immobile despite her growing agitation.

"This is my home. You are my people. I have lived here longer than anywhere else on this earth. I have been with you for over half of my life. I will not leave just because she summoned me. Just because now is the time for her. This was not our agreement. She knows that. You know that. I certainly of all people know that."

"This decision requires solitude."

Mere left Oroiti to balance himself while she went into the hut. She returned with his crutch, which he took from her and began making his way down the trail.

"I am not going," she said to his back.

He neither replied nor slowed his descent. Mere turned and entered her home. She paced the floor. She looked out the door. She sat in her chair. She stood and again paced. She lay on her bed. Finally she sat on the floor in front of her gift box.

"You didn't even send banjo strings."

She emptied the contents of the box into her lap. She opened the passport and stared at a photograph taken on the island two years ago.

"Were you planning this when you took this picture? And who is Mary Anderson? I don't like that name. It's not me. I am not an ordinary person with an ordinary name."

She closed the passport and dropped it back into the box. She took the currency from the envelope, recounted it, and spread it on the floor. She studied the bills for a moment before turning her attention to a second envelope.

"Pan American World Airways. Pan Am. This can't be possible. You have given me a ticket for me to be a passenger on a mail carrier. No. No longer just a mail carrier. You've spoken of this. You've told me that now many people sit strapped into seats in airplanes designed specifically for passenger flight. This is common, you have said. You have told me this. I've seen the magazines and the newspaper articles. You, yourself, you said, travel on these airplanes. You've described them to me. Jets, you call them. Pan American World Airways. Pan Am. This is a ticket for me to be a passenger strapped into a seat. I won't do it."

The envelope fell from her hand as she began rocking on the floor of her home. She held her head in her hands daring the pain to consume her. She swayed back and forth. She moaned until the moans turned into a humming familiar to Kaula who sat in the grass nearby. When finally Mere could sit in quiet stillness, she took the letter from the envelope and again read it and again read it and again until she knew in her soul every touch of the pen on the paper.

"I know nothing of your world. This is my world. This is where I belong. I came here to stay. How could you expect me to become someone else and return to a world so changed that it no longer has a place for me? And why must I become yet another person? No one remembers me. My name is forgotten and my place is lost. I will live out my life here, my bones will be buried under a mound at the top of the hill, and my soul will travel freely on the winds of this island. You have no right to summon me."

With those words, Mere returned her gifts to the box. She stood, stretched, and went outside for her morning ritual. She lifted the basket of rocks fifty times to her chest and twenty-five times above her head. She lay on the grass and did seventy-five sit ups. She used the worn tree branch to chin herself twenty times. Exhausted and breathing heavily, she lay back on the grass and felt the soul of the island enter her spine.

When she stood, strength and determination filled her being. She strode into her hut, picked up the box, walked outside and, with all of her energy, threw the box and its contents toward the ocean. She watched the passport and the one hundred dollar bills and the open ended airline ticket and the letter, much like her paper airplane of the evening before, catch separate thermals and waft their ways toward the sea. Satisfied of their courses, Mere returned to her hut and fell into an exhausted sleep on her bed.

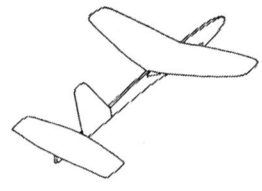

CHAPTER NINE

She did not awaken until the moon began its journey through the sky. She was covered with her quilt and a prepared meal was on the floor beside her. Oroiti sat facing her in her chair. She looked directly into his eyes. He did not look away. She sat up in her bed and ate her meal. She drank from her cup of water.

"Thank you," she said when the meal was finished.

"We nourish each other," he replied.

"Come to me," she said.

The old chief made his way across the room to lie beside her. She drew him to her. Throughout the night they breathed as one. As the morning's sun warmed the hut, she spoke.

"What did she hide?"

The old man turned on his back, sighed and asked, "Is this your concern? You have decided. Must this continue to pull your energy?"

"It's not pulling. I'm just curious."

"Curiosity requires energy."

With those words, he sat up, picked his crutch up from the floor, stood to meet the day and said, "You have entered your new year. How do you choose to spend your days? What do you choose for this day?"

"Do you know what she hid?"

He walked out of the hut, faced the ocean and did not turn to her when she spoke.

"Did you hide something for her?"

Even when Mere stood behind him on the mountain, still he faced the ocean. She moved to face him, looked deep into his eyes, and wondered if he were capable of deceit.

"What did you hide for her – from me?" she asked.

His gaze did not waver as he looked from the ocean to her face.

"Often that which was hidden becomes visible to us in its own time."

"Stop it!" she said, stamping her foot. "What did she hide? Do you know what she wants?"

"Only she knows her intentions."

Mere exhaled quickly and deeply, again stamped her bare foot into the rich earth, then turned away from the island's chief. Still stamping, she returned to her hut. She stood facing the inside of her home. Her back was to him.

It was to her back that he spoke.

"Amelia."

She had never before heard him speak the name by which she had been known until her arrival on the island. The sound of his voice saying that name seemed to stop her heart. She feared she would die before his breath ended that last sound of that name. A chill filled every part of her body so quickly and completely that she suspected her blood ran with ice and her stopped heart throbbed with the stabbing pain of frozen time. Her fingers tightened on her doorpost until her knuckles turned white. She felt him at her side.

"Breathe," he commanded and only then did she allow herself the common luxury of breath.

She turned to him and leaned against him and felt the ice

in her veins melt and her heart return to its normal rhythm. She inhaled and exhaled and felt her senses stabilize.

"My name is Mere," she whispered.

"Yes. You are the Star of all of the Sea. You are our Star. You are my Star. You are also Amelia. You came to the sea from the sky. You came to us from the sea. You did these things by your own design. If you return to the sea and leave us even for a journey from which you will return that, too, must be by your own design. If you go on that journey, you will take all that you are with you."

"I have returned her gifts to the sea. I am Mere. This is my home."

"You are Mere. This is your home. You did not return her gifts to the sea. Rua found them on the boulders near the bottom of the mountain. Their journey to the sea is not yet complete. Apparently the stabilizer was too short."

Laughing, she said, "Oh, shut up."

Ignoring her request for silence, Oroiti continued, "If you want them cast into the sea, we will take them in a canoe so far away you will never again see them. If there is doubt in your heart, the gifts should remain here."

As she straightened from him, he turned and left the hut. Mere did not look away from him until he disappeared down the mountain trail. She had not thought of her morning rituals. She felt too tired to even contemplate lifting a basket of rocks and for the first time questioned whether or not she mocked the passage of time with such activities. She considered the world she had left behind and compared it to the world to which her return was requested. She looked out on the world she called home.

"I hated that world," she said too softly for even Kaula's ears. "He used me for his own gain. He gained money and he gained fame. And I let him. Maybe I even enjoyed it at first. But then I hated it. I hated the crowds. I hated the limelight. And I loved you. I loved you but I hated that world. And now you ask me to return. That world no longer exists. It has changed more than I can imagine. Certainly your vague letters and chosen clippings haven't helped me understand that world. You have protected me from it, it seems. Either that or you have little actual knowledge of your world. Do you actually live in that world or do you float above it in the ethers of academia? This is my home and these are my people. And you ask me to leave my home! You ask me to leave my world and come to you in your world! I cannot do it. I will not do it."

With those words, Mere walked outside and forced herself to perform her rituals. She lifted the basket of rocks fifty times to her chest and twenty-five times above her head. She lay on the grass and did seventy-five sit-ups. She used the worn tree branch to chin herself twenty times. When she was finished, she paused to realize that she was not even breathing hard and took this as a sign that her decision was correct. She strode down the hill to the sea. She helped fishermen mend their nets. She visited women beating bark into paste. She wiped sweat from the brow of a woman about to give birth and slapped the father to be on the shoulders. She ate fruit for her midday meal and napped in the shade of a tree. Island life was slow and easy and Mere's rhythm matched that of the island and the people who lived their lives without care or curiosity about life beyond their world.

She awoke from her nap as the day was ending. She ate with the islanders and made her way back up the mountain to her hut and slept soundly through the night. When she awoke the next morning she greeted the day in her usual manner without hesitation. She lifted the basket of rocks fifty times to her chest and twenty-five times above her head. She lay on the grass and did seventy-five sit-ups. She used the worn tree branch to chin herself twenty times. She made her own calendar for the year 1978 and marked off the days already spent. She cut her 1977 calendar into squares and sewed the squares together. The task complete, she made her first entry into her new logbook. She inventoried her banjo strings and felt confident that the supply would doubtless last her the rest of her life. She played her banjo. She began a novel last read years before.

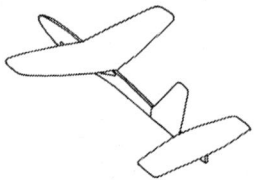

CHAPTER TEN

The days passed and her homemade calendar showed their passage with marks drawn through each completed twenty-four hour cycle. Often her thoughts returned to her gift from the sea and the letter requesting her return. When that happened, she forced her thoughts elsewhere. She reviewed the principles of celestial navigation. She named in alphabetical order the people she had nursed during the Spanish flu epidemic. She attempted to name all of the states of the United States of America and their capitals. If none of those exercises blacked out thoughts of the letter and its author, she played her banjo until darkness filled her hut. If darkness filled her hut she softly sang songs to herself. If nothing diminished the intensity of her thoughts, she allowed herself to see in her mind the handwriting and to remember as much of the letter as possible until she became too exhausted to continue. Soon all of her energy was spent trying to not think of that which filled her every thought. She could not escape the nagging sense that something on the island had been hidden from her and that the time for its discovery was slipping away. Unable to distract herself with physical and mental activity, she stopped trying. Inactivity broken by a restless dread began to inform and guide her days.

With the passage of time, the islanders noticed that their Star of the Sea had become thinner. The skin of her face had tightened. Her eyes no longer danced. They worried that her headaches distressed her beyond the ordinary. They knew she did not sleep well because during the night she talked to herself and paced the floor of her hut and sometimes very quietly played her banjo and sang songs that at one time had calmed and comforted her. Nights and days passed and her agitation and pain did not diminish. Hoping to calm her, the islanders brought her special teas. Hoping to diminish the pain in her head, they brought her herbs and offered special smokes and prayers. Women prepared a decoction of leaves of the Colocasia Esculenta plant, which they called votuki. This mixed with other plants they made into tea, which Mere drank with neither enthusiasm nor disdain. They heated the huge leaves of this same plant and gave them to her to place at her feet throughout the night. When her eyes were red from weeping, they extracted the plant's sap, diluted it in spring water and encouraged her to rinse her eyes in case the redness was not brought on by sorrow but by some other infestation.

Boys, hoping to entice Mere into joining them, began coming to her hut each morning to lift her basket of rocks and do sit ups and chin ups. At first she watched them from her doorway. Eventually, though, she did not even acknowledge their presence. She simply moved from her bed to her chair and back again to her bed interrupting the routine only to accept the ministrations of the islanders and to tend to her basic bodily functions in private.

Each day Oroiti, carrying some herb or trinket to perhaps interest her, made his slow journey up the mountain and each day he made his slow journey down the mountain carrying a heart growing heavier with each passing moment.

In other parts of the world where the passage of time is marked with changing seasons, spring's approach promises blossoms and hope. On Nani where seasons were not known and time required no markings, blossoms fell from the trees and a sense of sorrow settled upon the village. It seemed to the islanders that even the birds had stopped singing. The banjo remained in its case. Their Star of the Sea refused food and barely sipped the teas still brought to her. Life on the island stopped because her sadness was so great.

When next Oroiti came to her hut he brought no herbs or trinkets. He sat down on the floor near her feet. She did not acknowledge him even when he spoke.

"Pilapan believes that she is dying and yet you have become the one nearing the end of a journey."

She did not look at him and gave no indication of having heard. She sat in her chair staring at the photograph of the two young women.

Oroiti placed a hand on her knee. He stared intently at the drawn and pale face from which all energy had vanished.

"You were the one, Mere, who sat by me after the rocks crushed my leg. You held the knife in the flames. You placed it in my hand. You kissed away my screams to keep the others from suffering my pain. You bound my wound and fed me all that nourished me. You carried my spirit until I could once again bear its weight. You kept my face turned toward life even when I wondered if my journey would continue in that direction. You did not abandon me. Now I must ask your forgiveness. I have abandoned you. Please forgive me."

At last Mere's eyes focused on his face. When she spoke her voice contained hints of energy held captive for the past days and weeks.

"Ariki, you are an idiot."

The old man forced his face to not light up in a broad smile.

"That may be true. Nevertheless, I ask your forgiveness. And my name, as you well know, is Oroiti."

"Please tell me, Mr. Chief, how exactly you have abandoned me."

The emptiness in her eyes lessened as though they remembered having once danced with passions and energies.

"I abandoned you by indulging your desire for solitude. I did nothing while you refused food. I watched you remain inside for days and nights. You separated yourself from all that nourishes you, and I allowed you to do so. For that I ask your forgiveness."

"There is nothing to forgive. You showed the greatest respect for me. Besides, you know I would have bitten your head off had you tried to force me to do anything I didn't want to do."

The old man smiled and replied, "I have managed for all of these years to keep my head on my shoulders. Other parts of my body have not fared so well. My head, though, has remained intact. Still, you raise an interesting possibility. However, the teeth, as our ancestors might observe, are in your mouth."

She placed her hand on top of his and together they sat. The day wore on before either spoke.

"This is my home," she finally said.

Since she had spoken an obvious and accepted truth, Oroiti felt no need to reply. He trusted that in time she would speak again. In time, she did.

"The list of herbs is precise."

"Perhaps. That list, unfortunately, was not found on the rocks. I cannot return it to you. Again, I must ask your forgiveness."

"I didn't throw it away. It's here," she said and motioned around her.

"Ah. Just in case," he said and smiled. "And you've already gathered everything on the list?"

"No."

"They must be dried quickly."

"Yes."

Again the two sat in silence. The day passed and darkness began to fill the hut. A villager brought food and the two ate in silence. In silence they turned toward the doorway and gazed out at the night sky. In silence they made their way to the bed where they lay side by side each holding the other throughout the night. They awoke with the dawn.

"What if I've already waited too long?" she asked the dawn.

"Then we must hurry."

"Yes."

"In order to return to her, though, you must first return to yourself."

"I'm back."

"Your spirit, yes, is returning. Your body may require more time."

She gave herself two weeks marked off on her calendar. During those two weeks she forced herself to eat and to walk in the sand and eventually to lift her basket of rocks. At the end of those two weeks she gave herself one week more and at the end of that week she gave herself a final week. At the end of that week she could once again lift the basket of rocks fifty times to her chest and twenty-five times above her head. She could lie on the grass and do seventy-five sit ups. She could use the worn tree branch to chin herself twenty times. Finally when those rituals were complete, she did not feel the least bit tired.

"I am ready," she whispered to herself and the island heard her voice.

Throughout the next day they gathered herbs. Mere climbed the trunk to obtain scrapings from the bark of the salato tree for the treatment of pain in the lungs. Uncertain which part of the plant Pilapan requested, Oroiti broke off stems for the treatment of pain in the bones, joints and intestines. He gathered the small, white flowers of the taipoipo shrub just in case the salato stems failed to diminish any stomach pain Pilapan might experience.

"That wasn't on the list," Mere reminded him. "She was very precise in her request."

"And her teeth are in her mouth, too," he replied.

He then added the triangular shaped pakopako stems used for the treatment of a wide variety of ailments including ailments of the liver.

Mere looked into the basket and said, "You live a dangerous life, Ariki."

"What life is not dangerous if lived fully?"

"Nevertheless," she replied and gently snapped off several leaves from the small sanga plant.

She held the leaves in her hand for a moment than said, "Perhaps she also suffers from a fever," and dropped the leaves in the basket.

"These she requested," and Oroiti dropped leaves from the maga maga into the basket. "However, is she familiar with the methods of removing their juice? Only the juice will ease the stomachache. When I was a boy a child chewed on the stem and died. She must only use the juice."

"What she does with these is not our concern. I should just tell her to come and get them herself. If she wants to eat a stem, that's her choice. If she had chosen to live here for the past forty years perhaps she would know that only the juice of the maga maga cures."

Oroiti looked at her for a moment. He smiled and said, "It pleases me that you have once again found your teeth."

She threw her head back and laughed and her laughter echoed throughout the island and filled the hearts of the people with joy.

"For the moment, Ariki, they remain in my mouth."

"I shall maintain vigilance."

"That's best."

They continued in silence gathering plants and herbs. The stems from the toa tahi herb could be used as tea for pain relief. The bark of the nonu was well known for curing abdominal ailments. The leaves of the apele tree were not acceptable. They searched for leaves to reduce intestinal distress but could not make a satisfactory selection.

"We shall disappoint her," Oroiti remarked. "I shall look again at the apele leaves."

He returned to the tree to re-examine its leaves. Mere's gaze never left him and her body shook with sadness. When he returned she held his empty hands in hers and kissed them.

"Life is blessed because you exist," she said in the formal benediction of the island.

He leaned forward and rested his lips on her forehead in the traditional acknowledgement of the benediction.

All afternoon they kept the leaves and stems and pieces of bark and herbs near the fires. By evening they were dry. When they returned to her hut, Mere wrapped the dried gatherings into a large leaf and tied the leaf together with thread. She placed the parcel on top of her suitcase and turned to Oroiti.

"There was a time long ago when I believed myself to be brave. Now I feel only dread."

"Courage is an action, not a sensation, we are told. Are you asking that your gifts be returned?" he asked and his eyes filled with tears.

She walked away from him to stand in the door of her hut. She stared through trees to the sea. She leaned against the doorframe and forced herself to breathe slowly and deeply. When she turned again to face him she wanted with every part of her body and every part of her soul to cling to him for every heartbeat of the remainder of her life.

"Yes. Return my gifts."

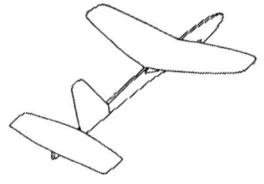

CHAPTER ELEVEN

The old man left her hut and did not speak. She did not turn to watch him go. Instead, she sat on the floor and stared at the suitcase brought by the woman for whom Mere was about to leave the island. The suitcase had been closed for so long. Mere traced the brand name with her fingers as though, sightless, she were reading it for the first time.

"Modernaire," she whispered when her fingers completed their tracings. "How modern could this be now, after all of these years?"

She unlatched and opened the suitcase. It smelled musty and forgotten. She looked from the suitcase to her hut and surveyed her possessions.

"I have so little," she whispered so softly that not even Kaula could hear. "And I have more than I ever dreamed I could possess. Now, once again because of you, I leave all that I have. I leave yet another life. This time it will be different. I will not lose this. I will return to this life that is mine."

She stood and began to carefully select possessions to place in the suitcase. She folded a pair of pleated khaki trousers. She crawled under the bed and returned with a pair of worn oxford shoes stiff with age, which she placed beside the suitcase next to the new penny loafers. She stood in front of her books. Shaking her head, she picked up the photograph of the two young women. She turned to the hat and the forked stick and again shook her head.

"No. I will not travel with any of this. I will not risk losing what little I have of importance. These things, these possessions, shall remain here. They are far too valuable. I will return to this place. I will return to this place. I will return to this place."

With each repetition, she turned in a circle. As she spoke the repetitions faster, the circles in which she turned become tighter and faster until she spun in place.

Her voice grew louder until she shouted again and again and again, "I will return to this place. I will return to this place."

She gestured as though she were speaking to someone, convincing someone, arguing with someone. She spun and shouted and gestured until firm hands on her shoulders stopped her.

"My Mere," he said and she fell into his arms.

He guided her to her chair and she sat. With a lumbering and careening grace all his own, he emptied the suitcase, closed it and returned it to its side and proper place.

"Yes," he said when finished. "You will return to this place. You will return to your home."

He leaned over the back of her chair and rested his head on her shoulders. He smoothed her hair. Then he set a bag woven from dracaena fronds in her lap.

"In order to return you must first depart. You need carry with you only that which you deliver and that which is required for the journey. The engine remains repaired and the men ready for the voyage. We shall all await your return."

Mere sat in the chair and looked around her. She felt the presence of Oroiti behind her and leaned back in the chair until her head rested on his chest. She closed her eyes and felt her pulse pound inside her head.

"How long has my head hurt?" she whispered to herself.

The old man leaned down, laid his face on the top of her

head and softly said, "You said that you brought this pain to the island with you. Perhaps on your journey you will find a place to leave it. Then when you return you will never again feel this pain."

"Brought it with me. You are correct, my dear one. I shall leave it on another island."

A slight breeze sent the airplane suspended on its cord in slow circles around the room. They watched its gentle journey.

"Maybe I should take my banjo," the old woman at last said.

Oroiti began to softly sing, "Oh, Susanna, oh don't you cry for me 'cause I come from Alabama with my banjo on my knee."

"Do you have any idea what those words mean?" and her voice contained laughter.

"They mean that you will undertake a journey from which you will return. When you return we will sing and rejoice."

"I underestimated you. That is exactly the meaning of the song."

The old man moved to the bed. She crossed the hut to join him.

"Mornings are the best times to begin journeys," she said as she lay beside him.

"The items returned to you, sent to you by her," he seemed to struggle for the exact words.

She did not attempt to rush him or to choose his words for him.

"They are important for your journey?"

"Yes."

"Will they also bring you back here?"

"I don't know."

"If not, how will you return?"

"I shall find a way because I will return."

"Yes."

In their silence the hut greeted the night and the moon cast familiar shadows.

"Are your provisions sufficient for the journey?" he asked.
"I don't know."
"Much is unknown."
"Yes."

They did not sleep that night nor did they speak. Together they watched the stars tell their stories to the sky.

As dawn approached she whispered to him, "Why am I doing this?"

"Because she needs you."

"Yes," she said.

Another silence settled over them like a worn, comfortable quilt. Finally, Mere sat up. She gazed down at him before bending to kiss his forehead.

"I shall miss you," she whispered in the language he did not understand.

Then she stood. He, too, stood. Together they walked to the hut's doorway and looked out at the day. He looked toward the sea. She looked into the sky.

When she strode onto the dock the men stood. She walked directly to the boat. She walked its length as though inspecting it. She stared at the engine. She looked out to sea.

"It's a big ocean. So much water."

She looked back at the shore. She took a few steps toward it and then returned her attention to the boat. Her bag woven from dracaena fronds hung from her shoulder. She wore the penny loafers and the slacks and the plaid shirt.

"We shall wait for him," Kahil stated.

"There's no need. He's doubtless resting."

"We shall wait for him," Kahil repeated.

The men sat on the dock. After several moments she sat down beside them. The sun was already beginning its climb in the sky. It warmed their shoulders. After several more moments she stood.

"We cannot wait. You must have time to return before dark."

The men looked at each other and then at her.

Again Kahil spoke, "We will not return until you sit among us."

She looked at them and her eyes filled with tears.

"How will you manage? Where will you sleep? What will you eat?"

"We shall manage as you manage. We will have tales to share when we return."

"Before we can return, we must leave. It's time. We can wait no longer."

As she climbed into the boat she was stopped by the sound of his footstep alternating with the sound of his crutch. Kaula rushed to stay beside him. Mere stepped off of the boat and ran toward them. They met midway on the dock. His breathing was heavy. Drops of sweat clung to his forehead.

"I worried you would leave," he said finally when his breathing calmed.

"I worried you would not come," she said.

"This took longer to locate than I had planned. It was well hidden."

He placed in her hands a round, tin container. Mere gasped when she saw it. Before her breath returned, she dropped it into the woven bag.

"I will tell her that you found it," were the only words she could manage.

She turned to look at the sea, already anxious to return.

"There is one other thing," the old man said.

As she turned back to face him, he took her hands and placed into them a leather flying cap. She stared at it in confusion and wonder. She took a step back and looked from the cap to him.

"Where did you find this?"

"Like you, it arrived from the sea. I have rubbed it regularly with the milk of the poniu to keep it soft and ready should you return to the skies."

She stared at the cap for only a moment before putting it on. "How do I look?" she asked and her face shone with joy.

Oroiti laughed and replied, "Your head is wrapped in glory. Now you can fly once more."

The roar of the old Pratt & Whitney engine shook the dock as Mere threw her arms around him. When they separated, their shoulders were each damp from tears shed by the other. With no more words possible, she turned and climbed into the boat. As she sped toward the horizon, Mere did not look back to see Oroiti and Kaula step from the rough, planked dock onto Nani's moist, warm sands and sit down already waiting for her return.

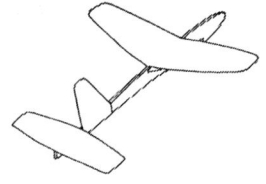

CHAPTER TWELVE

For most of the journey away from the island, Mere appeared to sleep. The oddly assembled boat allowed for shelter from the sun. The men had grown accustomed to traveling the sea in this craft although their natural choices utilized the strength of the wind or the strength of their arms. They indulged their Star of the Sea when the journey required more speed than those choices provided. They were used to the sea and used to this journey. They were not strangers to the bigger island and none on that bigger island betrayed the desire of their neighbors for secrecy. No questions had ever been asked. The nature of the neighboring islanders did not include inquiry.

She deliberately appeared to sleep. Mere could find no other method of containing her grief and her fear and her excitement. The journey had begun and something within her harkened back to days of constant journeys. Her feigned sleep contained the queasiness she felt in her stomach and in her entire being. She had not been on any moving vehicle since her arrival to the island. She did not want the men to feel more concern for her than they were currently experiencing. The next parting would be impossible should that occur. The day's heat had compelled her to remove her leather flying cap and place it in her woven bag. She held the bag close to her as though it were the only thing keeping her afloat.

Through the woven dracaena she felt the shape and weight of the tin container. She had no idea of its current contents. However, she knew its every detail. Perhaps an inch in height and three in diameter, the tin had once held candy imported from France. The words *La Seve de Pin – Epinal StDie, Gerarmer, etc.* circled the edges of the box. A drawing in its center pictured a beehive in the middle of a forest. *Bonbons*, she remembered, was part of a gold colored banner wrapping itself though the trees.

The tin recalled more. They were looking at the stars that night in a place they called their own – their secret on the roof of a building at Columbia University. Mere tried to remember which of the many accessible roofs they had claimed. She could not. Perhaps the smell of the engine and the rocking of the boat clouded her memory. The exact roof no longer mattered, though. What still mattered was that in 1919 they had been in each other's arms on that roof whispering and laughing and rearranging the stars to their own desires. Mere, with what even after all these years she believed to be more courage than she had possessed in her entire life before or after that moment, withdrew the tin of candy from her pocket and pressed it into the hands of the other young woman.

"These sweets are for you because you are the sweetest thing in the world," she had said and in the boat grimaced at her innocent awkwardness.

On the roof Amelia held her breath while the other woman looked at the tin.

"I shall treasure this always," she had finally said. "I will never lose it."

Then she opened the tin, placed a candy in Amelia's mouth and one in her own.

"Of course, we'll eat the candies now. The box, though, I'll keep forever."

They laughed and with mouths full of candy allowed for just a moment their lips to touch while the stars returned to their predestined order.

With her eyes closed and her stomach in constant motion, the sound of the engine filled her being and for long moments Mere forgot that she was a passenger in a small, strange sea craft. During those moments she felt not the dracaena bag in her hands but the metal of a control stick. With a slight movement of her hands the bow of the boat lifted or dropped. The men did not notice her movements and at times she was not aware of them herself.

Because this boat could travel fast, the journey from Nani lasted no more than half a day. Mere did not open her eyes until the engine stopped and the boat glided quietly and smoothly to a dock. Only then did she realize that she had no idea of her location. She had not come to Nani by water and she had not left the island since her arrival. Mere felt the boat's gentle rocking and listened to the sounds of the men securing the boat to a landing. They spoke to each other softly to respect her sleep. Then for the first time in years, Mere heard a voice unknown to her respond with similar softness. She did not want to open her eyes. She did not want to step off of this boat and leave her last physical connection to the place and the people she had grown to cherish. She listened as the sound of footsteps receded.

"All of these years," she whispered to herself with her eyes still closed, "I yearned for your return to the island. Now I only yearn for my own return."

The men saw her lips moving and understood that soon she would open her eyes and begin her journey. Like her, they, too, dreaded that moment.

Mere knew that if she did not leave the boat soon she would never do so. She would instruct the men to take her home. She would return to Oroiti the tin container hidden for so many years and he would once again put it in a safe place where it would never be found again. The roots and barks and herbs would be stored for future use. She would climb the hill to her home. Kaula would resume her vigil, which seemed pointless beyond reckoning but about which there was no arguing. Mere and Oroiti would once again welcome the day together or separately but always close in body and soul. With every fiber of her being she regretted her decision to leave the island. With every fiber of her being she knew that the journey was necessary because of an arrangement made lifetimes ago.

Finally she opened her eyes and said, "If I do not make this journey I am not myself."

All of the men on the dock turned to her.

Kahil said, "Then the journey must begin."

"Yes," she replied.

She stood stiffly, slung her bag over her shoulder, pulled her cap onto her head, and climbed from the boat to the dock. The men pointed to a larger boat.

Kahil spoke again.

"We have arranged for you to journey on that boat."

"We know the man who owns the boat," Peta further explained. "He is a friend. He will keep our silence."

Mere looked from their island craft to a much larger craft. The difference between the two crafts was almost laughable. The larger craft looked like an actual boat, built for water travel. Mere smiled and squared her shoulders. She turned to her companions.

"Do you think it will float?" she asked. "I don't see any large leaves holding the engine together."

The men looked from their boat to the bigger craft. As one, they smiled.

"Sometimes we must trust the journey," Afi said. "We did not build that boat out of gifts sent to us by the sea. Let us believe the leaves in that engine were placed there by someone as wise as our Star of the Sea."

He smiled and his eyes danced with delight at his joke.

"Indeed," Mere replied.

The second craft, the one waiting for her to board, was at

least three times larger than their makeshift boat. She stared at the craft for several moments before turning to the men. She looked around her. Both boats were tied to what appeared to her to be a deserted dock. She saw no buildings, no other vessels, and no other people.

"I thought you got supplies here," she said to Kahil.

"We do," he replied.

She looked around again before saying, "There's nothing here."

"That is true," said Peta.

Kahil took over the explanation.

"We dock here. Rua, because he is so strong, runs over the mountain to the other side of the island where there are boats and people and supplies. He returns with our friend and his boat."

"And you go back to the other side in the boat, get the supplies and the crate, bring them here, and unload them into the Pratt & Whitney?" Mere asked and informed. "What if your friend isn't there?"

"Then I borrow the boat of yet another friend," said Rua with pride.

Mere stared at the men and felt shame that she had never before wondered how her life for the past forty years had been possible.

Finally she asked, "Why do you go through all of that? Why not simply dock on the other side of the island?"

"This is the desire of Pilapan," Kahil replied. "We were told that no one must ever know of our Star of the Sea. We now must trust our friend with your existence."

"I see. Yes. I had forgotten that our simple lives on Nani are very, very complicated. This is surely the plan of someone who enjoys intrigue. When I return perhaps we can live our lives in a simpler fashion."

"These journeys have become our custom. There is nothing complicated about joy," Kahil said, but Mere had not heard him.

Her gaze was fixed on the larger boat.

"Am I expected on board that?" she asked.

"Yes," Kahil answered her. "Our friend awaits your arrival."

"Then I must arrive."

She embraced each of the men and each man in turn embraced her in the custom of their island. As she approached the larger boat, a man dressed in white walked down a gangplank toward her. He extended his hand.

"Welcome. My name is Hori. I am your friend."

He took her hand and shook it warmly. Hori spoke not the language of her island but a language understood by most who lived among the islands clustered around this largest of those islands considered insignificant by cartographers and merchants. Pilapan had personally taught Mere this language and Mere had grudgingly learned it well. Because this larger island was insignificant, its tiny clusters were invisible to all except their inhabitants. Only a few of those inhabitants ever ventured out into the sea toward larger bodies of land.

Hori did not ask questions as they walked together up the gangplank to the larger boat. Having grown up among the islands, he knew that questions about this woman were not allowed nor were they necessary. She was the Star of the Sea. No additional information was required. When they were on board, Mere turned to see Kahil and the other men sit down on the dock next to their boat.

"They will await your return," the man told her and Mere wondered if any of these men had the slightest idea of her destination.

"They may wait a considerable length of time," she replied.

"Then that is the length of time they shall wait."

She followed him along the deck and into the cabin.

"You have no luggage," he said when they were inside.

"Only this bag," she replied and shifted the woven dracaena fronds from her shoulder to her lap as she sat.

Hori stood in front of her. A silence fell between them. Mere looked away from his face to stare straight ahead.

Eventually Hori cleared his throat and spoke.

"There is an awkwardness here that must be remedied," he said in a formal tone.

She looked up at his face.

"I beg your pardon?" she said in English and, realizing he had not understood, repeated her question in their common language.

"This journey is long. We will travel this day and through the night and into the next day. Provisions and fuel…" he stammered, uncertain of how to continue.

Mere's face turned red. She nodded her head and reached into her bag. She was about to take out her money when she stopped.

"Did you quote a fee to my men?"

"No. They said that you would know best."

Mere felt her blood pound in her head as the old familiar pain returned. She stood and began to move back toward the deck before turning to face him again.

"They were mistaken. I do not know best. I have not traveled for some time. I know very little and what I do know certainly is not best."

"I see," Hori replied and looked as uncertain as Mere felt.

"Perhaps I should just return to the men now and shorten their wait considerably. I can be home by nightfall if we leave now."

She turned to leave the cabin.

"They say that you undertake a journey of honor."

His voice stopped her. She turned again to face him.

"They said that?"

"Yes. Such journeys must be completed. I will accept the fee of your choosing."

"Very well," and she again reached into her bag and pulled

out a single bill. "This is American money. It is one hundred dollars. I have no idea its current value. If we discover that I have underpaid you, I will give you more upon my return."

The man took the bill from her and put it in his pocket. Within minutes the boat had left the dock. Suddenly Mere felt a cold trembling shake her body.

"Excuse me," she said.

Hori turned from the wheel to face her.

"What is our destination, exactly?"

"You don't know?" asked Hori.

"I know I'm going to someplace with an airport. Oroiti gave instructions to the men and I assume they made inquiries of you before I walked onto the boat with you. I have not traveled for many years and never on a course charted by another. I should have asked, I suppose."

The fact that she had no idea to which island they traveled appalled Mere. While many things in her life prior to the island had seemed mandated to her, destinations were never beyond her knowledge or control. All other choices, it seemed, had eventually been taken away from her. But her ability to choose her ultimate destination had never been challenged. Not even a trained navigator dared question her decisions. Not ever.

"You are well cared for, it seems," Hori said.

His words ended her reverie and returned Mere to the boat and the cabin in which she sat.

"That is very true. I would still like to know our destination, if I may."

"We will dock at a small landing between Wau and Popondetta. There is no town. It is a hidden place."

Mere saw charts spread on a table. Lights swung overhead. Someone smoked a cigarette and the smoke seeped into the cells of her brain and caused them to pound against her skull. Her eyes blurred so that she could not clearly see the charts' lines.

"Could you be more specific, please?" she asked Hori.

"Wau and Popondetta are in the Morobe Province of Papua, New Guinea," he replied and she heard no impatience or condescension in his voice.

"I see. And where is the airport?"

"Where we dock has no airport. Neither do Wau or Popondetta. I shall make certain you have transportation from there to the airport."

"You are very kind. Where, then, is the airport?"

"The airport is not one hundred miles away. You will travel there on land. Hopefully the journey will take less than half a day."

Mere's vision cleared and she saw the charts on the table. Men had crowded around the table in this big, unheated airplane hangar. She felt herself grow colder as she traced her memory's finger north along New Guinea's northern coast.

"In what city is the airport?" she asked already knowing the answer.

"The airport is in Lae."

"Lae, New Guinea," she said and her heart stopped beating.

Her finger traced a line south back down the coast. Hori watched as she moved her hand through the air.

"Aren't Wau and Popondetta almost directly across the island from Port Moresby which has a much larger airport?" she asked and saw Hori's face cloud with confusion.

He studied her before he spoke. Under his gaze, she folded her arms across her chest. The bag lay in her lap.

"Do you doubt my navigation?" he asked without rancor. "I know the route well. I have made this journey many times first with my father and now, sadly, without him. You see no charts nearby. Forgive me if that causes you discomfort. I know these seas and the sun's path and the stars better than any chart. Besides, I have a compass and an extra compass, just in case."

Mere looked up from the chart she had seen so clearly on the table in front of her. For a moment she felt disoriented and ashamed. She rubbed her eyes and her forehead before she spoke.

"Forgive me, please. I was trying to recall a map I saw years ago. I have absolute faith in your navigational skills. My memory is what I question."

Hori's expression softened.

"They are north east of Port Moresby and, yes, in distance Lae is further away."

Mere thought a moment.

"I see. Forgive me yet another silly question. I'm only an addled old woman. But why, then, must I go to Lae?"

"There are roads to Lae."

Mere leaned her head against the cabin wall and sighed deeply.

"And none to Port Moresby," she stated because she remembered the answer. "None passable, at least. Probably not even now."

Again Hori studied her.

"You know Lae," he said.

"I was there once," she replied.

"And the memories of that visit trouble you?" he asked.

"Yes. They trouble me."

With those words, Mere closed her eyes and forced her heart to beat again. She hoped the man would think she had fallen asleep and, indeed, he did.

For hours she sat with her eyes closed lost in thought and consumed with battling combinations of terror and dread and excitement and regret. Her face gave no hint of the turmoil within. When food was presented to her, she opened her eyes and ate. When she grew stiff from sitting, she paced the deck. Always she returned to the bench in the cabin to sit with closed eyes yearning for the boat to reach its port and wishing that it could stay at sea forever.

"The galley, the head and small sleeping quarters are below,"

Hori had earlier motioned with his head to narrow stairs. "Feel free anytime."

Mere had felt free but chose to stay in the cabin. She spent a restless night laying on the bench thankful for the pillow Hori placed under her head and for the quilt he spread over her. He rarely left the wheel and never seemed to tire of guiding his boat. Even though his name meant "tiller of the soil," Mere saw that he was truly a man of the sea.

The sun was not half way to its highest point in the sky when Mere, standing in the boat's bow gazing at New Guinea's approaching shore, saw the outline of a dock. At almost that same moment, she felt and heard the boat's engine slow. Minutes later Hori cut the engine completely and the boat drifted to a dilapidated dock. Mere stared at rotted timbers and broken boards.

From behind her, Hori said, "It only looks weak. For my needs, that appearance is necessary."

He jumped from the deck onto the dock to quickly secure the boat. Back on board, he stood next to Mere and with her stared into the rain forest. Sunlight reflected off of the waters and danced through the heavy foliage.

"Where do you go from here?" Mere asked as the weight of silence and waiting pressed into her head.

"I retrace our route."

"You go back home?"

"This boat is my home. I go back."

"And forth?"

"Yes."

Mere smiled. She did not look at Hori.

"You have other cargo besides me on board, don't you?"

"Yes. Soon I shall transfer it."

"And load something else onto the boat?"

"Yes."

Mere turned to face Hori. He looked from the rain forest directly into her eyes.

"We both have our secrets," he said returning his gaze to the trees.

"Indeed," Mere said and followed his gaze because she, too, heard the sound.

Suddenly, as though shot from the forest by a large weapon, a United States Army surplus Willys Jeep skidded through the trees to stop inches before sliding off of the bank into the sea. Its fading camouflage did nothing to hide its presence. The sound heralding the Jeep's arrival combined a missing muffler and a cacophony Mere understood with alarm to be music.

"*Running on empty – Running on - Running blind – Running on – Running into the sun. But I'm running behind. Gotta do what you can just to keep your love alive. Trying not to confuse it with what you do to survive.*"

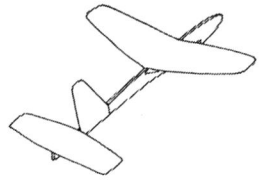

CHAPTER THIRTEEN

The Jeep's engine still running, the driver jumped out as though ejected and began to quickly remove a tarp from the small cargo area in the vehicle's rear. He wore nothing except swim trunks and a baseball cap. Long, interlocked coils of hair stuck out from the cap and hung almost to his waist. The man threw the tarp on the ground and lifted a sealed, metal, cargo box. Mere watched his muscles tense with the weight and counted six other boxes in the back of the Jeep. She turned, entered the boat's cabin, and sat down on the bench.

She heard the muffled words of Hori and the other man. She didn't know if they had deliberately lowered their voices or if the music was simply too loud.

"If it takes all night, that'll be all right if I can get you to smile before I leave. Running on – Running on empty –"

Alone in the boat's cabin, Mere wept.

When she heard them on the deck walking toward her, she wiped her eyes and stood. They brought the smell of sweat with them into the tiny space.

"This man will take you to the airport in Lae. He will do that for the sum of five dollars."

Without hesitation, Mere opened her bag. Hiding its contents from the men's eyes, she found and withdrew a five-dollar bill. She gave it to the man who, without examination, gave it to Hori who put it in his pocket.

"His name," Hori continued, "is Irawaru. Call him Ike."

"Ike," Mere repeated and extended her hand. "I am," and she paused to glance at Hori, "Mary Anderson."

Hori looked from Mere to Ike whose smile revealed a large gap between his front teeth. Ike took Mary's extended hand and enthusiastically pumped it up and down.

"With happiness I meet you," she said in the formal greeting of the cluster of islands left just the day before but already so far away.

Ike, still pumping her hand, stared at Mary Anderson and nodded his head so vigorously that his coiled hair threatened to bruise his bare skin.

"He does not speak our common language," Hori said and Mere withdrew her hand from Ike's exuberance.

"What language does he speak?"

"Only one language do you both share and that is English. Otherwise, he is a most trustworthy person."

Mere smiled.

"Ike, I am pleased to meet you. My name is Mary."

Ike, still nodding his head, replied, "Likewise. We gotta go. I got people waiting."

Hori walked Mere to the Jeep and, even though they both knew she needed no help, guided her into the still running vehicle. He leaned close to her and whispered, "Happy landings."

The tarp once again covered the rear of the Jeep.

Holding her bag tightly to her chest, Mere replied, "You have been most kind to me. I hope to make the return voyage with you soon."

"I will watch for you," he said, then turned and walked to his boat.

As the Jeep lurched into gear and pulled away, Ike reached over the windshield to the cassette tape player strapped with duct tape onto the hood. He turned the music's volume up even louder.

"*Yougotbloodonyouface. Youa bigdisgrace – Waveyour banner alloverthe place.*"

Mere struggled to make out the words. She was not even sure they were in English.

"*We will, we will rock you. We will, we will rock you.*"

Ike turned to Mere and over the engine and the music shouted, "Queen!"

Mere could make no sense out of his statement so she said nothing. Ike did not appear to care. His head bobbed up and down with the beat of the song and his hands added percussion onto the steering wheel. The Jeep careened along a vague path through the rain forest and soon slid and twisted down a hill to emerge on a dirt road, which appeared to be only marginally passable.

"Now we can make some good time," Ike proclaimed over the music.

Mere stared from him to the road ahead. When the music suddenly stopped, Ike braked so hard that the Jeep skidded in a complete circle. Mere grabbed the Jeep's frame and held tightly to the bag in her lap. As the circle slowed, Ike jumped out of the Jeep, turned over the cassette, jumped back behind the wheel, straightened the Jeep, and accelerated back to their previous speed.

"Another two hours," Ike shouted triumphantly.

"To Lae?"

"No. No. No. Of music. I recorded this myself. From records. I got more in back."

Mere stared at him with cold fury, heart stopping terror, and open-mouthed admiration.

"*Slip sliding away. Slip sliding away. You know the nearer your destination, the more you're slip sliding away.*"

"Very impressive," she shouted because she could think of nothing else to say.

Ike nodded in agreement then sang along in a voice even louder than the tape's deafening volume.

"We work our jobs, collect our pay and believe we're gliding down the highway, when in fact we're slip sliding away."

They careened into a village. The Jeep skidded around corners and barely missed dogs and naked children fleeing from its path. The road to Lae would curve sharply through steep jungle mountains. At times it would seem too narrow for even the Jeep let alone the overloaded and overcrowded buses it would meet.

So lost was Ike in his music that he at times seemed to forget he was the one at the wheel. He sang and drummed on the steering wheel or danced in place or shouted or waved at passing vehicles. The island from which she came and the island on which she traveled and the island that was her destination seemed like blurred images and forgotten memories. Only the relentless headache connected Mere to her increasing number of identities.

She thought of her morning ritual on the island and forced herself in her mind to lift the basket of rocks fifty times to her chest and twenty-five times above her head. The Jeep bounced over a rock and her image of seventy-five sit-ups disappeared. She could not reclaim her thoughts sufficiently to chin herself twenty times on the worn branch. The sadness filling her soul was replaced with comforting thoughts of Oroiti's arms around her until a large leaf whipped across her face. She slapped her knees five times and then with clenched fists hit her thighs five times.

"That's right," Ike shouted. "Now you got it."

Mere looked at him blankly before silently saying, "Stop it. Stop it. Stop it. Stop it. Stop it," twenty five times because that was the same as saying those words five times on five different occasions.

Nothing helped.

Finally, unable to tolerate the combination of the radio's volume, Ike's off key, strident voice, and the jarring unfamiliarity of her own language, Mere reached into her bag, took out her leather cap, and pulled it onto her head.

Ike threw back his constantly bobbing head and laughed. Without missing a beat or a word of the song, he reached into the back of the Jeep and, barely making a curve onto the road into the mountains, produced his own leather flying cap which he pulled down on his head over his baseball cap.

"You are a cool lady," he shouted and, giving his passenger another grin, resumed his singing.

He looked forward again just in time to skid and spin but avoid a branch that had fallen completely across the width of the road. When the Jeep finally finished fishtailing and spinning and stopped, Ike threw his arms around Mere.

"Mary Anderson, that was close," he shouted and, laughing, got out of the Jeep to inspect the branch.

His laughter stopped and his expression changed as he studied the tree. He walked to both sides of the road. There was no way around. He returned to the Jeep and shut off the tape deck. Mere closed her eyes and felt the silence calm the throbbing of her head. She did not see Ike's face soften as he looked at her.

"Time to eat," he said.

In the shade of the huge overhanging tree, sitting on the moist ground with their backs resting against the limb, they feasted on mud clam from a mangrove swamp in Milne Bay cooked in fern leaves, Dia made of sago, bananas and coconut cream, a variety of kumu greens, and rice wrapped in newspaper to keep it warm. Mere had not realized how hungry she had become. Like Ike, she ate with her hands and wiped them on her trousers.

"This is delicious. Thank you."

Ike nodded his head.

"I have a wife. Otherwise, my sweet lady, I would propose marriage to you at this very spot. My wife cooks and cares for me. We have a mumu pit at our home. We are very blessed. My daughter is learning to be a wife."

While Ike talked, Mere studied the tree and in particular the place where the branch had once been. There was no jagged torn place where the limb had attached to the tree. Mere quickly looked from the tree to Ike. She studied him for a moment.

"What is the meaning of your name?" she asked.

Ike looked blankly at her.

"Your name," Mere repeated. "Irawaru. What does it mean?"

"Got me," he said and shrugged his shoulders. "What does Mary mean?"

Mere stared blankly at Ike and, feeling a deep sadness, said, "I have absolutely no idea."

Ike's eyes darted to the Jeep, to the road, and to either side of them before he reached into the bag and gave Mere a bottle, then brought one out for himself. He snapped the tops off of both bottles with a tool so small Mere didn't see it. She stared, transfixed.

"Church key," he said, taking three gulps from his bottle and then continued. "Beer on a warm day, a beautiful lady, and a big branch blocking the road. What else could a man want?"

Mere worried that she had actually forgotten the language of her birth. From the moment Ike catapulted into her life she had struggled to understand him and the noises coming from his vehicle.

"I thought it would all come back to me so easily," she said in the language of Nani. "Obviously I was mistaken."

After considering her unintelligible words for no more than an instant, Ike leaned against the branch, closed his eyes, and still holding the bottle of beer, began to snore. Mere felt anxious and ill and uncertain. She yearned for activity. She wanted to leave this place in the road and this branch so clearly sawed off of the tree. She wanted to push the branch out of the road, fling the snoring Ike into the Jeep, and drive to the airport. She wanted to leave Lae as quickly as possible. She took a small swallow of the beer and immediately felt her head spin.

"Well, fool. Forty years without alcohol. What do you expect?" she said and could not immediately name the language of her voice.

To stop the spinning of her head, she too leaned against the log and closed her eyes. When she felt tears begin to streak the dirt on her face, she pulled herself to her feet and walked around the branch.

"Well, there's no doubt about this," she addressed the tree's fallen branch. "Yes. You are large and you do completely block the road."

She walked back to the Jeep. She stared at it as though it were an oracle. Gathering no divination from it, she walked to the edge of the road and vomited her lunch into the bushes. She backed away from the bushes until her back hit the Jeep. She turned as though the Jeep had struck her. She backed away from the Jeep until her back hit a tree just beyond the bushes. She pressed the length of her spine against the trunk of the tree trying to gather strength from its power and majesty. She felt nothing. She turned to the tree and wrapped her arms around it. Only then did she begin to feel its energy. Finally she was able to return to her place on the ground against the branch. A courtesy acquired on Nani dictated that she allow Ike to sleep until he awakened by himself. A brash impatience acquired long before she came to her island dictated that she shake him vigorously. She chose the latter course of action.

Ike jumped to his feet, whirled in circles, pumped his arms up and down and shouted, "What? What? What's the matter?"

Mere said nothing until he stopped spinning and pumping and was quiet.

"I do apologize for startling you. I wonder if you have plans for the rest of the day? You mentioned you have people to meet. I shall gladly help to clear the road."

Sweat beaded Ike's face. In his startled awakening he had thrown off his flying cap. His baseball cap was skewed. He breathed heavily. His expression, when he finally stared at her, was wild-eyed and primitive. Mere wished she had chosen the former course of action. He looked around and patted his pockets.

"It's on the ground over there," Mere said and pointed to his flying cap.

He stared from Mere to the cap and back to Mere. His deep set black eyes seemed to beckon her into them. She felt herself pulling away from him. The right side of his upper lip began to curl. Mere forced herself to stand facing him instead of turning and running into the jungle. When he spoke, his voice was soft and contained neither joy nor song.

"Did you do that to your man?" he asked through bared teeth.

As he spoke he took a step toward her. She did not retreat.

"Did you wake your man when he was sleeping? A woman serves her man. Or don't you know that? Have you been alone for so long you forgot your place?"

By the time he finished speaking he was standing so close to her that each breath he took and each word he spoke brushed her face with spittle and warm air. She stared into his eyes and remembered and reclaimed herself. She did not raise her voice. She did not clench her fists. She felt too angry to feel frightened.

"How dare you speak to me in that tone, in that manner, with those words. Look at me. Look into my eyes."

Ike did as she directed and said, "I was asleep. Now I'm not. Forgive me."

"Did you take this route because you knew the road was blocked?"

Ike's gaze dropped to the ground.

"I cut the branch myself on my way here. It had nothing to do with you. I didn't know you would be with me. Now we have to leave quickly before the others get here. There are some very bad people on this island. They turn on you quicker than a mad echidna, if you know what I mean. Now they will turn on me, too."

Ike's voice startled her. It was urgent and tense. As he finished speaking, he crawled under the Jeep. Mere heard him struggle with something.

"Do you need help?" she asked more to remind him of her presence than to actually assist.

"Piece of cake," Ike shouted from under the Jeep and Mere believed he forced exuberance back into his voice and his spirit.

Moments later he dragged out a metal toolbox and opened it. He quickly withdrew something that appeared to be a chain attached to a small engine. He pulled a rope to start the engine. Mere was transfixed as Ike carried his tool to the branch. She watched in wonder as the chain blades began spinning. She covered her eyes as Ike lowered the spinning chain onto the branch. She heard the tree scream as the saw began to cut into bark and pulp.

It took Ike almost an hour to cut the branch into four pieces. When he finally shut off the saw, silence wrapped around the limb and the tree like a shroud. Ike returned the saw to the toolbox and placed it on top of the tarp in the back of the Jeep. Only then did he look at Mere.

"Just a few more minutes." Tension had returned to his face and his voice. His eyes darted around him.

He began pushing and rolling one section of the branch to the side of the road. Mere went to another section and began to push and roll it. She welcomed the physical activity. Ike stopped to look at her. Once she had maneuvered her section of the limb to the side of the road, Mere looked up at the tree from which the branch had been sawed. It seemed defeated.

She embraced the tree and whispered, "It is possible for wounds to heal," then turned to see Ike roll the last piece of the branch to the side of the road.

"We're done!" he said. "Now let's get away from here."

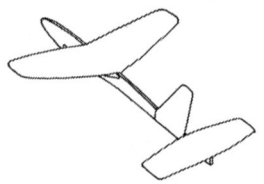

CHAPTER FOURTEEN

As they entered Lae, Ike pulled to the side of the road, got out of the Jeep, and checked the tarp. Satisfied that all was secure, he turned off the tape deck and said, "Can't be too careful."

Mere questioned neither his actions nor his statement. Her head threatened to explode with the pressure of her own secrets and with her return to a world so long ago abandoned.

"This all coming back to you?" Ike shouted.

Realizing he no longer needed to shout, Ike repeated his question in a softer tone.

"Does this look familiar to you?"

Mere shook her head and said, "I've never been here before."

"But Hori said," Ike began then stopped, satisfied with her statement.

Huts and shacks began to dot the sides of the road. Clothes hung from poles in front of some of the homes. Children played in front yards. Traffic on the road became heavier. Honking horns and shouting drivers shattered Mere's thoughts. She wanted to hear everything and she wanted to see everything and at the same time she wished she could see and hear nothing at all. The more she heard and the more she saw, the more overwhelmed she became. She wondered if Ike could see her head spin.

The first time she saw an airplane by the roadside she doubted her vision. The second plane seemed vaguely familiar. She pointed to the third and looked at Ike.

"War stuff," he explained.

"World War II?"

"Yeah. It's still a big deal here," he said and pointed ahead. "That's the War Cemetery. Three thousand people buried there."

The Jeep did not slow and the grave markers blurred in Mere's vision. Moments later they sped past another airplane.

"They just sit there and rot," Ike explained. "Not much of a tribute, if you ask me."

Just as railway towns of the American West grew around train stations, the city of Lae was built around its airstrip. People lived and worked in this central area. Even the railroad tracks delivered freight to warehouses close to the runway and close to the wharf at the end of one runway. Barges carried cargo unloaded from and loaded onto ships anchored beyond Lae's almost useless harbor. Storage sheds lined the train tracks. People rushed and shouted and waved and paid absolutely no attention to the Jeep, its tarp, its driver or its passenger.

The closer they got to the airport the heavier and noisier the traffic became. Shops selling things about which Mere had only read lined the streets. When Ike stopped for a woman carrying an infant on her back and bags in her arms, Mere looked into a store window and saw the small box with its moving pictures. She had read about televisions and imagined something quite different. Music blared from the shops. Mere didn't know whether she should be comforted or terrified when she realized the words to the songs were becoming easier to identify.

"*I want to fly like an eagle to the sea. Fly like an eagle. Let my spirit carry me. I want to fly like an eagle till I'm free.*"

She turned to Ike, smiled, and said, "That makes sense."

"Right on," Ike replied which made no sense to Mere.

When he stopped the Jeep in front of the Air Niugini terminal, Ike turned to face her.

"Where do you go from here?"

Mere stared at the buildings and the automobiles and the people and the terminal and beyond that a runway. Unable to focus on any one thing for more than a fraction of a second, her eyes darted back and forth around her. She gasped as the noise of a jet engine shook the Jeep and stared wide-eyed as the airplane climbed steeply from the runway. She held her breath until it disappeared into the sky, mesmerized by the trail it left behind.

When she could breathe again, she turned to Ike and gasped, "This is not what I expected."

"Maybe you were thinking of Nadzab," he said. "It's new and people say it's beautiful. I don't think so. I like this airport."

"This is not how I remember it. Everything is so changed."

Ike studied Mere for a moment.

"So you have been here before."

She lowered her gaze.

"I flew in years ago. Then I flew away. Now I recognize nothing."

"That happens."

Ike, once so frenetic, seemed content to sit in the Jeep with her. Vehicles barely recognizable to Mere as automobiles drove by them. Smells and sights and sounds and memories hammered her until she felt herself driven into the seat of the Jeep. Finally she pulled herself away from the fabric's safety and turned to face Ike.

"You have been most kind to me," she said.

Ike turned from her gaze.

"Well," he began, "I'm not a kind person. I just like you. You're cool. That's all."

"And I like you," she said.

Still looking away from her, he continued.

"I was going to kill you back at that branch and take all of your money. But I couldn't. Besides Hori would have killed me once he found out. Or at least never given me any more jobs."

Mere stared at him and did not allow her face to show any emotion. Her eyes, though, became black and hardened with rage and had he looked into them he might have fled for his life.

"I thought as much," she said in a voice flat with control. "You were also expecting friends."

Still looking away, Ike said, "They weren't my friends. I blocked the road so they could steal the stuff and give me half when they sold it. When you woke me up I knew I couldn't do that to Hori. He's a good man. I was so angry I wanted to kill you. I couldn't do that, either."

Only then did Ike turn to face her.

"I am not the man I believed myself to be."

Mere studied Ike for a long moment. Her anger was gone. He did not turn from her gaze.

"No. But you are the man I believed you to be," she finally said and stroked his cheek wet with tears.

Ike took her damp hand and held it in his before he kissed it.

Mere searched in her bag until she identified another five-dollar bill, which she placed on Ike's bare leg. She patted his leg to smooth the bill onto his skin. When she removed her hand, they both stared at his leg until he reached down, took the bill, and put it under his seat.

They did not speak as Mere climbed out of the Jeep to face the terminal. She did not look back to see Ike pull onto the street and quickly disappear into traffic.

Mere stood in front of the terminal entrance forcing deep and slow breaths. With each breath she felt the heaviness of her feet diminish. When they finally felt light enough to lift, she walked into the Air Niguini terminal.

There were voices down the corridor. I thought I heard them say – Welcome to the Hotel California.

The soft music filled the terminal's vastness. Mere staggered under the glare of bright lights and wondered if she hadn't already left Lae. For a moment she couldn't see through the light's reflection. She stood motionless until her mind calmed and her vision returned. She looked around her at counters and shops. A man on the far side of the terminal shined shoes. People of all ages and dress sat in rows of brightly colored seats. Suddenly desperate to sit down, she saw an empty chair in a corner of the terminal and walked toward it as quickly as possible. As she walked, Mere noticed, standing near the chair, a completely motionless person. Walking closer, Mere realized that the person was a statue. She fell into the chair forbidding herself to look again at it until she became oriented to her surroundings and time and life became slightly more manageable. Finally, stuffing her flying cap into her bag, Mere stood to face herself, frozen in time.

Except for the fact that her skin was metallic brown, she appeared exactly as she remembered.

"You've held up well," Mere said, then read the plaque at the base of the statue: "Amelia Earhart – July 2, 1937 – Last took to the skies from the Lae Airfield never to be seen again."

Mere stepped back from herself to study the statue more carefully. She circled it and found no fault. When again she stood face to face with herself, she placed a hand on the statue's face. It felt so cold she trembled. She removed her hand and placed it on her own face.

"I am alive," she said to herself.

To her statue she asked, "Did you ever live?"

Her statue did not reply.

Mere stared at her cold hands so young and strong. She held her own hands in front of her face. She studied their lined, age-spotted, skin. She spread her fingers and looked through them past herself to a reflection in the window of a shuttered shop. A white haired woman looking through her spread fingers stared back at her. The statue stood motionless between them. Mere waved at her reflection. Her reflection waved back.

Mere circled herself five times. After the fifth circle she forced herself to walk away.

"Again," she said, "I leave you."

She repeated those words until she stopped in front of an Air Niguini counter.

"I have a ticket on Pan American," she said in English to the man behind the counter. "My name is Mary Anderson. I have an American passport."

He replied in English.

"No Pan American here. You have to go to Port Moresby and then to Sydney for Pan American."

"Fine," Mere said. "In that case I wish to purchase a ticket to Port Moresby."

'That's not possible. There are no more flights to Port Moresby today."

"I see," Mere said and felt failure's weight press down on her shoulders.

"Don't quit now," her voice said from behind her.

Mere turned to see Amelia point a scolding finger.

"What?" Mere shouted.

"There are no more flights today to Port Moresby," the startled man behind the counter said. "They leave only in the morning. In the afternoon they return."

Mere looked from Amelia to the man behind the counter then back to herself. She saw only cold, motionless metal.

"What did you say?" she asked the statue.

The statue did not reply. Mere looked to the shop window. The woman who had waved to her was gone. The pounding in her head sounded like the passing of a freight train. Forcing herself to not leap under the counter to escape the train, Mere turned to the man behind the counter.

"I want to go there today."

"That is not possible, Mrs. Anderson."

Additional Air Niguini staff gathered and each additional person added emphasis to the initial statement that all planes leaving Lae bound for Port Moresby had already left and would not fly there again until the next day. The voices pierced Mere's mind like needles.

She covered her ears with her hands until a man with more ash than cigarette hanging from his mouth said around his chapped and tightly clenched lips, "Go find Malum."

The Air Niguini staff immediately scattered. Finding herself alone, Mere saw an empty chair and sat down. She stared into one of the terminal's bars. Listening to bar noise, she closed her eyes to remember when they walked from the Lae runway to check into the Hotel Cecil. Fred had gone straight to the bar.

"A hotel, Amelia, is only as good as its bar," he had said.

"Perfect," she had thought.

By the time she returned from dinner, he would be too drunk to find his way to bed much less navigate the next leg of their flight.

She had slept well that night. She remembered that the bed had been extraordinarily comfortable. Not as comfortable as this chair but definitely memorable.

Hearing footsteps, she opened her eyes to see a man so overweight she wondered that he could walk. The man who had given the earlier directive walked beside him.

"Mrs. Anderson, this is Malum."

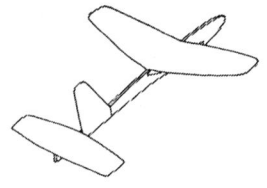

Chapter Fifteen

The movement of his lips sent ash and cinder onto his shoes. He seemed not to notice.

"This is Malum. He will fly you to Port Moresby for fifty American dollars." the man said then turned to walk quickly away from them.

Mere stood to face Malum.

"You're a pilot?" she asked and before he could answer she asked another question.

"Are you going to kill me and take all of my money?"

The man looked confused and said, "I hadn't thought of that."

Mere looked from Malum to her younger self and saw that it was, indeed, a statue. She felt completely alone. She wanted to push her horrid, frozen image onto the floor and break it into pieces. She wanted to roll on the floor with her shattered self and scream. She wanted to go home if only she knew home's location.

Mere, instead, forced herself to speak to Malum.

"Do you understand English?" she asked.

She immediately remembered that they had been speaking English and felt like a fool.

"I don't understand half of what I say," Malum replied.

"I don't understand much of what I say, either," Mere replied and couldn't keep herself from smiling.

"Well, we cleared that up. Good. Now, if you want to go to Port Moresby, we've got to get a move on. I don't fly after dark. I got no instruments. Let's go."

He turned and lumbered toward the door of the terminal. Without turning for a final look at herself, Mere followed him. Together they walked out of the terminal onto the runway.

"Mrs. Anderson is just a little too formal for me. Do you have a first name?"

At first they walked side by side. Then Mere let herself drop behind two steps while she sorted through her response. Her response chosen, she regained her place by his side.

"You should call me Mary. I'm Mary Anderson. I have a United States passport."

They crossed the runway and continued walking past a maintenance shed and then past a hangar. They walked past a graveyard of airplane and automobile parts overgrown with weeds and littered with empty beer cans and oil drums. When they walked around the corner of an abandoned building with faded letters unrecognizable on its unpainted boards, Mere stopped and stared at a row of light airplanes tied down to eye bolts fastened in concrete buried in the dirt. She wondered if she would soon see her own footprints. Malum realized she had stopped walking and turned to her.

"Pretty nice, huh? Mine's the old Luscombe. Needs a paint job but I don't care. Paint doesn't keep an airplane in the air. Come on. We gotta get going."

He motioned her to follow him and he walked the length of the line of planes to the very last. He smiled when he spoke.

"My pride and joy," he said, opened a side door, and motioned for Mere to get in.

Instead of climbing into the cockpit, she looked the plane up and down. She walked to the tail and gently moved the rudder back and forth. She bent down and lifted the elevators up and down. Malum stared at her as she walked to each wing and pulled on the struts. When she felt his eyes on her, she stopped. Her face turned red.

"Go ahead, Mary," he said smiling. "Two pre-flights are better than one. Besides, it's kind of hard for me to bend down lately. I've put a little on. In fact, I don't normally take on passengers. I'm enough for this old thing to carry but they said you probably didn't weigh much and seemed pretty intent on getting to Port Moresby."

He stopped talking and watched Mere complete her walk around the plane.

"Can't be too careful, huh," he finally said when she once again faced him. "What do you think? Will she get us there?"

As he spoke, Malum saw that her eyes were filled with tears. He put a hand on her shoulder.

"It's a good old plane," he said and hoped his words were reassuring.

After he had with great difficulty and many groans climbed to the top of the cockpit to insert a stick into the gas tank to check the fuel and then had somehow gotten himself back on the ground, he clapped his hands, dusted his pants and proclaimed that they were ready to go.

"Let's untie her," he said and unsnapped the ropes from both wings while Mere released the tail.

"How about if you get in while I prop her?"

So it was that Mere climbed into the cockpit of the ancient Luscombe 8A tail dragger. She looked at the instrument panel and saw only an altimeter, tachometer, compass, and artificial horizon. The number of instruments seemed sparse even to her memory. She placed her hands on the stick between her legs. She breathed deeply and smelled the musty interior of the airplane. She looked through the windshield to the cowling and wondered what type of engine it protected. She looked down at the rudder pedals. She looked again at the instrument panel and at the single throttle in the middle of the instrument panel.

As Malum placed his hands on the propeller, Mere shouted from inside the cockpit, "Where are the brakes?"

"Little pedal between both sets of rudder pedals," he shouted back.

She found the little pedal and pushed it down with her left foot, hoping she had chosen correctly.

"It's chocked," he said. "Don't worry too much."

Malum then slowly turned the propeller several times before standing back to shout, "Brakes?"

Mere pushed the pedal harder and shouted, "Brakes."

Malum pushed on the spinner. The plane did not budge backward even a little. Mere smiled and felt a rush of accomplishment.

"Switch on," Malum shouted.

Mere scanned the instrument panel until she found it.

"Switch on," she said first for herself then a second time for Malum.

Malum shouted, "Clear?"

Mere looked around the front of the airplane. She saw the dirt runway to the right of the plane rutted from rains and overgrown with weeds. She knew that this runway ended at the water. She could smell the salt and hear the waves hit the very edge of New Guinea.

Malum shouted "Mary! Clear?" a second time.

Mere returned her attention to the front of the plane and shouted back, "All clear!"

Only then did Malum place his weight into the propeller to easily spin it. The engine immediately started and before he jumped away from the blade's whirling blur, he smiled broadly at Mere and gave her the thumbs up sign. As he got into his side of the cockpit, Malum reached down and pulled the chocks away from the wheel and handed them to Mere. She stowed them in the small cargo space in back of his seat. With Malum in the plane, it seemed almost as if the Luscombe would tip onto its side. Mere fastened her seat belt and pushed as far as she could into her door just to give him enough room to reach forward and take the throttle. As he pushed the throttle toward the instrument panel, the plane heaved and struggled and complained until finally it began to roll forward.

Once it was rolling toward the runway, he turned to Mere and said, "I don't generally have passengers."

"So you said."

As the plane turned at the end of the runway to ready for takeoff Mere shouted, "Do you know the date today?"

"No idea," Malum shouted back at her.

"Good," Mere said and breathed a sigh of relief.

She watched the numbers on the tachometer rise as Malum slowly pushed in the throttle. Finally when it seemed that the old Luscombe trainer would vibrate into pieces, he released the brake and the old plane lumbered forward down the runway. Mere's heart raced as Malum pushed the stick forward. She felt the nose of the plane dip toward the ground as the tail rose. She knew this face into the ground feeling of forcing a tail dragger to pick up enough speed to finally pull the nose up and fly. She saw the edge of the runway rapidly approach. She saw the water beyond and the waves lapping at the runway's edge. As Malum at the last possible moment pulled the stick back toward him, Mere laughed and felt the plane leave the ground and barely clear a low bush growing precariously at the place where water and runway met.

Believing she recognized the still growing after all these years bush, she said to it, "Hello, you stubborn little twisted not quite green refusing to let go shrub," and hoped she had not spoken aloud.

The plane dipped again and water splashed against the cockpit windows as wheels touched waves. Mere closed her eyes because she knew this takeoff. Instead of being heavy with the weight of Malum and his passenger, the plane became heavy with fuel. One big fuel tank was what that Lockheed Electra had become. Those gathered to watch wondered if she would pull free of the lapping waves and gain enough speed and altitude to remain airborne. She, too, wondered then and now she wondered again if the water would claim her at the very edge of this wretched island. For several long seconds the plane struggled against the lure of the water. It rose above the waves only to have its wheels once again brush against them.

As Malum struggled with the throttle and the stick Mere placed her hand on the other stick and, matching her pull against that of Malum, felt the Luscombe tear free of the waves and hesitantly climb toward the sky. When they had climbed no more than two hundred feet, Malum took his hand off his stick and applauded.

"Well done, Mary! Well done," he shouted because shouting was the normal mode of conversation in a Luscombe 8A with its side by side seating for two. "You've flown a Luscombe before, haven't you?"

Mere laughed. "I've never been in one before. How much horse power?"

"Sixty-five big ones."

"Well, that explains our take off," she said smiling and feeling completely happy.

"Hey, this baby can carry five or six hundred pounds. We don't total any more than four hundred, I'd say, unless you've got a lot more in that bag of yours than I think you have."

"There's nothing in it of interest to you," she said as she took out her flying cap and pulled it onto her head.

Malum looked at her and smiled.

"Okay, then, take us on into Port Moresby, sister."

Only then did Mere realize Malum had not only taken his hand off the stick but his feet off the rudder pedals and his other hand off the throttle. The plane's nose began to dip back toward the ocean. She looked at him and, as she snapped the flaps of her cap together, assumed control of the plane. She banked gently and slightly eastward to begin a one hundred eighty degree climbing turn back toward New Guinea's coastal mountains and on to Port Moresby.

They landed in the day's last light. Now it was almost completely dark. Mere felt drained of physical and emotional energy. She gladly relinquished control of the Luscombe back to Malum after they climbed over the mountain and began their descent. The mountains between Lae and Port Moresby invited capricious currents. Mere remembered them well. Now on the ground, she turned to him and smiled.

"Rumor has it," Malum later said in a normal voice when the engine had been shut down at Jackson's Airport in Port Moresby, "that this airport was safer when the Americans and the Japanese were taking turns bombing it in World War II. Wherever you're going from here, you be careful while you're in this airport. You hear me?"

"I shall be on the lookout for all dangers."

She took off her flying cap, stuffed it in her bag, and ran her fingers though her hair damp with sweat. Together she and Malum tied down the Luscombe and put the chocks around the tires.

"You'll be wanting the Air Niguini terminal, I suppose. That's the main one. Straight on down there."

Mere looked from Malum down the row of light airplanes, past buildings becoming increasingly large in size, until she saw a building the size of the biggest hangar she had ever seen. In bright bold letters Air Niguini flashed from dim to bright to dim again. She looked back to Malum and from him to his faded yellow Luscombe and yearned just a moment for a time long before when life seemed to have no limits.

"Where is the Pan American Airways terminal?" she asked.

"I think you have to go to Australia for that. You've got some traveling to do, I suspect."

"I suspect you are correct," she said and pressed two twenty dollar bills and one ten dollar bill into his hand.

Malum opened his hand and looked at the money. He extended his hand with the money back to Mere.

"I was coming here anyway. I should pay you for doing some of the flying. Maybe when you come back we'll fly some more."

He opened his arms and engulfed Mere into him. She leaned her head on his massive shoulders and hugged him as hard as she could. When they separated, Malum took a grease-stained handkerchief from his pocket, blew his nose into it, and waved it toward the terminal.

"You better get on your way, now, before I decide to fly away with you."

They looked at each other for another moment before Mere turned and, her bag thrown over her shoulder, walked away.

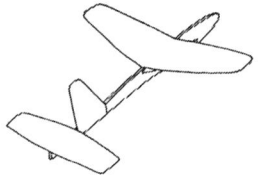

CHAPTER SIXTEEN

When she walked – finally – into the Air Niguini terminal, Mere felt completely throughout her body the lack of food and rest. She collapsed into the first place she saw to sit – a bright red chair in a row of plastic chairs some with abandoned paper cups of coffee beginning to soak through the container, some with unfinished lunches. The cavernous terminal seemed, when she had adjusted her eyes to the bright lights, almost abandoned.

Mere forced herself to calmly take stock of her surroundings – to listen and to observe – and not lose her ability to think and plan. She could understand little of the overhead announcements and couldn't even recognize their language. Signs scattered throughout the cold cavern pictured young, smiling men and women embracing or walking hand in hand on beaches or sitting in what Mere assumed to be automobiles. Black boxes secured to walls puzzled her until she saw a man insert coins, lift a handset and begin talking. She nodded her head in confused recognition. An elderly man pushed something across the floor. In his wake the floor seemed damp and glowing. His machine made a terrible noise. Round objects covered each of his ears. Whatever they were, if they dulled the machine's screaming, Mere yearned for a set of her own. At least the music in this airport terminal didn't speak of distant hotels. "Perhaps Mozart," she thought.

Several televisions hung from the ceiling, suspended by pipe and cables. Mere stared transfixed as soldiers appeared to perform surgery on a wounded colleague. A man wearing a nightgown and a feather boa rushed into the operating room. A broader view showed the soldiers worked out of a tent instead of a hospital building. It was raining. When the man wearing the nightgown stepped out of the tent, he slipped in the mud and fell. He did not appear to be injured. Mere blinked away from these confused images.

A woman holding an infant in her lap sat in a far row of equally cluttered plastic chairs. They both appeared to be sleeping. A teenager – a boy perhaps seventeen years old – paced back and forth near a counter. He wore earphones and held a small box in his left hand. With his right hand he seemed to be keeping a rhythm in the air. His lips moved as though he were speaking to himself. Mere heard nothing and had no idea that he was doing anything except talking to himself. She watched him with a combination of fascination and alarm. She worried that he was under the influence of a spell cast by perhaps a scorned girl friend. She took a mental inventory of the herbs in her bag and rejected each one as having any value for combating such a situation. She considered going to him to obtain more information but was distracted by the baby's cries. Both infant and mother had awakened and seemed at a loss for methods of comforting one another. The mother rocked the baby in her arms. She stood and with the still crying baby on her shoulder began pacing and rocking up and down the aisles between the rows of plastic chairs.

From the corner of her eye Mere saw a woman approach the mother and her crying infant. The woman wore a red cape and carried a forked chief's stick, which beat a rhythm announcing her approach. The woman was short, Mere thought, no more than five feet two inches tall, and heavy – too heavy for good health.

Mere remembered when she had given voice to concerns about weight and health.

"Let's get some exercise," she would suggest.

Each suggestion received a similar response.

"You know, you surely remember, that I was sickly as a child. I was always warned against excessive exertion," came the predictable reply.

"Running on the beach is not excessive exertion. Come on."

Then Mere would perhaps laugh and kiss her on the forehead.

"Well, perhaps a walk on the beach," the other woman might reply. "And you can certainly take your run, if you must. And chin yourself and whatever else it is that you do. Never will I understand why you lift those rocks."

Still laughing, Mere might say, "Because when we are both old women, I will still be able to lift them. My body will expect to lift them. You, on the other hand, will barely be able to lift that typewriter of yours."

And immediately Mere would regret having spoken those words even though this type of discussion always ended with regret.

"I always say stupid things," she said aloud. "I just don't think things out like I should. I just don't think things out like I should."

She repeated the phrase five times pounding her knees with her clenched fists with each repetition. At the end of the repetitions she felt calmed enough to watch the woman in the red cape reach out to the now almost hysterical, screaming infant. The moment the woman's hands touched it, the baby calmed. The mother without question or hesitation relinquished the baby to the woman.

The woman wearing the red cape held the baby in one hand and her forked stick with the other. Within seconds the baby was sleeping peacefully on the woman's shoulder. Turning toward

Mere, the woman smiled that smile seemingly reserved only for children.

Mere stood and started toward the woman.

"It's you," she said and reached out to take the woman to her and feel the softness of her skin on her lips.

"Excuse me," a woman said in a strident, unfamiliar voice.

Mere stopped and felt her arms lower foolishly to her side. She looked at the woman with the sleeping baby on her shoulder. This woman wore no red cape. She held no forked chief's stick. She stood almost as tall as Mere and seemed to be very fit. She did not smile. Mere backed away from the two women and the sleeping infant. She offered no words of explanation or of apology. She had none.

When she had moved a distance away sufficient for safety, she looked around her. She knew that more than anything she wanted to find a way out of this huge cold and completely strange building. She also knew that she would not, could not, escape from this obligation. She stood in the middle of the almost deserted terminal and forced herself to focus until finally she was able to calm herself enough to see a uniformed man standing behind a counter. Holding her woven bag tightly to her chest, she approached him.

"I have a ticket for an airplane called Pan American Airways."

She spoke English and he appeared to understand her words although he did not say anything. They stared at each other until Mere suddenly realized that he was not responding to her because she had given him information but had requested nothing from him. For him to speak would have been the height of bad manners. She felt foolish and reminded herself that on this journey feeling foolish would become a frequent experience.

"Please tell me, if you can be so kind, where I might find the Pan American Airways airplane."

The man responded immediately with courtesy and respect.

"Pan American Airways does not fly out of Port Moresby. You must go to Sydney, Australia, to fly that airline."

"I know. But … forgive me … I am an old woman. I do not know how to get to Australia."

The man smiled.

"We have flights to Australia."

"I see," said Mere. "How much does a ticket cost?"

"One way or round trip?"

Mere paused. She had not considered these choices.

"How much does it cost to purchase a ticket in American dollars?"

"A one way ticket to Sidney is," and he paused to do calculations on a pad of paper, "six hundred forty two dollars and thirty-seven cents. A round trip ticket is one thousand eleven dollars – American dollars. You actually save money when you purchase a round trip ticket."

Mere felt her heart and her knees sink. She backed away from the counter. She approached the counter. She backed away from the counter. Finally she approached the counter and spoke to the man."

"That's a lot of money," she said and backed away from the counter again.

"Yes, it is. For that, I am sorry. Please understand that I do not set the fares," he said when again Mere approached the counter.

"Will you be so kind as to sell me a one way ticket?" she asked and remained at the counter.

Mere began counting money onto the counter. With each bill she placed in front of the uniformed man she felt her return to Nani slip away.

When she had finally counted out the price of the one-way ticket, she asked, "Where is the airplane?"

"You need your ticket."

"Of course," she replied and reminded herself to allow herself to be a fool.

"What is your name?" the uniformed man asked.

Mere reacted as though she had been slapped.

"What?" she shouted and took several quick steps away from the counter.

"What!" she repeated, looking around her as though searching elsewhere for the perpetrator of such an inexcusably outlandish question.

The man waited for her to return to the counter before speaking.

"I need your name for the ticket. Any name will do. However, if you have any type of identification, the name on your ticket should match the name on your identification. It will be easier, that way, for you to leave Australia.

While backing away again, Mere whispered to herself, "Don't count the times you are a fool. Don't count. Don't count."

The man behind the counter maintained his respectful silence. When Mere returned to the counter, she held the passport in her extended hand.

"My eyes have dimmed with my years. I am certain you can find whatever information you need in this."

The man examined the passport.

"So you are going home to New York City, Mrs. Anderson."

Mere stared at him for a moment then repeated his words.

"Home to New York City, Mrs. Anderson."

"Yes," he replied in support of her statement and gave her the ticket and her passport.

"Where do I find this airplane?" she asked, staring at the ticket and making no sense of it.

"Gate three. Tomorrow morning at eight. Be here by seven thirty unless you are checking luggage."

"Tomorrow?"

"Tomorrow morning at eight."

Stunned and saddened and too tired to ask more questions,

she simply moved backwards until her legs touched the seat of a chair and there she sat.

The terminal became cold and Mere tried to remember when she had felt so completely chilled. Her stomach ached from hunger but since she saw no place where she might purchase food, she willed the hunger away. Sometimes she slept but never soundly and never for very long. Once or twice she drank from a water fountain and after each of those visits to the water fountain she forced herself to walk from one end of the terminal to the other and back to her seat. The man who had been behind the counter and who had sold her the ticket had apparently gone home during one of her naps. The counter was dark. One or two people kept vigil with Mere. The adolescent with the headphones, the woman, the baby and the possible grandmother of the baby were not among those wretched souls spending the night in the terminal. Mere located a restroom. Desperate to wash her hands and face and possibly smooth her hair, she could only dumbly stare at a sink with no faucets. She left the restroom and returned to her chair. When she finally saw a woman enter the restroom, she rushed in behind her and waited for her to come out of the toilet stall and wash her hands. After the woman left, Mere approached the sink and, just as the woman had done, she pushed down on the top of a capped pipe. Water came out of what she now saw was a faucet. Just as she put her hands under the flow, the water shut off. Mere looked quickly around her. She was alone. No one would know that she had broken the faucet. She pushed down on the cap again. The flow of water returned. Mere waited until it stopped.

"Well," she said to the faucet, "you are interesting."

During one walk Mere noticed a man eating a sandwich and wished she were either sufficiently rude or sufficiently brave to ask him for part of his food. She was neither so the question remained unasked.

The night wore on with Mere repeating her routine of dozing, using the water fountain, walking the length of the terminal, sitting, running water over her hands, and dozing. Once she lay on the floor and did push ups. Mostly, though, she sat yearning for daybreak and warmth and home.

When the counter opened for a new day, people began coming into the terminal and blessed, glorious heat began to enter her bones. Mere stood and walked on legs weakened by fatigue to the counter.

"Where is the plane? The one to Port Moresby?" she asked the new man behind the ticket counter.

He looked at her and on his face Mere saw courteous confusion.

"This is Port Moresby."

Mere looked around her.

"Yes. I remember now," but began to worry that she no longer remembered. "I have a ticket to Sydney."

Mere's words sounded strange to her and she worried that she was not making any sense. The man, however, seemed to understand and pointed to a nearby doorway.

"Gate three. The plane leaves in one hour."

"I'll board now and wait," and she strode toward the gate.

Security at Air Niguini Terminal has a reputation for inattention to detail. The Port Moresby Airport overall has consistently throughout the years been rated as one of the least safe airports in the world. This safety record does not apply to the planes taking off and landing. Once on board, the safety record becomes much higher. The appalling lack of safety has to do with passengers inside the terminals. People are robbed frequently and regularly. The fact that Mrs. Mary Anderson managed to spend an entire night in the practically deserted Air Niguini terminal and greet the dawn with both her person and her possessions intact was most certainly in large part a reflection of her appearance and her behavior.

Since leaving her island she had spent hours on the makeshift boat she had designed. She had spent one night on the larger boat traveling to a desolate dock somewhere southeast of Lae, New Guinea. She had hung onto the frame of an old Jeep and had cut wood and had flown a Luscombe 8A and now she had spent the night in an Air Niguini terminal.

She had eaten nothing since the food shared with Ike and had retained nothing of that meal. The clothes she wore when she left the island were the clothes she wore in this terminal. Her slacks were streaked with dirt and mud. Her new penny loafers were dusty. She had wiped her hands on her shirt and it had retained more of that jungle lunch than she. Her hair was matted with sweat. In the restroom she had rinsed her face in the basin and believed it to be clean. She was mistaken.

As people entered the terminal and Air Niguini began its usual business day, Mere felt the stares. In this terminal on this day, those stares combined with a growing anxiety and excitement and fear compelled her to announce doubtless louder than the situation warranted, "I'll board now and wait."

As she strode purposefully toward a gate, the famously inattentive Air Niguini Port Moresby Airport Security Department became, without explanation or reason, alert.

"Hey! No you don't!"

Three uniformed security officers blocked her path. For a moment she turned as though to flee then stopped to face the men.

"I have a ticket. I bought it so I can be a passenger. I must get to Pan American Airways in Sydney."

For a moment the men looked from one to the other, at Mere, and back again to each other.

Finally one security officer spoke, "You have to wait for your flight to be announced."

All three security officers then escorted the old, bedraggled woman back to a plastic chair where she sat for a moment in subdued confusion until her excitement and dread and confusion and horror and hunger and fatigue rendered sitting in a plastic chair impossible. Deprived of all the orienting activities that had sustained her for forty years, Mere began muttering to herself in the language of her island. She knew people were staring at her and that knowledge only intensified her need to enact some sort – any sort – of comforting ritual.

    She stood up and took three steps forward, stopped, turned around, took three steps back to the plastic chair, stopped, turned around, sat down, muttered an incantation understood perhaps to her but certainly to no one else, stood up, took three steps forward and the ritual repeated five times, sat down exhausted but calm. The airport security and waiting passengers soon became bored and either left or stared at something more interesting.

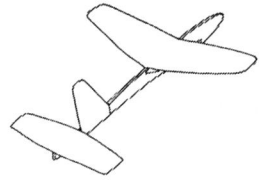

CHAPTER SEVENTEEN

Sitting with her eyes closed, Mere jumped in alarm when she felt a hand on her shoulder.

"Mrs. Anderson," a man in a uniform announced and asked.

Mere looked at him in wild-eyed alarm.

"What?"

"Mrs. Mary Anderson," he repeated. "I can walk you to your plane now."

And with those kind words, the airline clerk helped Mere to her feet and together they walked into the bright Port Moresby, New Guinea, day. Mere blinked her eyes both from the heat rising visibly from the asphalt and from the sight before her.

"What is it?" she asked, stopping to stare.

The clerk, his arm wrapped through hers, stopped, too.

"It's the last of an era, isn't it?"

"I've never seen anything like it. What era? What end?"

"We're phasing out our fleet but there will never be another plane like it. Best airplane ever made," the man beamed as he helped Mere up the moveable stairs and into the old tail dragger DC-3.

Despite her excitement over being in such an airplane as she had never even imagined, the moment she buckled her seatbelt

Mere fell asleep and did not awaken until the descent into Sydney Airport. As she awoke, she noticed bags of peanuts and two cans of apple juice in her lap. She stared at the items with suspicion.

"You slept though snack service so I took the liberty of putting them in your lap. I hope you don't mind," the stewardess said as Mere turned a can around and upside down.

The stewardess took the can from Mere, opened it with the flip top tab, inserted a straw and returned it to Mere's trembling hands.

"There you go. We're descending so you should have your snacks now."

By the time the stewardess was seated and buckled, Mere had finished her peanuts and both cans of juice. After the plane taxied to and stopped at the gate and after all the other passengers left the plane, the stewardess again approached Mere.

"Is this your final destination?"

Mere looked blankly at the stewardess for a moment before answering, "I must find a Pan American Airways airplane."

"That terminal is close by. I can walk you there if you like. I don't have another flight for a few hours. It will be pleasant to go for a walk."

Mere seemed to withdraw into her seat. She tightened her hold on her bag.

"Are you going to kill me and take my money?"

The stewardess laughed.

"No. I'm going to walk you to the Pan Am terminal."

Even Mere's eyes seemed to sink further into the seat.

"I have to find a Pan American Airways airplane," she said.

"I know. Come. Let's go."

And the stewardess took Mere's arm and helped her stand. Together they walked down the boarding stairs, through the Air Niguini terminal, onto the sidewalk, and toward the Pan Am terminal of the Sydney International Airport.

"My name is Amy," the stewardess said.

Amy put her hand on Mere's arm to guide her toward the terminal. Car horns and truck horns honked. The sidewalk seemed to Mere to be overflowing with people. Everyone was rushing and shouting. Amy did not release Mere's arm. Twice Mere stumbled and each time Amy caught her. When they finally entered the relative calm of the Pan Am terminal, Amy guided Mere toward a chair.

"Where are you going, Mrs. Anderson?" Amy asked when Mere was settled with her bag in her lap.

Amy's voice calmed Mere.

"I must find a Pan American Airways airplane," Mere said and her words sounded so familiar she wondered if she had become her own echo.

Amy sat down beside her.

"You've been traveling for a long time, haven't you?"

Mere nodded her head up and down.

"Where are you going?"

Mere struggled to make sense of all that had just been said to her. Amy asked for her destination. Hadn't she already filed her flight plan? Didn't the whole world know her destination? And why did this one person want to know?

"Are you a reporter?" Mere asked, desperately trying to make sense of the situation.

"No. I'm not a reporter. I was the stewardess on your flight from Port Moresby to here. Sydney, Australia."

Mere looked directly into the eyes of the stewardess and said, "I didn't think you were a reporter. There are no photographers. Reporters need photographers."

"They certainly do. Were you hoping for photographers?"

Mere continued to look directly into the eyes of the stewardess and the stewardess, when looking back into the eyes of the old woman, saw them fill with tears. Mere felt the tears spill from her eyes and run down her cheeks. She did not look away from Amy nor did she wipe away her tears.

"No. No reporters. No photographers. I never wanted either. Everyone thought I did but I didn't. I just wanted to fly."

"And where in the world would you like to fly today?"

Mere's eyes left those of the stewardess. She looked around the terminal as though in search of a destination. She saw newsstands and a bar and something called McDonald's out of which people walked carrying bags from which they ate food that looked simultaneously so disgusting Mere thought she would again be ill and so deliciously inviting that she thought she would again weep. In response to those two completely contradictory reactions, she held her stomach and tasted the tears stream down her cheeks and watched them drip on to her clenched fingers which held her bag so tightly her knuckles had turned white.

Amy leaned forward, patted Mere's shoulder, and gave her a tissue, which Mere held in her hand.

Unable to determine the purpose of the tissue even after examining it at length, Mere finally asked, "What is this?"

Amy began to fully appreciate and comprehend that special circumstances surrounded this odorous, disheveled, exhausted, hungry and confused old woman. Determined to help in some way or in every way possible, she finally asked and observed, "You don't travel much, do you? By the way, you can blow your nose on that."

She motioned to the tissue in Mere's hand.

"Thank you," Mere said and folded the tissue and put it in her bag.

"You don't travel much, do you?" Amy repeated in her kindest, most professional manner.

"Not as much as I used to," Mere replied staring towards the McDonald's fast food restaurant. The stewardess followed her gaze.

"I'll get you something to eat. Then you must tell me where you are going so I can get you on your plane and get myself back to mine."

"I don't have a plane anymore."

But Amy didn't hear. She was already walking to the McDonald's.

Mere thought her Big Mac as disgusting as it looked and in spite of her disgust ate the entire burger. She had tried – she had intended – to eat slowly lest she become ill again but she could not restrain herself from taking big bites and eating rapidly. She sipped on her strawberry milkshake only because drinking it quickly gave her terrible headaches. Even as familiar as she was with headaches, the milk shake headaches were spectacular.

"Ice cream headaches are the worst, aren't they?" Amy asked rhetorically while chewing on a French fry. And then, "All finished? Feel better?"

Mere wasn't sure. She suspected she did feel better but didn't think she was finished.

"Now. Where do you want to go?"

"You don't know? I thought everyone knew where I was going."

"Maybe others do know but I don't."

Mere looked at the young stewardess so full of kindness and optimism and did not want to take further advantage of her innocence.

"Do you know who I am?" Mere asked looking directly into the eyes of the young woman.

The stewardess smiled. "Of course I do."

Mere relaxed, relieved at last of the need to hide and pretend.

"You are," the stewardess continued, "Mary Anderson. I saw your ticket when we were in Port Moresby."

Mere looked at Amy and smiled. A visible twinkling returned to her eyes.

"That's where you are mistaken, my young friend. I am not Mary Anderson."

While Amy considered this potential new development,

Mere heard and saw and felt and knew with every part of her being that the short, heavy woman in the red cape had somehow also arrived in Port Moresby. She looked from the face of the stewardess to the sound of the counter rhythms of footsteps and chief stick rapping on the tiled terminal floor. The woman was walking toward Mere urgently – not angrily but urgently. The woman's short hair had turned white and for a moment Mere did not recognize her. Then she stopped directly in front of her. Her expression was stern – not angry but stern. Mere felt again that world famous presence that caused crowds to part as she walked through them. Right in front of Mere the woman stopped and stared down at her.

For a moment Mere expected her to say, "Now I'm taller than you."

Then she would stand to tower over her and they would both laugh and fall into each other's arms.

"What are you thinking? That was never the arrangement. You confide in no one. You know that. Have you any idea what will happen to us both if you say the name on your lips?"

Mere met the gaze of the legendary temper and for a moment said nothing. What she wanted to say, what she had wanted to say so many times, was that she had been the only one to honor the arrangement and the arrangement no longer had meaning. She wanted to scream those words. She wanted to jump up and down in anger and frustration. She wanted to shout that this arrangement had not worked out the way she had imagined.

She wanted to scream, "Where were you all of these years? Oh, yes. You were doing work important for the whole world. You were doing this and that and what was I doing? What was I doing? I was living on the island we planned together. I was home. I was home without you. But I was home."

As her silent rant subsided, Mere looked into those eyes magnified by glasses always slipping out of place. She looked past the flashing anger and into the memories of two young women lying on that roof top of a university dormitory gazing at the stars and claiming each one of them for the other and remembered that more than anything she yearned to please this seemingly simple but immensely difficult woman. She wanted to protect her and, yes, protect herself from all that would befall them should she speak the name on her lips yearning to be spoken.

"Then who are you?" Amy asked with a note of caution in her voice.

Mere turned to look at the stewardess. She sighed before she spoke.

"I am Mrs. Mary Anderson. If I don't announce to the world that I'm married, I'll have to beat off the gentleman callers with a stick."

Mere laughed. Amy, relieved, laughed too.

"You are right about that. You would definitely have too many gentlemen callers."

Amy might have said more. She probably said more. Mere did not hear her. She had turned her attention back to the woman wearing the red cape. She was smiling now. That smile. It had captured her heart so many years ago. It delighted Mere and filled her soul with excitement and hope. For that smile anything was possible.

"I'll get there. Wait for me."

"Excuse me?" Amy asked, confused again.

"What?" Mere asked and looked at the stewardess.

"Who is waiting for you?"

"What?"

Mere looked back at the space so recently occupied by the other woman. She looked at empty space. At silent space. Not even an echo of a chief's staff or of footsteps. Just silence and emptiness. Just emptiness and aloneness. She looked again at Amy.

"Sorry. I didn't hear you," Mere said.

"Is someone waiting for you? Do you want to tell me where you're going so I can get you to your gate?"

"Here," Mere handed Amy her Pan Am ticket dug out of her bag.

Amy stared at the ticket then, as though she held a precious jewel, gave it back to Mere.

"That's open ended. Do you realize what that means?"

"It means I am going to New York City. Again."

"Yes. And they hold a seat for you. On every flight."

Amy, with this new information, became to Mere a confused blur of efficiency. They walked to a Pan Am ticket agent. Amy said something to the agent and then guided Mere down a wide hall. They stopped at a gate where people already waited to board.

"Look, Mrs. Anderson. There's your plane." Amy said as she pointed through a floor to ceiling window to what Mere would have believed to be a winged building on wheels.

Mere stared in horror and wonder at the awkward metal thing that could not possibly be anything capable of defying gravity. The tallest building in the Atchison, Kansas, of her childhood was not as tall as this white structure with the blue stripe on its side. She stepped closer and saw windows in the stripe. She stepped even closer to the terminal window and lifted her head to see the top of the huge tail. Painted on the tail was a blue circle intersected with navigational lines indicating latitude. The letters PAN AM stretched across the middle of the globe. Near the tip of the tail, Mere recognized the United States flag. Some sort of tube connecting the terminal building to the whatever it was hid the cockpit from her view. She hurried around the counter to another window. Amy followed her. Together they stared up at the nose and the hump like raise of the cockpit.

Mere backed away from the apparition saying, "What on earth is that?"

"It's a 747. Lucky you. I've never flown in one."

Amy's voice stopped Mere from backing away from the gate, out of the terminal, and into the streets of Sydney.

"That can't fly," she said. "Can that fly?"

Amy laughed.

"It's the best plane ever made. You'll be fine."

With that she walked Mere to the counter.

"This is Mrs. Mary Anderson," she said to the ticket agent. "You've been waiting for her."

Chapter Eighteen

Mere, with a representative from Pan American Airways on either side, walked cautiously down the long tunnel tube and into the 747 jumbo jet. She stopped in the entrance. More uniformed men and women smiled at her.

"Welcome, Mrs. Anderson," a uniformed woman said.

Mere wondered how the woman knew that name then remembered it was on her ticket. She took another step into the airplane. To her right she saw more rows of seats than she remembered having been in that motion picture theater the afternoon of everyday pleasures they had stolen for themselves.

"What was the name of that movie?" she tried to remember while urging her mind to focus on present concerns instead of on useless memories.

She looked to her left expecting to see the cockpit at the plane's nose. She saw nothing except more rows of seats. She tried to remember what this contraption looked like when viewed from the terminal window. Her mind filled with racing images. She became nauseous and disoriented. What if she weren't on an airplane? If not an airplane, then what had she stepped onto?

She took a step backward out of the plane and into the tunnel and felt the gentle pressure of hands on her arms.

"Is everything okay, Mrs. Anderson?" a uniformed someone said to her from someplace.

Mere's eyes darted about the vast cabin until they finally settled on a woman no longer smiling but still wearing the uniform of Pan American.

"I've made a mistake," Mere managed to whisper.

"Everything looks good to us, Mrs. Anderson," the no-longer-smiling stewardess replied. "What can we do to help you?"

The question confused Mere even further. What could these uniformed strangers do to help her? Her mind raced with possibilities. None of them seemed pertinent to this particular situation.

"Would you like us to help you find your seat?" asked another no-longer-smiling uniformed young man who looked as though his heart would break if he could not be of some service to this strange little old lady.

"My seat?" Mere repeated and tried to fathom the number of seats on this plane without a cockpit.

"Shall we go find your seat?" the stewardess offered.

"No," Mere heard herself say. "This is all wrong."

She backed further into the tunneled tube.

"There's no cockpit. This can't fly. I'm not pretending it can. I have to go home."

The stewardess stepped toward her and again smiled.

"Of course there's a cockpit and this does fly. It's the best and safest plane ever made. Would you like to see the cockpit? Perhaps chat with the pilot? Come. Let's go."

The gathered crew members walked Mere down an aisle, up several stairs into another area full of rows of seats and up several more stairs to stop and motion for Mere to look to her left.

She did look to her left and was neither comforted nor calmed. What she saw was no airplane cockpit. It was a room. A room in this white, metal, winged gargantuan. No. It was the cockpit of an airplane. No. It wasn't the cockpit of an airplane.

Her eyes and her mind couldn't take in the dials and switches. There were too many of them. They surrounded the cockpit windows. They were on the cockpit ceiling. They were on the sides of the cockpit. They were between the seats. How many seats were there? Two? No. Four seats. One seat faced the side of the cockpit. Whoever sat there sat at a small counter and faced more instruments than stars in Nani's night sky. All those cockpit dials were blinking and flashing at her. Mere suspected they were trying to tell her something. She turned from the cockpit to face the smiling, uniformed people.

"What is it?" she asked with obvious alarm.

"Is there a problem, Mrs. Anderson?" a new uniformed man asked.

"This," Mere began but could think of no words with which to ask and demand and plead information and reassurances.

She shook her head in confusion. She clasped her hands, put them to her face, and began rocking back and forth in place. Her bag hung from her neck like a shield.

"This," she tried again and again could speak no further.

"Mrs. Anderson," a tall uniformed man spoke in a calm, confident voice. "My name is Frank Goodwin. I'm the captain of this flight. Why don't you stand next to me and we can chat."

As he spoke, he took her still clasped hands and guided her into the cockpit to stand beside him. It seemed to Mere that his complete attention was on her. He bent close to her face so only she could hear.

"Is this your first time in the air?"

She shook her head rapidly back and forth. Finally she was able to say, "It's been years."

Captain Goodwin smiled. "I'll bet you've seen a lot of changes through the years."

"No," she said. "Not through the years. Right now."

"Well," the captain continued, "I'm happy to answer any questions you have. A little basic information might help. Today we've got 350 confirmed passengers. Our capacity is 366 but we're not full today. To take off we'll need to get to a speed of about 180 miles per hour. We're going to climb to a cruising altitude of 35,000 feet and once we get there maintain a speed of about 555 miles per hour. After takeoff I'll let the controls do most of the work until we begin our descent into Honolulu. I hope that information reassures you, Mrs. Anderson."

Mere also hoped she was reassured. She stared at the captain trying to organize his information. She knew she could not possibly have heard him correctly. An airplane could not hold more people than a motion picture theatre. It could not be this big and go that fast. The captain looked so earnest that she wanted to communicate to him her reassurance even if she lied and even if he lied.

"Have you already done your preflight?" she asked.

"Certainly."

"You've walked around this, this airplane?"

"No. I trust the mechanics to do that."

Mere stared at him.

"You trust mechanics with the preflight?" Her hands tightened around her bag.

"These instruments tell me everything I need to know," he said and gestured toward a panel.

The instruments continued blinking and flashing at Mere. She thought the throttle waved at her.

"What do they tell you, exactly?" she asked.

"All sorts of things. For example, those over there," he said pointing in the general direction of a bank of flashing lights, "keep track of fuel use for each engine. We take off with about 48,000 gallons of fuel. Those over there monitor our weight. We can't go over 735,000 pounds or we can't take off. Over there," he pointed to another blur of instruments, "are navigational tools. We know exactly where we are every second of the flight."

"And, I assume, others know where you are, too."

"Absolutely. Every second of the flight."

Mere looked into the eyes of the captain and wondered if he wondered. After a moment she again looked around her. There was little left to ask. Soon, she knew, the pilot would dismiss her. Her mind raced.

"This has been very helpful," she said finally. "I have only one more question, if I may, Captain Goodwin. How many engines does this airplane require?"

"Excellent question, Mrs. Anderson," he said patiently. "We've got four of the finest engines Pratt & Whitney ever made."

Mere felt the entire airplane vibrate. The noise from the shaking became the roar of engines straining and pulling and tearing from their mounts. She closed her eyes because she dared not see the water hit the airplane's nose. She felt herself fall only to be caught. When she opened her eyes she looked into the concerned faces of the flight crew. Captain Goodwin held her in his arms. She stiffened and forced herself to stand.

"I do apologize," she said. "You've been most kind and I've taken up far too much of your time."

She allowed a stewardess to guide her back down stairs and practically the entire length of the plane to a window seat in the huge cabin.

"We're not full today," the stewardess said as she gave Mere a pillow and a blanket. "You'll have this whole row to yourself. It's almost as good as first class."

Mere stared at a wing bigger, she felt certain, than the entire Electra. The wing's two engines looked nothing like the Pratt & Whitney engines she had known. More proof, she decided, that Captain Frank Goodwin was not telling her the truth. She listened carefully to the safety instructions and disregarded each one. She knew a seat cushion could be of no use if an airplane went down in the ocean. A Mae West wouldn't help, either.

"Ours only got in the way," she whispered to herself. "Of course, they'd only been around for about a year then. Nevertheless, these don't look so different."

Mere looked up the rows of seats. Every passenger seemed to pay careful attention to the safety demonstrations. A stewardess was actually demonstrating proper use of the Mae West. How could she, Mere wondered, be the only one aware of their danger? How could everyone else be completely oblivious?

Her heart beat so rapidly she expected it to rip from her chest. Her stomach formed a tight knot around the hamburger eaten such a short time before. The milkshake froze into a solid chunk of ice near the knotted hamburger. Her occasional breaths were shallow. Every muscle in her body tightened. She felt herself ready to either kick out the glass and crawl out the tiny window next to her or push aside the incoming passengers and run as fast as she could out of this airless metal box across the water to home. Knowing neither of those possibilities possible, Mere prepared herself for death.

As the plane was pushed backwards away from the terminal, she recognized Captain Goodwin's voice echo in the cabin.

"We're going to taxi to our takeoff position. Flight crew, please buckle up now."

Mere yearned for a harness. The seat belt seemed so superficial. Nevertheless, she tightened it, reached into her bag, pulled her flying cap onto her head and waited for fate to play its hand as the plane slowly taxied into position.

Finally the plane stopped its slow forward motion. She gripped both armrests as it began to shake in place. The noise of the engines began as four separate whines then built into a single, unified roar. When it seemed the plane could tolerate no more stress, it shot forward. As Mere's head snapped backward then forward she felt horrific pain and feared her neck was broken. The plane gained speed. Every pebble on the runway felt like a boulder. The buildings along the runway disappeared. Trees blurred. The noise was deafening. It filled the cabin. A baby screamed. Mere felt pushed back into her seat by a terrifying, invisible force. There could not possibly be much more runway left and still the ground held them hostage.

"The Petrified Forest!" Mere wanted to shout.

She laughed because in her last moments alive she had been able to remember the movie they had seen. Then silence filled the cabin. Mere watched the runway grow tiny beneath her and felt her head realign itself on her spine. She released the breath she had held since first the plane began to move and felt suddenly giddy as though she were floating.

"All this evening I've had a feeling of destiny closing in," Leslie Howard had said to Bette Davis.

With a voice so soft it was barely a whisper, Mere had said to her, "No one can see. Hold my hand."

In that darkened theater she not only held her hand, she sunk down in her seat to lay her head on her shoulder as Humphrey Bogart's Duke Mantee curled his lip in villainous disdain.

Having survived the takeoff and the climb to their unbelievable cruising altitude, Mere ate a meal presented on a tray and wrapped tightly in aluminum foil and still hot and wiped the tray clean with her bread and ate her bread and drank her juice and marveled at the passage of time and technology.

Flight attendants regularly checked on her well being. When she accepted the offer of a magazine, she stared at the cover into the eyes of a handsome young man with dark hair. 'Time' she recognized as the name of the magazine. The words 'Mr. Hollywood' confused her. The name Warren Beatty meant nothing to her. Her eyes shot to the small inscription almost resting on the large 'T' of Time – July 3, 1978.

"Excuse me," Mere signaled to the stewardess. "What is today's date?"

"Today is July the second."

Mere rolled the magazine into a tube and gripped it until her fingers hurt. The stewardess turned to walk away.

"Wait," Mere said, slapping the rolled magazine against her thigh. "Will we by any chance fly over New Guinea?"

"Absolutely."

"When?"
"I don't know exactly."
"Please ask the captain."

The stewardess called from the rear galley phone then returned and said, "It'll just be a couple of minutes. He says you're on the right side of the cabin. If you look down you might see it."

The stewardess leaned over Mere and both women peered out of the window.

"Will we refuel in New Guinea?"

"Heavens, no. We won't need fuel until Hawaii and then not again until Oakland. Then we go straight on to John F. Kennedy Airport in New York City. How about that, huh? We don't even change planes."

After a moment the stewardess straightened.

"I can never make out anything down there. All of those islands are just tiny spots on the water to me."

"Not all of them," Mere whispered as the stewardess returned to the galley.

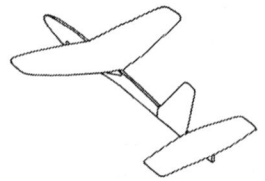

Chapter Nineteen

Mere saw the rugged mountains of New Guinea. She recognized the northern coast where strong surf and angry waves threatened to pull the Lae runway into the sea. This route pulsed in every fiber of her body. She knew the exact location of a mile long stretch of land that dared to call itself an island. She also knew the exact location of the other island known to only a few and felt her heart ache for that place, its people, and her home. She knew the sky and the water between Hawaii and Oakland and the location of and approach to every dirt strip between Oakland and New York. She had never heard of John F. Kennedy Airport but if she could find her way from there to Idlewild Airport she could find her way into New York City.

"Hang on," she whispered. "Don't let go until I come."

Having pulled free once again from the grip of the New Guinea sea and feeling only slightly ill from whatever strange food she had eaten, Mere pulled the Pan Am blanket around her and fell immediately asleep. In her sleep they laughed together. They danced together. They were free, daring, willing to make promises and do outlandish things just to please the other. In her sleep they lay together. They loved together. They yearned for the privacy neither could have and both believed they wanted. In her sleep the stolen times spent together no longer sustained. They each knew they could never have the life together they wanted if they continued to live in the harsh glare of the lights of public life. In her sleep they planned and dreamed and finally dared.

"I'll go first," she had said in her practical way of looking over her glasses to make a point about which there could be no argument. "I go so regularly no one will suspect. Only this time I shall go further away with fewer people. When you arrive everything will be ready."

"You will wait for me?" Mere had said then and now asleep aboard the jumbo jet.

"Why else would I be doing this? Of course I will wait for you."

"And then? How will we explain?"

"We won't explain. People disappear. Oceans are big and mysterious. Things happen. Trust me."

"I do trust you."

"Good."

And in her sleep she slept with her.

Somewhere south of Hawaii the jumbo jet encountered turbulence, which entered Mere's sleep. She felt the rapid descent and saw the water approach. She had circled the island all the while calling in distress signals so scrambled the origin was impossible to determine. To land an airplane not equipped for water in the shallow surf was nothing more than a planned crash. Mere knew this and believed she was pilot enough to bring the plane in and get them both out of it before they drowned. The rest was up to everyone else. Pull the plane onto the beach and get it into the pit and out of sight. Not that anyone would come looking this far off course, but one never knew. Caution cost little. Disconnecting the trailing radio antenna and changing frequencies had surely purchased enough time to burn fuel. Now the tank was almost empty and there was no more circling the island. This was the moment. Still drunk from his night at the bar in the Hotel Cecil, Fred had passed out and couldn't argue with her. Amazing thing about drunks, Mere had thought at the time. They can never really stop being drunks. Just like her father. Even when they try and give it their best, it never takes much of a push for them to fall off of the wagon. Fred had fallen and hit hard. Not that he was in the dark about the whole thing. Oh, no, he knew all about it. Thought it was a great idea. Be the king of a tropical island. It just helped that he never refused an offered drink. She had no time to answer questions or to argue. Sometimes, just like her father, old Fred liked to argue. Better he slept.

Another patch of turbulence and Mere knew her approach speed was too great. Slow it down by pulling the nose up and then risk stalling if the speed drops too much too fast. Who could have guessed there would be this much turbulence this close to the shore? More power for more control with the nose up might help. Lucky thing she had burned up fuel because this airplane had been nothing but a flying gas tank. No happy endings if she blew up the island.

"Come on. Think."

She said those words aloud as the Pan Am jumbo jet's wheels touched Hawaii but no one heard her or if they did hear they ignored her. Except for the islanders. They must have heard her. She could see their horrified expressions. And where are you? Yes! There you are! Running toward the shore. Actually running. You will be exhausted for days and then you will write in your journal about how you ran but without purpose because no one must ever know that this thing is happening.

The Lockheed hit the sand, water, and surf more smoothly than she had hoped. Almost a perfect landing if tearing off the wheels on initial impact and spinning around several times because a wing got caught in the sand can be called perfect. But perfect it was until the spinning stopped and somehow the door flew open and water started rushing in all before she saw the boulder in front of her and slammed into it with more speed than she thought she had maintained. Later she would remember feeling certain, seconds before the impact, that they had come to a complete stop. Clearly they had not.

In the middle of it all she thought, "So this is what a crash feels like," and then decided to never under any circumstances call this a crash because she was about to walk away from it and that is called in any pilot's book a good enough landing.

She would not walk away from this unbelievably successful landing, though, before calling out to him, "Wake up. Get out."

No sound. Nothing. She climbed toward the back of the fuselage over the fuel tanks and pipes to unbuckle him and try to pull him toward the door. The fuselage was filling with water.

She shouted his name again and again. She slapped his face. She shook his chest. She pulled on his shoulders. She couldn't budge him. She knew she couldn't and yet she kept trying. Water blurred her vision. Still she would not stop pulling on him and pushing metal and floating debris away from her. When the plane shuddered she felt it begin to slide deeper into the sea. Through its only window she saw her on the shore wringing her hands.

"I will lose you because I cannot stop trying to save this man," she shouted and her mouth filled with the salt water of sea and tears.

Then at that last moment of the Lockheed's clinging to the island's edge, naked men rushed into the cabin and back through the debris to push her out of their way and cut him from straps and cushions and life vests to carry them both out of the sinking plane onto the shore. She almost but didn't quite see other men wrap vines around the plane and pull it toward the hole where it quickly disappeared – all of it including those loose pieces that threatened but never quite managed to wash out to sea and betray this now almost completely and successfully executed madcap plan.

Within seconds, it would later seem when she could replay the scene in her mind, the island bore no evidence that anything larger than a bird had ever landed on its shores since it blew out of the waters eons before during some alarming but oh so gratifying geological phenomenon. Even the sand was raked smooth before the next wave kissed the shore.

No. She saw none of that. She saw only the face of the woman who had prepared and waited for her.

On the beach she lay in her lap breathing her scent while she stroked her face and removed the leather flying cap and ran her fingers through her sweat soaked hair and said, "I love you."

"I love you, too," was the only reply possible.

Only then did she entertain the notion that her landing had not been perfect after all.

Mere barely knew when the jet left Hawaii to assume another route she knew well. For one disorienting moment she thought she saw a movie playing on a screen far away from her down the cabin's long aisle but quickly returned to more pressing matters on Nani when she saw the monster Frankenstein wearing a tuxedo and tap dancing.

He never became king of a South Pacific paradise. The islanders buried him on the hill with their ancestors. Even though he had sustained no visible injuries, he died.

"Sometimes that happens," a young man named Ariki had remarked.

Mere agreed that sometimes people did die without rhyme or reason. Often, though, she had wondered if a combination of too much alcohol, too frail a heart, too rough a landing, too hard a collision into a rock, and generally speaking way too much of an adventure had not at least in some way contributed to his death. Throughout the years she continued to wonder and had regularly visited his grave to ask, to beg, to implore, to demand his forgiveness. He never gave it and she never stopped wondering. At times in the middle of the night or in the middle of turbulence while strapped into a seat on a jumbo jet carrying her to yet another adventure she both wondered and regretted.

They buried him and gradually exhumed parts of the plane

including the one salvageable engine. Other parts were eventually hidden throughout the island piece by very small piece. The islanders never asked why this thing from the sky had fallen into their lives. They welcomed the Star of the Sea and made her their own at first for no other reason than their beloved Pilapan wished it.

The two women were at last together in the hut on the hill. Mere had her banjo and books and a model airplane to remind her of flights yet to come if only in her imagination. They lay at night remembering times when they wanted nothing more on earth than to lie at night remembering times before this time when such times were forbidden. Now those times so yearned for were theirs and in them they gloried. The islanders rejoiced to see such happiness. Days and nights melted into weeks and months marked only by the calendar hung with her usual precision on the wall. Months became one year. Always during their time together she left the island in some sort of boat that to Mere seemed unlikely to stay afloat long enough to sink. She had to leave she said because the world watched her and she had to be places and write about those places even though Mere had understood the agreement differently.

"I thought we were both going to disappear," she once said and received no answer beyond a puzzled smile.

Finally Pilapan left and did not return for so long that even the years blurred into misery until the misery became not a stranger but a routine within many routines that allowed Mere to call the island her home, not their home, and her hut her own. Then, of course, always the old year was bade farewell and the new year greeted by the gifts for all and for her because they had, years before they even dared to imagine an island, claimed that time as their own. Then, of course, she returned again and again but never often enough and never for long enough. None of that was their agreement. This, however, this return to all Mere hated, was part of their agreement.

"When you need me I will come," they had sworn to each other that night on the beach when they had danced and sung 'Pennies From Heaven' softly each into the ear of the other because by their love they were both rich beyond imagination.

That and much more they had sworn to each other. They swore to each other and formulated an agreement sealed, they giggled, with a kiss. Mere honored the agreement even when the turbulence threatened to throw her from her seat and rip this 747 thing into tiny pieces and cast the pieces into the heavens to perhaps be on some dark night mistaken for stars.

When the jumbo jet made its approach into Oakland Mere imagined a time forty years prior when she might have made a similar approach clearing the Golden Gate Bridge perhaps tipping a wing for the crowds gathered to see just this landing. That wing-tipping, crowd-pleasing, world-exhilarating landing never happened in Oakland or any place else, though.

The plane did land, in a manner of speaking, on an island, in the surf, with water filling the cabin-fuselage special-made gas-tank space slamming into the boulder end of story witnessed by only a few who never spoke of it to anyone not even now when the jumbo jet slid onto the tarmac of the Oakland Airport. If she hadn't been staring out the window monitoring and comparing, Mere would never have realized the plane was no longer airborne.

"Smooth," she heard someone else say and while she did not comment she did not disagree.

Even though other passengers going on through to New York chose to exit the plane and wander the terminal for the time it took to refuel and board new passengers, Mere remained in her seat pinned into it by indecision and unfamiliarity and, yes, by fatigue and also by an increasing awareness of the fact that she had not bathed or changed clothes for quite some time. Under those circumstances, her seat seemed to be the best place for her.

So she slept and once again only vaguely felt the plane again become airborne. She ate the meals provided and drank the juices and the waters and the sodas. She slept some more. She ate more of whatever foods and drinks were put before her. She looked at her fellow travelers. Their dress and behavior seemed different from hers but she could not fathom in what ways. Finally, long before the captain announced it, the jet began its descent into the bright crystal clear sky above New York City. That the captain delayed his announcement was one more proof to Mere that things were not as she was told.

"You can't fool the seat of my pants," she said and no longer cared if others heard.

When Mere looked out the window and saw the skyline, she gasped and asked the heavens, "What on earth?"

The stewardess, who had barely taken her eyes off of this strange and inexplicably special passenger, heard her question and sat down beside her to gaze with her in wonder.

"Isn't that the most amazing thing you've ever seen?"

"I've never ... everything has changed ... so tall ... how on earth..."

"It's the World Trade Center. Just finished last year. We call them the Twin Towers. Tallest buildings in the world."

"Taller than the Empire State Building?"

"Way taller."

Then the jet banked and Mere could no longer see the skyline of the city she once knew so well. Even though she knew – really knew and accepted with gratitude—that there would be no ticker tape parades after this landing, a part of her yearned to not be a stranger in this strange place.

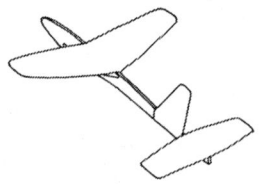

CHAPTER TWENTY

As she walked down the aisle toward her exit, Mere thanked the flight attendants for their assistance and their courtesy. They smiled and assured her that she had not been a problem. Mere, wearing her flying cap, did not ask for explanation but with head held high and bag clutched tightly to her chest strode into the crowded chaos of John F. Kennedy International Airport.

She stood near the gate for a long moment attempting to get her bearings then finally decided that there were no bearings to be obtained. People rushed by her dragging luggage and children. They all seemed to know their exact destination. Mere's eyes followed them toward a sign marked 'Baggage' but since she had only her woven bag she felt no need to follow that particular crowd. Her need was to get herself to Idlewild Airport and then to Manhattan. The entire terminal, Mere realized, was decorated with American flags. A man walking on stilts, dressed in red, white, and blue, and wearing a top hat walked by her.

"Happy fourth," he said and extended a miniature American flag on a tiny pole to her.

She automatically took it. The man released the flag but continued to hold out his hand. She stared at his palm as though about to interpret its lines. He wiggled his fingers and extended his hand further. She looked from the outstretched hand to the man's face. Their eyes locked for a moment before the man snatched the flag from her.

"Bitch," he said as he turned from her.

Mere watched the man offer the flag to several more people. Each person declined with a shake of the head. Finally a mother wrestling two distraught toddlers accepted the flag. Mere watched while the woman produced coins from her purse and dropped them into the man's hand. The man produced a second flag from his coat and gave it to the woman. Both children laughed and waved their flags as they climbed into their stroller built for two. The man turned, saw Mere, and raised the middle finger of his left hand to her. He quickly disappeared into the constantly moving stream of human chaos that filled the terminal.

"Excuse me," Mere said to someone in uniform.

The uniformed either did not hear or ignored her and kept walking purposefully in a direction not guided by the word 'Baggage'. The smells of Dunkin Donuts and hot dogs and coffee assailed her and she felt grateful for the meals and snacks she had eaten on the plane even though this new food left her feeling more than a little ill.

"Excuse me," she said to another person in uniform and that person at least slowed his pace. "How do I get to Idlewild Airport from here?"

"You don't," he said moving quickly away from her.

"I don't?" Mere shouted after him.

She quickened her pace to catch up and when she did grabbed the person's arm. He pulled free and rushed away.

"What's the problem," a policeman asked as he approached Mere. "Did that guy hurt you?"

She stared at the officer and shook her head.

"No. He confused me. He said that I couldn't get to Idlewild Airport from here."

"That's because this is Idlewild. Don't you remember that they changed the name after JFK got killed?"

Mere did not remember because she had never known.

"Oh. Of course," she said to the officer. "Thank you for reminding me. Apparently traveling is more challenging than I thought."

"Well, you sit awhile and if you need more help just call me. I'm around."

The officer left and Mere sat trying to make sense of the madness around her until she began to wonder if perhaps she had gone a little mad herself. A television screen hung from the ceiling nearby. Mere stared at it. The voice was one she believed she had heard years before in another life. She stood to stand closer to the television.

"Burns and Allen," she said aloud and was startled when a woman she didn't know was standing next to her spoke.

"Weren't they great?" the woman stated more than asked. "This is a wonderful movie. My grandson loves it."

Despite the fact that Mere's mind screamed, "You have no time for this!" she found herself asking the woman, "Is Gracie in this motion picture?"

The woman, assessing Mere from head to toe, allowed a long moment to pass before she responded.

"Dear, Gracie has been dead for years. Only George is in this movie. He's God."

She spoke to Mere as though she were speaking to someone just declared a threat to public health. By the time she stated the deity status of George Burns, she had backed so far away Mere only thought she heard her declare him to be God and reminded herself she had been too long without rest and exercise. Wanting to quickly address the situation, she moved to the wall, took off her flying cap, put the cap in her bag, put the bag on the floor, dropped to the floor and began doing push ups. Unable to do her entire exercise routine, Mere forced herself to do three more push ups than her normal number then allowed herself to roll onto her back to breathe heavily, surprised at how exhausted she felt. When finally she stood, she considered lifting a trash can above her head several times then decided, when she saw the policeman's concerned look, to simply reclaim her seat. Noise and motion and smell assaulted her. Despite her best efforts, she could maintain neither visual nor auditory tracking. The noise became a hammering sensation. All she saw was a blur swirling around her with increasing speed. Her head separated from her body. Just in time she caught it and stowed it in her bag. She clutched her bag tightly to her chest and did not notice the passage of time nor did she notice the officer again approach her.

"You okay?" he asked.

From inside her bag, Mere looked around to see about whose welfare he might be inquiring. She saw no one except herself. She placed her head back on her shoulders.

"I'm fine. Thank you so much for asking."

He stepped away from her as though to more accurately appraise the situation. His face was a face that could only be found in New York City. He had been a member of New York's finest his entire adult life. He was thirty-seven months from retirement and was certain he had seen everything and heard everything. A thin, dirty, smelly, wild-eyed old woman dropping to the floor to do push ups and then sitting with some sort of woven bag to her chest as though it held her heart all the while claiming to be fine was definitely not telling the truth.

"If you're fine, I'm Mickey Mantle. What can I do for you?"

Mere blinked her eyes and tried to meet his gaze but couldn't because there was so much to see and so much to guard against.

"You waiting for someone or what?"

Her mind raced with possible responses and finally settled on, "I'm here to visit a sick friend."

"Right here in this terminal?" the officer asked and sat down beside her. "I don't think so. So where you headed?"

"New York City."

"Yeah. I get that. You got here. Now where to?"

This exchange seemed to Mere to be so rapid fire she could barely follow the questions much less formulate responses. She did her best under the circumstances.

"I don't know where she lives."

"She's sick. She in a hospital?"

"I don't know," Mere said and realized for the first time that she really didn't know. "I haven't heard from her for awhile. She told me she was ill. Seriously ill."

"And you don't know where she lives and you don't know if she's in a hospital. She still alive? That would be an important thing to know."

Tears filled Mere's eyes and the officer's face softened.

"Sorry. Look, what do you know about her?"

"I know where she works."

"Great. Where's that?"

"I don't recall the exact address."

Mere stopped. Her mind raced through questions such as, "How much can I tell him? What if I say too much? What if I destroy everything? What if you are dead? What if I betray you? What if ... what if ... what ... what ... if ... if..."

She ended the questions by blurting out, "It's at Seventy-seventh and Central Park West. That's the place. I remember very well. I don't think I shall ever forget."

"Okay. That's good. She works near the museum. Okay. Now we're cookin'. You know how to get there? You got money for a cab? Nah. Even if you do, you don't want to waste it that way. Here."

He reached into his pocket, pulled out what appeared to be a coin, and pressed it into her hand.

"Use that subway token. I got more. Now, I'll get you pointed in the right direction. Here's what you do."

He stood and guided Mere to a window. As he pointed and explained directions, Mere nodded her head vigorously retaining not one word of instruction. When at last he finished, he looked at her dazed expression then shook his head.

"Never mind. My shift is over. I'll drive you to the train. But after that you gotta remember to do exactly what I tell you."

So it was that Mere found herself sitting on the Eighth Avenue Express headed toward Manhattan. She sat and she repeated and repeated endlessly to herself the officer's instructions to get on that specific train and if she forgot its name to just remember that the signs for that train were dark blue.

"Dark blue. Dark blue. Express. Blue. Express. Express. Blue. Dark Blue. Dark express. Express dark. Blue Express. Express. Express. Eight. Eight. Eight. Blue. Blue eight." Over and over she said the words even though she was already on the train.

She also said, "Get off at Seventy-second Street. Get off. Get off. Seventy-second Street. Eight. Blue. Express Street. Seventy-second eight."

The words became a circular continuous amalgam that soon became meaningless even to her. She wondered if it was her vision or her mind that blurred. Almost every stop made by the train was preceded by some sort of garbled, unintelligible announcement which she suspected had something to do with the name of the stop. Since she could make no sense of those announcements she tried to read the names of the stops but frequently she could not locate even part of a name. So she sat as the train became increasingly crowded. She remembered or she thought she remembered seeing words such as Norwood and Cleveland and Rockaway and Fulton. The train stopped at each of those words, she believed, and at the time it stopped she looked through the growing crowd to make out letters. The train passed by the words Park, Canal and Spring with no stops. When the doors closed at Fourth Street, Mere stood to look at a map across the car from her.

"I am good at maps," she announced much louder than she had intended and she had not intended to announce anything at all.

Looking around, she realized no one had heard her or if anyone had heard her no one paid her any attention. She also noticed when she looked around that she had lost her seat to a young woman who chewed gum and appeared to be listening to something on earphones banded over her head. The doors opened and closed at Fourteenth and Thirty-fourth Streets but Mere had failed because of the crush of people to read the names of the stops. Unable to contain her anxiety, she pushed her way to the doors and when the train stopped at Times Square she leaned out to read the sign. When she did so she was caught in the crowd leaving the train and swept quite literally onto the platform. Completely confused and disoriented, she followed the crowd up the stairs until she remembered that she had not wanted to exit the train but only determine her location.

She circled a pillar five times to calm herself, then looked around her all the while repeating what she believed to be the instructions given to her by the policeman but which were actually by that time complete gibberish which to passers by sounded something like, "Bark Dark. Ex-ue. Blue. Blue. Five. Six. Seven. Eight. Dark. Sperk. Berk. Exfast no slow. Blark. Get off. Get off. Seven. Seven. Seven. Smark. Fast. The fast one. Not to die. No never. Love you too much. Express love. Blue. Blue. Blue," but which to Mere sounded just like, "Look over there. It's the blue line."

She walked to the Eighth Avenue Local lettered in a blue somewhat lighter in color than the Eighth Avenue Express and boarded the first available train which, in theory would have gotten her eventually to her desired destination had she remembered to exit at Seventy-second Street and had she then known to walk east to Central Park West and then north. Neither that memory nor that knowledge, however, was necessary at that particular time because she had boarded the Eighth Avenue Local going away from Manhattan to Brooklyn. Even getting on the wrong train took an effort of pushing and shoving and squeezing in at the last minute. Once aboard, a direct path seemed to open for her to take a seat offered by a large, black woman.

"Get out of the way," said the woman to everyone whether or not they wanted to hear. "Don't you see that she's old? You show respect to old folks you more apt to get respect when you old."

The woman then did some more pushing and shoving of her own until she could reach out, take Mere's arm, and pull her through the remaining crowd to the seat into which Mere, completely confused, sank. Her darting eyes immediately sought out locations. She saw Christopher Street and she saw Chambers Street and when she saw Wall Street she could practically feel the ticker tape floating down onto her like gentle snow in an adoring blizzard. She could hear the crowd chant her name again and again and again except it was not the name by which she had been known for the past forty years. It was another name she had not heard spoken aloud in public not once since that less than perfect but certainly passable island landing.

When she saw Atlantic and Franklin and Winthrop and Church and Beverly the sudden suspicion that she was not going uptown after all began to seize her. Then Beverly and then Newkirk and then the train stopped at Flatbush and did not move again. The car emptied.

Mere sat until the engineer said, "End of the line. You gotta get off."

She stepped off of the train and followed the exit signs through the turnstile. As she walked onto the sidewalk, she realized that she had made a terrible mistake. She had used her only subway token and could not re-enter the train tunnel. A nagging in the back of her mind asked why she didn't take a taxi into the city.

"You've got money," the nagging nagged. "Raise your hand and get into a cab. Good grief! How difficult could that be?"

Mere never in her life had responded to nagging in anything resembling a positive manner. She chose to ignore the nag. She regretted her mistake in the subway. She also regretted her inability to listen to the nag she knew to be wise and correct.

"Stupid. Stupid. Stupid." she said and turned around in circles and careened up and down the sidewalk and crossed the street against a light and honking horns all the while calling herself, "Stupid," until she felt too dizzy to continue so she stood perfectly motionless and upright. People moved out of her way or stepped around her and stared before moving on. When her head stopped spinning and her eyes could focus, she found that she was staring into a small pizzeria. The smell wafting from the open door was so powerful and compelling her entire body shook.

"How much money? How much money?" she asked herself repeatedly because she realized she had absolutely no idea how much money remained in her bag.

She immediately started digging into her pockets and into the bag until she had in her hand all of her money, which she then started to count.

"Ten. Five and ten is fifteen and twenty is thirty five and one, two, three, four five is," she counted.

So focused was she on her counting she did not see the man staring at her and licking his lips and leaning toward her and finally bounding toward her and pushing her down and gathering up most of her money that had fallen onto the sidewalk and running away before anyone could register what had happened if they had even seen anything at all.

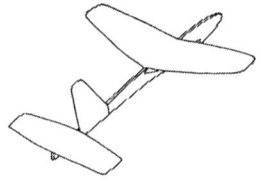

Chapter Twenty-One

Mere felt the sidewalk's moist warmth on her face and wondered how long or if she had been unconscious. The edge of the candy tin dug into her side. The pain reassured her that her bag was still in her possession. She slowed her breathing until she felt her heart beat return to something within the range of normal. Finally she forced herself to sit up. Blood dripped from her left elbow onto the sidewalk. When she touched her forehead, blood dampened her fingertips. She looked around her. The street swirled in front of her. Traffic noises became waves washing onto the shores of Nani and the buildings mountains green with lush foliage. When she shook her head to clear her senses, she gasped because the pain was so intense. As her hands opened to hold her head, Mere realized they were empty. The money so recently held was gone.

She rolled to her knees then slowly, stiffly, and painfully stood. She stared around her. She looked into the darkening sky. She looked down at the ground. She looked at her skinned, scraped and bloodied knuckles. She felt blood dripping down her knees. She looked at her torn pants. She felt her bag, which still hung around her neck. She clutched it to her chest.

Then she screamed and screamed and screamed until she felt like her throat would rip open, and then she screamed some more and then she sat down on the sidewalk with her back against the small walk in pizzeria which just moments before had seemed so inviting. No police officer came to her rescue. A man wearing a white crew neck t-shirt and some sort of white head covering came out and inquired of her well being but when Mere did not stop screaming he went back inside. Moments later he came back out and, sitting on the sidewalk beside her, offered her a diet soda and a slice of pizza. She stopped screaming and looked from the food and drink to the man.

"You are most kind," she said in a voice and manner that bore little resemblance to the wretchedly screaming woman of a few minutes prior.

Sensing that she was doing better or at least moving slightly away from madness to a safer place, the man stood up and returned to the pizzeria. Mere was left alone to eat her meal. She cherished every bite of food she could neither name nor recognize. When she finished the pizza and the drink, she looked around her in abject sorrow and desolation. As she was struggling to stand, a hand reached toward her and helped her to her feet. Once standing she looked into the dark eyes of a man who seemed to her to be just slightly better off than she. She tried to back away from him but couldn't. Her back was already pressed against the window of the pizzeria.

As the man stepped toward her, Mere said in her strongest possible voice, "If you are going to rob and murder me you'll have to be satisfied with just the murder because someone else has already done the robbing."

"Well, Mama, I guess I'll have to make other plans, then," the man said.

His voice seemed kind. He continued to hold her hand. For a long moment they stared at each other. Finally Mere spoke.

"I'm not your mother."

"My mistake. Where you live? I'll walk you home."

"Why?"

"Maybe you'll invite me in for a shower or a nap on the couch or something."

Mere looked carefully at the man. She could almost see her reflection in his black skin. His hair stuck oddly out from beneath a Yankees baseball cap. The cap's bill was missing a piece as though an animal had attempted to eat it. The man was thin. His clothes – an odd arrangement of torn canvas shoes and combat type pants and a denim shirt riddled with holes under which could be seen a striped shirt of some sort – hung from his lanky frame.

"So you can murder me." she stated rather than asked.

"Chill, Mama. You got murder on the mind."

Her thoughts beginning to clear, Mere considered her situation. She had little if any money. She was not certain of her exact location but knew it was not Manhattan. The long summer day would soon end. She would have to sleep someplace and then sort out methods of getting to Manhattan. She ached from fatigue. Her head hurt so badly she thought it would explode. Of course, she acknowledged, she generally thought her head would explode. She feared the pain would soon force her to sit with closed eyes to concentrate on relieving this consuming, debilitating pain. She was not, she determined, in a position to afford the luxury of sitting or concentrating.

"I don't live here," she finally said to the man.

He considered this new information along with his options. He was a man used to considering his options. Lately he had few so consideration was simple. Whatever few options he had, they had not previously included extending a hand to an old woman. This old woman, though, seemed different. She reminded him of places and times and faces he tried with all of his being to forget.

"Okay. That's cool," he said over his shoulder as he turned to walk away.

After taking no more than a dozen steps toward Flatbush Avenue, he stopped and returned to face her.

"You need me to walk you home or something?"

Mere stared at him.

"You are kind to offer. However, my home is too far away. There is no walking there."

Mere saw the man's expression change from confidence to confusion before he again turned, walked to Flatbush Avenue and disappeared into the crowd. Mere refused to allow the despair she felt consume her. With eyes closed, she slumped against the pizzeria window. She did not hear the man return to again stand in front of her.

"You need a place to sleep?" he asked and immediately wondered why he had done so.

Mere, startled, opened her eyes and looked at him with suspicion before cautiously asking, "Why? I thought you were looking for a place to sleep?"

"I have a place to sleep. I was just messing with you. I was just talking hip. I'm not really so cool, you know. That other stuff is just street talk. It's not me."

"I see," said Mere even though she doubted she did. Then she said, "Yes. I need a place to sleep."

She immediately wondered why she had made that statement. Nothing about this disheveled man inspired trust. She felt certain she would regret letting him into her life but something about him reminded her of someone else. Perhaps with sleep she would remember. Perhaps if he did not murder her while she slept she would remember in the morning. While she wondered if she would remember, the man disappeared into the pizzeria.

"Well, that's the end of that," she said to herself.

Alone again, Mere immediately began charting her own course. Brooklyn College was to her right and Flatbush Avenue to her left. This seemed correct. However, when she turned to face the pizzeria, the college was to her left and the avenue to her right. Uncertain of which direction she should next take, she turned her back to the pizzeria and then turned to face the pizzeria. Once again she turned her back and then turned her face. She turned and turned and turned until the man placed his hand on her shoulder to stop her turning. Standing still her vision continued to spin. She backed away until the wall again stopped her.

"Close your eyes," he said.

Her spinning world slowed as she felt dampness wipe her scrapes and cuts. When he had finished tending her wounds he stepped back to look intensely into her eyes. After a long moment, seemingly satisfied with work well done, he nodded his head.

"Okay, then. Off we go."

With most of the blood wiped from most of her wounds, the unlikely couple walked the few feet back to Flatbush Avenue then turned left to walk toward the setting sun. They walked past discount shops and grocery stores with bins of fruit and vegetables set out on the sidewalk and drug stores and Kosher bakeries. When a sudden thunderstorm dropped buckets of rain on them, Mere reached into her bag to pull her leather cap onto her head.

"Way cool, my mama," he said motioning to her hat while guiding her under the awning of a thrift store.

"Once again," Mere replied, "I'm not your mother, my young man."

As she spoke she almost smiled and her eyes almost danced.

"I'm not your young man," he shouted over the deafening drum of raindrops on the tightly stretched canvas. "I'm Elijah Copeland. And I'm not all that young."

As he spoke he almost smiled and his eyes almost danced.

"My name is Mere. It means Star of the Sea. I'm not young either," she shouted back.

Still shouting, Elijah said, "Star of the Sea. I like that. Names should mean something. My name means 'prophet' though I gotta tell you I am lousy at telling the future."

Mere looked into the eyes of Elijah the Prophet a long moment before shouting, "Prophets don't necessarily tell the future. Sometimes they just know about life – its dangers and its delights."

"Well, I've seen a lot of both of those. So I guess I do know a thing or two," Elijah shouted back and wondered why the old woman smiled.

By the time the rain stopped and they stepped back onto Flatbush Avenue, fatigue threatened to consume Mere. She could barely shuffle along fast enough to stay beside Elijah. When finally she stumbled and reached for his right arm she wrapped her hands around an empty sleeve. As she fell she heard the fabric of his denim shirt rip. As she fell he wrapped himself around her in such a way that she landed gently in his lap. Together they sat on the still damp sidewalk just beginning to cool from the hot Brooklyn day. A strange yet familiar comfort settled over them. Finally Mere spoke.

"You're missing an arm."

"I know," he said.

After another long silence, Mere asked, "So, my young man, where do you live?"

He replied without hesitation, "My Mama, I live in the most beautiful place on earth."

Mere smiled as she brushed dirt from Elijah's cheek.

"No. That's where I live," she said, struggling to stand.

It was immediately obvious to both Mere and Elijah that she could walk no more. He motioned her to climb on his back, and so she did.

"I haven't had a piggyback ride since I was a child," she said as they began to make their way again on Flatbush Avenue.

"I haven't given one since I was a child," Elijah replied and then remembered that he didn't want to remember that he had not too many years before carried a friend screaming from war wounds through a far away jungle to a waiting helicopter. He shuddered from the memory and Mere feared he would stumble and fall.

"I must be very heavy. I'm so sorry."

"You're light as a feather."

"You are too kind. How far are we going?"

"Not far. Another mile or so."

If people marveled at the sight of a one armed man carrying an old woman on his back, they did so silently or later in the privacy of their homes. As the day ended, and they entered Prospect Park, Elijah felt Mere's spirits lift.

"It's beautiful," he heard her say.

"You ain't seen nothing yet, my Mere."

She did not know why his words tore at her heart nor did she know why she ached as they passed a sign welcoming guests to the Brooklyn Botanic Garden. When he stopped, Mere slid off of his back to walk beside him along a chain link fence. They stopped at a break in the fence.

"We have to wait out traffic," Elijah said to a question Mere had not yet formed but to which she replied, "Of course."

The evening had slipped into darkness and the sidewalk where they stood was not even in the penumbra of a streetlight's glow. Elijah looked up and down the sidewalk. Mere followed his gaze. Neither saw another person. Elijah looked up and down the street. Mere again followed his gaze even though she was not at all certain for what she looked or why.

"Now," he suddenly whispered and pulled back the tear in the fence.

He guided and almost shoved Mere through it and then he lay beside her in the heavy growth on the Garden side of the fence. A slight movement of his hand pushed the brush back into position. They were completely hidden from any pedestrian or motorist on the other side of the fence. For several minutes they sat in silence before Elijah stood and helped Mere to her feet.

"We're almost there," he whispered and led her toward a trail.

Mere staggered not from fatigue or confusion but from the beauty of the place. She trotted to keep up with Elijah.

"So beautiful," she whispered.

"It's closed now. You don't have to whisper."

They walked past rose gardens and paths almost completely overgrown with trees. Behind them a fireworks display in Prospect Park turned the sky into millions of streaking sparks of color. They turned to watch a Roman candle briefly light up the night sky.

"Happy Independence Day, if you go for that sort of thing," Elijah said.

Even though she understood that the fireworks were not in her honor, Mere took them as a message sent directly to her.

"Thank you," she said.

Fireworks continued lighting the sky behind them as they walked farther into the garden's darkness. When they came to a small building made almost completely of glass, they stopped.

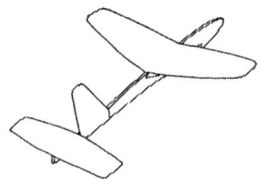

CHAPTER TWENTY-TWO

"We're here," Elijah announced as he opened the door of the greenhouse.

Mere stepped into what, in her mind, could have been a miniaturized duplicate of Nani. The greenhouse was small and never open to the public. It housed excess tropical plants and extra supplies. Tools and wheelbarrows and hoses along with plants in varying stages of growth filled the cramped space. To Mere, though, it was paradise. True, there was no beach and there was no mountain and there was no nighttime breeze coming in off of the ocean to cool and comfort and there was no Oroiti and there was no Kaula to guard over her and there were no islanders to rejoice and dance with her. There were, however, five men sitting against potted ferns and huge dracaenas. Mere blinked as she tried to absorb her situation but her head hurt and her legs trembled. The men appeared to be dressed in rags similar to those worn by Elijah. Some had beards. Some had tattoos on their bare arms. Each man wore an expression of blank acceptance.

"This is Mere," Elijah announced to the others as he guided her away from the gathering to a cramped area canopied by elephant ear ferns and towering sago palms. He helped her lie down in the soft shredded redwood where she immediately fell asleep.

In her sleep she heard Elijah's voice say things like, "I don't know. I just couldn't leave her. We'll figure it out." She smelled food and she smelled coffee and she heard laughter. She heard other voices say things like, "It's okay. Semper fi. You did the right thing." And then, "We ought to see if she's got family. They're probably real worried." And then, "She says she's not from around here." "Where's she live?" "I don't know. I don't even think she knows." And finally, "It'll work out." She felt safe and, almost but not quite no possibly never again, content. When she awoke, Elijah slept at her side. She remembered his heavy breathing in her dreams. She sat up and saw food in front of her, which she ate while listening to the snores of the others. Then she lay back down and slept until Elijah's gentle shaking of her shoulder awakened her.

"We gotta get out of here now," he said.

She did not ask questions but merely gathered her woven bag to her chest, stood, followed him out of the greenhouse, out of the garden and back eventually onto Flatbush Avenue where they watched sleeping Brooklyn awaken for another day.

Side by side they walked. Mere's injuries felt raw and her muscles stiff. Already the Brooklyn day was sticky with heat and humidity. Dried blood stained her pants leg. Her only reality was the sidewalk and the man with whom she walked. She began to wonder if there had ever been a place called Nani and if she had ever been the person she for so long pretended did not exist.

"Go away. Go away. Go away," she said to her thoughts.

As she spoke, she waved her arms as though pushing away a rabid dog or a swarm of wasps. Elijah, emptying a plastic bag into a dumpster, turned to her.

"You okay?"

"Very well," she replied and forced her arms to her sides.

Mere soon imitated Elijah's inspection of dumpsters and trashcans and the coin receptacles of pay telephones. Together they filled a plastic bag with stale Kaiser rolls, half eaten candy bars, fries, pizza crusts and not quite empty bottles of soda. Mere was appalled to realize that she hoped they would soon eat the garbage they gathered. Between them they collected over one dollar from the pay telephones and that, combined with the seventy-five cents Elijah found in the middle of the street, gave them enough to consider their financial options.

"We could sit in a diner and have coffee like real people," Elijah offered, "Or we could grab a burger at that McDonalds down the street."

Mere stared at the McDonalds and remembered that, "I ate at one of those in, was it Australia, I think."

"Australia," Elijah repeated. "That home?"

Mere smiled and said, "No, I was just passing through."

Without even seeming to consider Mere's statement Elijah said, "Let's just pass through the McDonalds, too. I gotta pee and you probably want to wash up."

Using first one hand then the other to keep a steady flow of water through the spring-load restroom faucet, Mere tried to remember every drop of water in the pond on Nani in which she had daily bathed but she could not feel even a single drop of memory's water. Her inability to remember terrified her. As she dried her face with the rough paper towels, she stared into the mirror and saw a frightened old woman looking back at her. The woman's forehead was raw and bruised. Mere reached into her bag and pulled her flying cap onto her head. The old woman did the same.

"Don't mock me," Mere shouted to the mirror.

The mirror did not reply.

"Who are you?" Mere asked the mirror.

Still the old woman said nothing. Mere ran from the restroom and into the parking lot where Elijah waited.

"Whoa, Mama," he said and caught her just before she ran past him.

Mere stared at him until she remembered that they were

gathering trash even though gathering trash seemed an activity unrelated to her original reason for coming to New York.

"It's as good as anything else, though," she said not apropos to nothing because she suddenly realized that she had no idea of why she had left the only place on earth for which she yearned.

Elijah studied her for a moment then said, "Okay, then."

A notion nagged at Mere as they continued on Flatbush Avenue. That notion had something to do with the only person on earth for whom she would risk losing that place for which she yearned. At the moment, though, she could put neither a face nor a name on that person which increased the nagging notion that she was missing something important. She vowed to remind herself later to give the matter more thought.

They continued on Flatbush Avenue until they came to Atlantic Avenue, which Mere remembered from her alarming subway ride the day before. They turned left onto Atlantic Avenue. As they walked they both looked for food or money. By the time they reached Hicks and turned right Mere could feel the heat of the day through her feet and up her back to her shoulders. It did not soothe her aching muscles. The city had come to life with screeching brakes and honking horns and the crash and bang of delivery trucks not too carefully unloading and loading boxes and crates and lumber and bags of concrete and bales of scraps that once had been clothing or bed sheets. Just before they turned left onto Remsen, Elijah stopped at a trashcan. After sorting through empty cartons and crumpled bags he produced a torn in places and faded in others and discolored possibly from spills in others leather jacket which with a not quite but almost ear to ear grin of pride and generosity he held out to Mere.

"I bet this fits you," he said and placed the jacket over her shoulders.

It did fit. Even the sleeves were long enough. And even in the already hot and humid day, Mere felt the coat's once luxury. She felt its weight on her shoulders and felt its hem touch her thighs just above her knees and remembered a time when she had worn a coat like this new and smelling of leather and remembered the photographers and the crowds pressing toward her and wanting to run and run as fast as she could to a place where tranquility could be a fact of life and where no one cared about world records and promotional tours and speeches and smiling just the right way.

Mere put her hands in the deep pockets and pulled out a wad of tissue, a gum wrapper, forty-seven cents in loose change and a one hundred dollar bill at which she and Elijah both stared not with greed but with absolute astonishment at the miracles of which life was capable when least expected.

Not knowing what else to do or say, she dropped the tissue and gum wrapper back into the trash and extended her hand holding the money toward Elijah. He shook his head.

"Put it back in your pocket. The coat is yours and so is whatever you find in the pockets."

As they resumed their walking, Mere's footsteps felt lighter and she felt stronger. She no longer worried that she would collapse from fatigue but soon began to suspect that she might collapse from heat wearing such a magnificent coat on such a hot day. She took the money from the pocket of her coat and put it in the pocket of her pants where she felt more loose change and perhaps more one or five or ten or twenty or maybe fifty or maybe even hundred dollar bills because she had forgotten when she took her money out of her bag the day before and when it was taken from her as she was pushed down on the sidewalk that she had put some money in her pocket. She did not mention to Elijah this reclaimed memory. No. Not now. Definitely later. She did not know this man. She barely knew herself. What she did know, though, with absolute certainty was that she would tell him about the extra money. There were so many other things she wanted to tell him and she couldn't. The least she could do was tell him about the money. Elijah was not a person from whom she desired to keep secrets.

"Once in our lifetimes, if we're lucky, we meet someone like this," she said to herself and then remembered that she had already met a few such people.

"I am indeed fortunate," she said aloud. "How did you know this was in that trashcan?"

She took off her jacket and folded it over her arm. Elijah beamed because everyone likes to be considered a specialist at something.

"You get a feel for stuff, you know. So I just knew there would be something good in that can. That's all. You'll get good instincts, too."

As they walked, Mere suspected that she might already have good instincts but that nagging notion at the back of her head kept her from trusting her instincts about the quality of her instincts.

"What on earth," the notion nagged, "are you doing here?"

Then she gasped and reached for Elijah's empty sleeve and held it as though it contained an arm and staggered toward the closest bench and collapsed. She could not take her eyes off of the skyline of Manhattan Island once so familiar to her and now so changed and alien and foreign that she could not even imagine finding the place of the parades or of the speeches or of, "Yes, didn't I live somewhere over there once or twice or maybe even several times?"

Her thoughts raced with such speed and in so many different directions that she stopped trying to follow or sort through them. Even though she had seen this so changed skyline just the previous day, the view from a window seat of a jumbo jet could not compare to this view with only a river between her and so much she had once loved and hated. She simply sat and stared wide mouthed and wild-eyed. Elijah, following his empty sleeve, sat beside her. In silence they stared over the wrought iron fence of the Brooklyn Heights Promenade and across the East River as though neither had ever before seen such a sight. When the music finally distracted her, Mere allowed her gaze to shift from the skyline to the activity around her. Parents or nannies pushed babies in strollers. Old men played chess and spoke in languages Mere did not recall ever before hearing. Dogs, euphoric over the prospects of walks, pulled at their leashes. And, yes, further down the Promenade, a band performed. A man sat on the ground and played bongo drums. Two men played guitars. Another man sang a song. Mere suspected she knew that song. She remembered lyrics seeming to make reference to a hotel in California. She could not recall where or if she had actually heard it. The fifth musician played a banjo and Mere's heart suddenly ached for so much left behind in so many places. She stared at the musicians. Their faces seemed familiar as though she had seen them in a dream. As she shook her head to clear the dream, she realized that Elijah was speaking.

"Every morning, just about, I'm right here looking across the river."

"And every night you sleep in the garden?"

"Just about," Elijah said with pride and contentment.

"You are one of the luckiest people alive."

"I know that. You better believe I do."

The music ended and Mere turned to see the musicians approach them. As they approached, she remembered their faces.

"We slept with them last night," she said with an excitement that surprised her.

Elijah laughed and moved to the grass behind the benches to begin emptying their collected food onto the grass. When the musicians arrived, they, too, emptied bags of salvaged food. The meal lacked any type of coherent theme. Half-eaten bagels. Stale donuts. Pizza. A grapefruit. Peaches considered in some kitchen to be too old for the table were perfect for this gathering. Six hard-boiled eggs. An entire peanut butter and jelly sandwich. Several candy bars in various stages of consumption. The food was carefully divided and each person received a fair and equal share.

"You all remember Mere," Elijah reminded the men.

They nodded their heads but did not interrupt their eating. The only sounds made were of food consumed with delight.

Eventually Elijah spoke again.

"Mere, I want you to meet my band: Nick is the guy with the drums. Lyle and Bob both play guitar. Jack has the banjo and Bud tries to sing."

Mere stared and smiled at each musician. Each musician stared and smiled back at her. After a long moment of smiling and staring, the musicians gathered their instruments, walked several yards down the Promenade and returned to songs of handymen and tonight being the night. Mere returned her gaze to the skyline. Even though it was just across the river, the city began to feel very far away and far less urgent than it had seemed when yesterday's jumbo jet began its descent into today's swirling uncertainty.

The promenade filled with tourists and regulars and nappers and lovers and writers and artists. Many stopped in front of the musicians to watch and to listen and to sometimes drop coins in an open guitar case.

"What do we do now?" she finally asked when the sun began to dip from the middle of the sky.

Elijah started awake.

"Huh?"

"What do we do now?" she repeated.

"Oh," he said rubbing his eyes. "We gather up the money, we buy stuff for tonight, and we go home. Just like a regular day in the life of a regular person."

"They've earned the money. Doesn't it belong to them?"

"Well, they kind of work for me. I always make sure we've got a place to sleep. I keep a look out for trouble. I'm the manager. Besides, I write the songs that matter. We're gonna make it some day. You'll see. Besides, I look out for my people."

Mere considered this for a long moment.

"Do you have many people," she finally asked.

"Nah. Just them. And you."

He looked directly into her eyes and smiled.

"You are responsible forever for what you tame. You are responsible for your rose. That's from *The Little Prince*."

Suddenly Mere felt a comfort she had not known since leaving her island. In her mind she saw the books in her hut and the worn copy of the Antoine de Saint-Exupery, dog-eared and stained and in her mind she returned there to another and oh so different time.

"Who has tamed whom," she asked her as they lay in bed reading the book aloud.

"Sociologically speaking ... "

"Oh, shut up!" she said and both women laughed.

Then she was gone again from that place.

"The author was an aviator," Mere said.

"Yeah. I know," was Elijah's reply.

Mere studied Elijah before she asked, "Are you also an aviator?"

Elijah shook his head.

"Not me. I just got dropped in and airlifted out. Helicopters. You know."

Mere looked into his dark eyes and then back to the skyline and could not remember why it beckoned to her. Elijah stretched and stood as the street musicians walked toward him.

He turned to Mere and said, "I want you to go on with them. I gotta do some stuff and we'll meet at the park. We always hang there until, you know, we can get into the greenhouse."

As though they already knew, the musicians smiled at Mere as she watched Elijah walk past them, touching each on the shoulder but not speaking. She and the musicians stood awkwardly for a moment before Bud motioned to her to join them. Then they all walked back toward Flatbush Avenue. The evening's walk seemed to Mere easier than that of the morning and she knew her strength was returning. After a time she put her coat on because wearing it was easier than carrying it. After some more time she put on her leather flying cap because the evening had begun to chill and because she was feeling too good to not look her best.

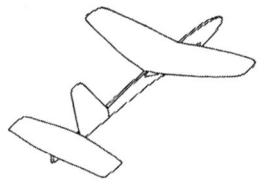

CHAPTER TWENTY-THREE

As they entered Prospect Park and walked directly toward its center, Mere saw even at a distance that Elijah was waiting for them at two picnic tables pulled together. When they were closer she saw food. Pizza. Salad. Juice. Mere laughed to see such a table.

"I never before yesterday in my entire life ate this pizza pie and now two days in a row I'm eating it. I love it. How do you obtain such a wealth of food?"

The musicians looked at Elijah and Elijah looked pleased so they relaxed and laughed, too, and said things like – "This is great. Man. He feeds us good."

"I have a deal with Max at Luigi's," Elijah explained around bites. "Twice a week I buy from him. He knows how to treat steady customers. He always throws in something extra. Like tonight we got extra salad and a couple pies that he didn't think turned out so good so he saved them for me. That sort of stuff."

"Two nights a week?"

"Sure. I don't want to start feeling like a mooch. So I go other places other nights."

"Besides," Nick added, "we like some variety, you know."

To which Lyle added, "That way we aren't eating the same old garbage."

And they laughed. And after a moment's consideration, Mere

laughed too because she remembered that breakfast had, indeed, been garbage.

"How long have you been doing this?" she asked after taking a long swallow of cranberry juice.

The musicians looked again at Elijah. He stared off into space as though counting the moments in the hours and the days during which he had eaten garbage and slept on the ground of a greenhouse.

"Where we're at, now? I think maybe seven months. We started when the weather was warm enough."

"And before that?"

"Well, you know," Bob said no longer looking to Elijah for permission because they now understood and accepted that Mere had at least for the time being joined their ranks, "We had some jobs. Sometimes stuff gets in the way, though. You know."

"Stuff?" Mere asked.

Bud coughed before saying, "Two steps forward. One backward. It's kind of hard sometimes. Sometimes we slip a little, I guess."

"We always manage. Elijah makes sure of that. I guess we all make sure of that," Jack added.

"Yeah," Nick joined the conversation. "Before the greenhouse there were the subways and before that…I don't know… We'll get ahead of the game someday."

"Where will you be when you get ahead?" Mere asked.

Elijah answered that question. "We'll own a house and we'll have recorded our songs and we'll get paid real money not money thrown into a hat or a case for playing. I write songs but I don't want to give them away on the Promenade. We got plans, Mere."

"I see that," she replied as she watched a cat perch on a trash can searching for food.

Because she watched the cat, the others did also.

"Kind of like us, isn't she?" Bud said.

The group fell silent watching the cat dig out the remains of what was surely once a tuna sandwich.

Mere resumed the conversation by asking, "Have you been friends long?"

The men looked from her to each other. Bob finally broke the silence.

"You know. 'Nam'."

Mere did not know 'Nam'. She did not know that almost a quarter of all the homeless in the country were veterans and that over half of that quarter served in Vietnam. Mere did know, though, that eating garbage could not make for long-term dignified living. As her heart broke, she turned from the men to again look at the cat.

When the cat stopped eating to stare at him Jack said, "Tomorrow morning that's us. Maybe when we get a house we'll invite that cat to live with us."

Nick whistled at the cat. The cat returned to the sandwich.

"An Ash Can Cat," Mere suddenly said. "I've been an Ash Can Cat."

Elijah and the musicians looked at her and hoped for a good story because nothing passes the time when you're waiting to sneak back into a place where you shouldn't be in the first place than a good story.

"Apartment 21. 606 West 116 Street. That's where I lived."

"That's up by Columbia," Elijah said.

"Yes. We were students. She and I. And we lived there. All of us. I remember."

They waited for the rest of the story. At that moment Mere did not know the rest of the story. She raced through memory's empty corridors searching for clues. She silently opened doors to more empty rooms. The silence lasted so long that the musicians began to fear there was no story. Finally Mere forced herself to return to the benches in Prospect Park.

"I'm not accustomed to talking about myself," she began. "I

don't know where to start or how much to say. I don't want to bore you."

"We love hearing about stuff," Lyle said. "Tell us more about the Ash Can Cats. And about her."

Mere opened one more door. The room was not empty. Dusty sheets covered perhaps furniture? She wasn't certain.

"I think we all lived together. Perhaps we were students."

"At Columbia?" Jack tried to help.

"Yes. I believe we were at Columbia. I remember now. I didn't graduate."

The sheets were dusty. Mere tried not to shake up too much dust for fear her sinuses would become infected and her head would resume its throbbing. She pressed her fingers to her forehead. She opened a photograph album and studied the happy faces smiling at her through the years.

"Looking back, I imagine my life would have been much different had I remained in school."

"I hear you on that one," Elijah said.

She nodded her head in agreement with his statement and with her statement and thought it odd that she had never before entertained that thought.

"Why didn't you graduate?" asked Elijah.

Mere raised her head to look through the floating dust to Elijah. His face seemed kind and old beyond years.

"My parents separated. My father moved to California. My mother joined him and all of a sudden I had a family again. I so wanted that family to be whole. Apparently I believed in that fantasy about wholeness depending on family so I left school for California. I fully intended to return to Columbia, finish school, and live my own life. Instead I became a rolling stone for many years until I claimed, declared, a home for myself. The arrangement had been that I would share that home with another. Things don't always work out the way they are arranged."

"With her? Were you going to share the home with her?" from Bud.

The directness of the question shocked Mere. She closed the album. She pulled the sheet off of a rocking chair. It was empty. She raced to a bookshelf. The titles seemed somehow familiar. She turned to search the rest of the room and in so doing her coat caught something and knocked it to the floor.

"Yes. With her," Mere said spinning to find what had fallen.

"She double crossed you?" Bob asked with what appeared to be genuine anger.

Mere bent to pick up the fallen chief's stick. She stroked the smoothed with age wood and thought for a moment.

"No. I believe she cheated herself. Oh, but we had such wonderful times on West 116 Street and at Columbia University. We used to lie on a roof at night and look at the stars and imagine our lives and the meanings of everything the sky offered. We believed in a limitless sky. Those were wonderful feelings in magical times."

The stick had no clues to offer. Mere leaned it back against the wall. She looked one more time around the room. The dust had once again settled. She left the room, closing the door behind her.

"But that is ancient history. Here we are now having finished a wonderful meal. You have let me into your lives and for that I thank you. For as long as we journey together…"

"Which will be forever," Elijah interrupted.

The musicians stared at him. He knew his face flushed even though the color of his skin hid his involuntary response to having possibly made a fool of himself. He wasn't sure why he had made the statement aside from the fact that he could not bear to see another white-haired woman scream in abject agony as napalm melted her skin. Mere stopped, looked at Elijah, and smiled. Although at that moment she wanted nothing more than to live out her days with these gentle men, she felt the familiar stirring in her chest and knew that she was about to once again become air borne.

"All journeys one day end, you know. That's the nature of the journey. It's so easy to forget that but we must try not to forget. So. Did you know that I play the banjo?"

The members of the band opened their mouths but no one spoke.

"Think of this, Elijah, as my audition. For as long as we travel together, I'd like to help out. Maybe I could play a few pieces while you rest. Who knows? People might pay quite a bit to see an old woman play the banjo. Besides, playing the banjo nourishes my soul."

She motioned for Jack's banjo. When he gave it to her, tears filled her eyes.

"It's a tenor," Jack said as apology.

Mere closed her eyes and held it to her.

"I know."

Finally she played. The songs were as old as her youth and she sang them with the energy and passion and disregard for personal dignity of her youth. She played a John Phillip Sousa piece. She played and sang old folk songs and spirituals. She almost played *Pennies From Heaven* but stopped herself because of the stabbing pain that filled her being. She could play no more.

In her sleep on the greenhouse floor, Mere returned to the empty hallway. She opened the door to the sheet draped room and stepped inside. The door snapped shut behind her. The chief's stick still leaned against the wall. As her eyes surveyed the room, Mere noticed that the stick had collected no dust since she had held it to her soul. She entered the room to sit in a chair near a window. She looked out the window and saw on the street below two women looking up at her.

"I'm not on ground level," she said aloud.

Her voice awakened Elijah. He sat up to look down on her.

She again looked at the books. Something about them seemed so familiar. The photograph album, once again covered in dust, lay on the table where she had returned it a life or an eon or a moment before. She again opened it to stare at so many unfamiliar faces.

"Please come. I need you," one of those faces spoke and said to her.

Mere stared into the photograph until she entered it. Dust immediately filled her sinuses. Her head throbbed. She reached toward the woman who had spoken. The paper of her face was brittle with age. A tear ran under her glasses.

"I'm sorry," the woman said. "Forgive me. Come now. Please."

"No! No! No!" Mere screamed as she ran from the room.

She slammed the door shut behind her. As she ran down the empty corridor, Mere heard the chief's stick fall onto the floor with such force the building began to shake.

No!" she screamed.

Elijah reached out to touch her hand as the building crumbled around her. Bricks and broken glass and walls of silence shattered behind and in front of her. Thunder shook the greenhouse. Lightning streaked through the Brooklyn sky. Rain hammered on the greenhouse glass. Mere sat up. She jumped to her feet. She turned in circles in the small greenhouse. She covered her head with her hands. All the time she shouted and moaned and wept.

"I'm too late. I have to get to her. Why did you do this to me? Don't die without me. I love you. I'm coming. Wait for me."

Over and over she said these things even after the thunder was silent and the rain spent. Elijah and the musicians did not interrupt her with questions or comforts or assurances. They knew all too well sleep's terrors.

When she was finally silent, Elijah spoke.

"Do you need to find her?"

Her entire resources spent, Mere whispered, "Yes."

"Okay."

Night trudged toward morning. No one slept.

Finally, as dawn peeked through the windows, Elijah asked, "Do you know where she's at?"

Mere, holding her knees to her chest, shook her head and whispered, "No."

More silence and then, "Where would we start to look for her?" from Elijah.

More silence and then from Bud, "Does she live in that apartment with those Ash Can cats?"

"I don't think so."

Elijah stood and began to pace back and forth in front of Mere.

After a moment, he stopped pacing and asked, "Does she have a job? Do you know where she works?"

Mere raised her head to look at Elijah. Defeat fled from her face.

"The Museum of Natural History. She works there. But she's sick. I don't know."

She lowered her head under defeat's returning weight.

When was the last time you saw her?" Lyle asked.

"Two years. Perhaps longer. I may have lost track of time."

"Okay. So where did you see her then?" Elijah asked.

The question alarmed Mere. She considered Elijah's question carefully before answering.

"We met elsewhere. Not here. I no longer live here."

Elijah, the man of plans and direction and action, seized the situation with his usual sense of calm purpose.

"So. Mere and I will go to the museum and look for her friend. You guys go on to the Promenade and bring in the bucks."

"We'll have breakfast together before we go, right?" Mere asked and Elijah and the musicians smiled and agreed that no adventure should begin without a good breakfast gathered from dumpsters and trashcans.

If he thought the project to be the result of lunacy, Elijah gave not even the smallest hint. He had never even asked Mere where she came from and what brought her to Brooklyn and how she had become homeless and why she frequently wore a leather flying cap. He liked her. He didn't need to know the hidden details of her clearly long and eventful life. If she needed a lift on his back from time to time he was thankful for the strength to do so. He was not a man who required much information. He didn't need to know that those were the characteristics so enormously appreciated by this old woman who seemed to have come from so very far away that she knew little of life and at the same time from so close that she knew every crack in the sidewalks upon which they wandered.

They quickly left the greenhouse. Already they were late in leaving. Mere worried about her hair and smoothed it with water from a sprinkler. She wondered whether or not to wear her flying cap and finally decided to wear it and her jacket despite the already rising heat of the not yet fully formed day. Making their usual visits to the dumpsters and the garbage cans along the way from the greenhouse to the Promenade, Mere chose three empty cans which Elijah returned with his usual respect and gentleness. She also chose a banana peel and he suggested they keep their eyes open for a banana which they could encase in the peel and congratulated her on such a wise find. At the Promenade, she stared vacantly across the East River and barely ate. When she spoke, Elijah and the musicians suspected that she did not speak to them.

She said things like, "We made an arrangement. No one must ever find out. Don't leave me. I will wait for you. The world does not necessarily need you. Oroiti, I must return. Ariki, I am your leg on which you stand and without you I fall."

Her voice was soft and mechanical. Her eyes never left the skyline of Manhattan Island.

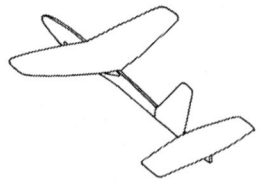

Chapter Twenty-Four

Finally Elijah stood and announced, "Okay, folks. We gotta get going. We'll be back before you know it. But if we aren't we'll meet back at the greenhouse."

With that he extended his hand and helped Mere to her feet. Together they left the Promenade and the musicians. They paid for the subway ride with money from Mere's pocket and got off at the American Museum of Natural History. Mere made mental notes of the musicians on the subway platforms and in the trains and wondered why Elijah and the band didn't spend some time below ground and then mentally compared the Promenade to subway platforms and moving subway cars and wondered no more. Out of the subway tunnel and onto the street they walked purposefully toward Central Park West on Seventy-Seventh Street. When they came to the south side of the museum Mere stopped and stared up at the two turrets on either end of the building. Elijah stopped and stared with her, following her gaze from one turret to the other. Mere felt convinced that he could hear the pounding of her heart. For what seemed to her like hours, she stood at the southwest corner of Seventy-Seventh Street and Central Park West without ever taking her eyes off of the museum and without ever slowing the sweep of her gaze from one turret to the other.

When finally she spoke she felt to herself and appeared to Elijah to gasp for breath.

"I don't remember which one," she said without slowing the sweep of her gaze.

Feeling no need to ask questions or venture opinions, Elijah said nothing until he was certain Mere had regained strength and breath.

"Why don't we just go in and see if she's here," he finally suggested.

Mere forced herself to cross the street despite the traffic and the honking horns. She walked as though to her own execution toward the entrance to the museum stopping before ascending the wide steps to the doorway in front of the statue of President Teddy Roosevelt on horseback with what appeared to be an American Indian standing beside him. Mere stared at the statue.

"I never met him," she said turning to Elijah. "I knew his cousin, though."

If Elijah read anything more into that statement than a natural delay before battle or adventure or long awaited climax he did not give even a hint of that to Mere. He stood in silence while she stared at the statue and became convinced that he saw her shoulders square and her bearing become stronger.

"Anytime you're ready," he finally said.

She stared at the statue for several minutes oblivious to the visitors streaming into and out of the museum many of whom stopped to stare or at least to furtively glance at this unlikely couple standing in front of the statue.

Finally they walked up the steps and through the huge doors. When they entered the museum Mere said, "You know, I used to come here often."

Elijah nodded and pointed to the information desk. Together almost in perfect step, they walked to the line and stood waiting their turn to ask questions and seek guidance. When people moved away from them, neither Mere nor Elijah wondered if it was because his matted hair still had redwood chips and leaves in it or if it was because in the middle of summer she wore a leather jacket ripped and discolored and a leather flying cap pulled down over her ears or because the man with the matted hair had only one arm or because the woman's wide eyes darted back and forth across the vast museum entrance as though she at any moment expected the most important person in her life to walk directly to her and throw her arms around her never dropping the chief's stick which had become almost as famous as she.

When their turn at the information desk finally came, Mere found herself unable to speak. She simply stared at the woman behind the desk who seemed to her like a child and backed away and then approached the desk and then backed away again and before she completed the next approach heard Elijah's voice.

"Good morning. Perhaps you can help us. My friend is looking for her friend. She works here."

The not actually but seeming to Mere child behind the information desk looked from Mere to Elijah and back to Mere who had by then completed her cycle of five retreats from the desk and five advances toward it and was feeling calmer and more focused.

"I've been to her office many times. Perhaps we could just go there. I know the way."

"What is your friend's name?"

"I can't tell you."

From behind the information desk came a stare designed to wither. Elijah leaned close to Mere.

"I think you pretty much have to give her your friend's name. It's okay. I'm here."

Mere turned from the information desk to the cavernous, crowded lobby. She turned again to face the not actually a child behind the desk. Mere took a deep breath. She swallowed and felt herself begin to stall.

"Nose down," she said.

"I beg your pardon?"

Elijah's hand on her shoulder stopped the stall.

Finally Mere spoke.

"We're here to see Margaret Mead. We can go right to her office. I know the way."

Mere felt Elijah's eyes widen. She no longer felt his hand on her shoulder. She had passed the point of no return. And still silence behind the information desk.

"Really," continued Mere and her voice rose in pitch and volume and her words came out faster the longer she spoke, "All you do is get to the Plains Indians Hall and then you go through that room with all the meteors and then I'd get in the elevator to the fifth floor and then we'd walk down that long hall past those glass cases you know the ones with all the sculptures and plates and bowls and costumes and jewelry and I believe some primitive weapons and many other artifacts I can see all of them as though I were there yesterday and that hall seems to go on forever but when it ends you go up that staircase and then past some shelves and other rooms and then there it is practically in the roof. I know how to get there. We can just go and wait for her. She'll be here any minute. I know. She's expecting me. She's expecting us. She sent for me … us…"

So intent had Mere been on convincing the not-child behind the information desk that she knew the way and so intent had Elijah been on watching Mere as though his sheer concentration and power of will would keep her at the desk that neither of them had noticed the not-child pick up the telephone and dial a number.

Mere stopped speaking, however, when the not-child spoke into the telephone with a voice too soft and too quiet to be heard by anyone standing on the other side of the desk. Both Mere and Elijah began to back away from the desk but the not-child stopped them by motioning to a bench presumably a safe distance from the information desk.

"Someone will be with you in a moment. Please wait over there."

Mere and Elijah walked to it and sat. Elijah did not challenge the name of Mere's friend. After a few seconds Mere stood and returned to the information desk. Elijah stood but did not follow her.

"Thank you. You have been most helpful," Mere said smiling.

Then she returned to the bench and sat back down. Elijah smiled and waved to the not-child and fully expected to spend the rest of the day waiting for the moment to arrive when someone would be with them. He seriously doubted if that someone would be Margaret Mead. In his mind, he incorporated Mere's banjo playing and singing into the street band. Unless he could find her family, he knew that he could do nothing except care for her for the rest of her life.

The not-child's moment, however, arrived very quickly in the form of a young man perhaps in his late twenties who introduced himself as Dick A Research Assistant. Dick A Research Assistant sat on the bench beside Elijah and for what seemed to Elijah to be several long moments said absolutely nothing. Elijah felt Mere's increasing restlessness and placed his hand on her knee. Her leg began to shake and he patted her knee. Finally Dick A Research Assistant cleared his throat and spoke.

"Is Dr. Mead expecting you?"

"Yes. She requested this meeting," Elijah said having no idea what he was talking about but feeling confident that his lack of insight mattered not at all.

"I see," replied Dick A Research Assistant and both Mere and Elijah knew that he did not see at all.

No one spoke again for several more moments until finally Mere took Elijah's hand off of her knee, kissed it, stood up and walked in a large circle away from the two men still sitting on the bench. She walked until she returned to her point of origin plus or minus a few degrees because now she stood directly in front of the research assistant.

"Young man," she began, "I have traveled more miles than you can imagine to keep this appointment. My friend, here, has left his professional responsibilities to accompany me. In this bag which you clearly see hanging over my shoulder are items requested by Dr. Mead. You certainly know her complete inability to tolerate incompetence or buffoonery and since you are currently displaying both characteristics, I suggest you run upstairs and let her know we are here or step out of our way so we can tell her ourselves."

Elijah stood to be beside Mere. Dick A Research Assistant appeared to sink into the concrete of the bench even though all three suspected that to be an impossibility. Mere glared directly into his eyes and held onto Elijah's empty sleeve for fear she would actually enter his eyes and emerge holding bits and pieces of his brain. The unlikely tableau ended when the research assistant coughed nervously and looked around the lobby until his gaze connected with that of the person behind the information desk. Comfortable that he had verified he was not alone, Dick A Research Assistant stood.

"If you have something for Dr. Mead, I will be happy to make sure that she receives it."

As he spoke he extended his hand toward Mere. She immediately took a step backwards and away from him. Elijah stepped back with her. Mere clasped the bag tighter to her chest.

"You know," Elijah began and with each word felt himself wading further and further into a scenario about which he knew nothing but into which he felt no hesitation to enter.

"You know," he continued searching for words that might sound calm and sensible, "Dr. Mead has asked that these things be delivered to her personally and not by an intermediary. I'm certain you can appreciate the importance of exactly honoring her request."

Mere was impressed.

"Have you ever done anything to displease her?" she asked and by the changed expression on the face of Dick A Research Assistant knew that he had, indeed, walked on at least one occasion into the dark, raging, terrifying, black-eyed fury of Dr. Margaret Mead when irritated.

Dick A Research Assistant felt himself suddenly riding two horses about to go in different directions. Elijah, keen observer and interpreter of human nature, saw Dick's dilemma.

"I guess this kind of puts you in a tough spot," he began. "If you let us go upstairs to her office you might be breaking some sort of rule and we might be full of shit and you could get into trouble with the museum and your boss. And if you don't let us go see her, you're risking getting her really upset because you kept her from getting the stuff she sent for. Man. You are in a tough spot."

Dick A Research Assistant stiffened, glanced at the information desk, and then looked at Mere and Elijah.

"Not really. Dr. Mead has left strict instructions. She will see no one unless we have that person's name on our list. So, tell me your names and if you are on her list, I can certainly let her know that you wish to make an appointment to see her. That, however, will not take place today."

Mere's eyes narrowed and her face became an unmoving mask. She took one step toward the research assistant and then turned and walked across the lobby to the far wall and then turned and strode quickly back to the research assistant. She did not stop walking until their faces almost touched. Then she turned and walked back across the length of the lobby and returned and turned and turned and with each turning the distance decreased until she stood in one place turning in circles. Dick A Research Assistant stepped backwards until his legs touched the bench and he could move backwards no more unless he fell over the bench.

Elijah looked from the spinning Mere to the increasingly uncomfortable research assistant and then around the lobby. Museum visitors and museum employees had stopped to stare.

"You have that list with you?" Elijah asked the research assistant.

"I can get it," he said without taking his eyes off of the old woman spinning in front of him.

"Why don't you do that," Elijah suggested. "And look for the first name of Mere on the list. You might want to rush that along."

Dick A Research Assistant hurried away. When he had disappeared into the museum, Elijah turned to the still spinning Mere and placed his hand on her shoulder but she spun away from him. He stepped closely to her, put his arm around her, and held her tightly to his chest and immediately felt her weight press against him and felt and heard her rapid breathing and pounding heart.

"It's okay," he said. "We'll just see how this plays out and then we'll figure out what to do next."

So they stood motionless in the middle of the lobby of the American Museum of Natural History. Visitors resumed their activities. Employees returned to work. After glacial minutes Dick A Research Assistant returned and walked directly to them. He held a list in his hand.

"What name did you say?" he asked.

"First name Mere," Elijah answered.

A quick glance on the list which did not appear to be very long and Dick A Research Assistant shook his head back and forth and then as though no one knew the meaning of a head shaking back and forth said, "No."

Elijah kissed the top of Mere's head and whispered to her, "Any other names?"

Mere whispered back, "Mary Anderson. Mrs. Mary Anderson."

"Mrs. Mary Anderson," Elijah said loud enough for the research assistant to hear.

The research assistant again scanned the list and simultaneously shook his head back and forth and said, "No."

Before either man knew she was going to move, Mere stepped out of Elijah's embrace and moved close enough to Dick A Research Assistant to grab the list from his hands. When he pulled it away from her the list ripped. He held the bigger piece of the list and Mere held only a corner which she briefly studied before throwing it into his face.

"That's not her writing. I know her writing. That's not her writing. You fraud. You imposter. That's not her writing. She didn't write that. If she had, my name would be on the list. My name would be on the list. How dare you keep me from her. How dare you keep her from me. How dare you keep us apart."

Mere's voice had gotten louder with each word until she screamed at the research assistant.

"You see this bag?" and she took the bag off of her shoulders and held it in front of the white-faced research assistant. "Do you see it? Do you see it? She asked for this bag. The contents are exactly to her request. You know nothing. You know nothing."

When he thought she would strike the research assistant with the bag, Elijah took it from her hands and she allowed him to do so. Relieved of her bag, Mere seemed also to be relieved of any ability to remain in one place. She began running in ever increasing circles around the lobby.

While she ran she shouted, "Oroiti. Oroiti. Ariki? Where are you? What have they done to me? Where is she? You brought me here. You brought me here. You brought me here. I love you. I will help you. Don't die. Don't die. Don't die. Death is not our arrangement."

As the security guards approached, Mere's ability to communicate her exact thoughts became significantly compromised. Even she knew that she made no sense. By the time the first security guard placed a hand on her, Mere had stopped trying to articulate her thoughts and had, instead, began roaring like a lion. Soon, however, the lion's roars diminished into the meows of a kitten and Mere was understood by Elijah and Dick A Research Assistant and those near enough to hear to be saying something about Ash Can Cats.

Few people are comfortable in the presence of a person who has so obviously moved beyond the barrier of rational behavior. Certainly the museum's security guards had no comfort whatsoever and tried to calm her with threats of arrest or incarceration. Their best efforts only fueled the fire already fed by forty years of waiting. Mere jumped up on the bench and began waving her arms as though her hands held burning torches with which she could keep the crazed mob at bay.

"G. P. will take care of this. He can be good for something. All you … none of you … have any idea who I am. Do you want to know who I am? Well I can't tell you who I am because we made an arrangement."

Elijah walked to the bench and extended his hand. Mere misunderstood his gesture and assumed he wanted to stand on the bench with her. She pulled him upward and toward her and wanting neither to offend or agitate further, he joined her on the bench. Mere looked around her and wondered why the short woman in the red cape would not at least step into the lobby, rap her chief's stick so loudly that its echo would fill the entire museum, and tell everyone to be quiet so she could return to her writing. The short woman did not appear. Not even to warn Mere to not say under any circumstances what she said the minute she saw the New York Police Department officers with guns raised race into the museum lobby.

"You have no idea who I am. But I will tell you who I am and she will be angry. She will be so angry these walls will shake in terror. I am Mere. Yes, I am the Star of the Sea. And I am apparently Mary Anderson. Mrs. Mary Anderson because that is the name she gave me. But I am also now and always Amelia Earhart," she shouted at the top of her voice and knew immediately that she had not spoken loudly enough because the police officers continued their approach.

"My name," she repeated even louder, "is Amelia Earhart. I am here to see Margaret Mead. We have an arrangement. She is expecting me."

As though they had not heard a word she had just spoken, four police officers pulled her down from the bench and onto the floor. She kicked and she screamed and she bit one officer on the arm as her hands were cuffed behind her back and her ankles were bound together and still she continued to reveal her identity even though her identity had begun to sound again like various animals some of which had never set foot on the island of Manhattan or on any other island on the face of the planet.

Elijah moved close to Amelia and sat on the floor next to her. No one objected to his presence because his presence seemed to calm the crazy old street person who had apparently just experienced some sort of psychotic break in the lobby of the American Museum of Natural History. When the ambulance arrived, Elijah stood while Amelia was strapped to a gurney and then he put the bag over his shoulder and walked beside her onto the street.

"Bellevue?" he asked an attendant and the attendant nodded yes.

Elijah bent down and kissed Amelia on the forehead and as he did so he heard the attendant comment to the ambulance driver that this one thought she was Amelia Earhart.

"I'll get you out," Elijah whispered to Amelia so softly that no one except her heard or even knew that he had spoken.

The driver laughed as he started the rig and the ambulance pulled away from the curb to join the south bound traffic on Central Park West.

"Another wacko claiming to be Amelia Earhart. Must be the

weather. Brings all the crazy dykes out," Elijah thought he heard the driver say and hoped he had misunderstood.

Elijah turned from the ambulance into the still ashen face of Dick A Research Assistant.

"How hard would it have been, you academically achieved asshole, to have at least pretended to believe her?"

As Elijah took another step toward the research assistant, the research assistant took a step backwards and away.

"I'm not going to hurt you. I've got one arm and bugs in my hair. You've got a white shirt and a necktie and, oh yeah, a telephone so you can call the police when old ladies get a little excited."

Dick A Research Assistant took another step away from Elijah.

"You know, jerk off," Elijah continued in the most reasonable tone imaginable, "You take one more step away from me and I'll bite your nose off."

The research assistant stopped. His shirt was drenched with sweat.

"Now," Elijah continued, "You tell your Dr. Mead that you kept her from seeing an old friend and you kept that old friend from delivering whatever it was that Dr. Mead requested. If she doesn't shove that stick of hers up your ass, I will."

"Dr. Mead," the Research Assistant said with the arrogance of one who has privileged information, "is ill. She isn't even in the city. She's resting on Long Island. She does not want to be disturbed."

Elijah considered this information for just a moment.

"Okay. In that case I'll find my own stick and shove it up your ass. You got that?"

Dick A Research Assistant vigorously nodded his head up and down and in his redundant manner to which Elijah had become somewhat accustomed whispered, "Yes."

"Okay, then. I'll be in touch."

With that, Elijah turned and joined the pedestrian traffic headed south on Central Park West. As he walked, he asked himself many questions.

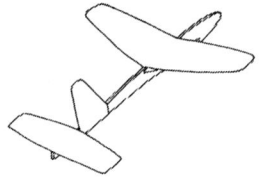

Chapter Twenty-Five

In order to wind up in a locked psychiatric facility involuntarily, certain criteria must be met. The first criterion is evidence of a mental disorder. The person must behave bizarrely or have a history of some sort of mental illness such as Major Depression or Bipolar Disorder or Schizophrenia. Doubtless the first suspicion of the visitors to the museum and the staff of the museum and the security guards and the police officers was that the old woman wearing the tattered leather coat and the leather flying cap running in circles and talking to herself and shouting and jumping up on concrete benches and claiming to have an appointment with Dr. Margaret Mead and claiming to herself be the famous and long lost aviatrix Amelia Earhart was mentally ill. They made no secret of their suspicions.

They said things like, "She's nuts." or "What planet did she come from?" or "She must be crazy."

They said things like that and the more people said them the more other people who had not necessarily observed the events in the lobby said them the more widespread the conclusion became. No one seemed to believe that the ragged, smelly, wild-eyed old woman really had an appointment with Dr. Mead and certainly no one believed that she was Amelia Earhart. Unusual beliefs and statements and not bathing or changing clothes are not sufficient for involuntary hospitalization in a locked psychiatric facility, however. In order for that to happen there must also exist a factor of risk. Thus the second criterion that must be met is being a danger to either self or others. Suicidal or homicidal ideations plus the existence of or the appearance of a mental disorder is just the right ticket for a ride to Bellevue Hospital or for that matter thousands of other psychiatric facilities throughout the country.

Amelia's behaving in a threatening manner toward Dick A Research Assistant might not have been high enough up on the danger meter to deprive her of her rights to come and go as she pleased but certainly biting the policeman's arm while claiming to be Amelia Earhart did the trick even though most women in their early eighties can't really hurt anyone too much unless they have a weapon and Amelia had nothing except her outrage and, unfortunately for the police officer, her teeth. Nevertheless, it was to Bellevue Hospital on First Avenue that the ambulance headed.

Bellevue Hospital, founded in 1736, is said to be the oldest public hospital in the United States. First a 'Public Workhouse and House of Correction' Bellevue changed sites and focus a few times before 1811 when the organization purchased the land upon which the hospital now stands.

On that hot summer afternoon in 1978, as the ambulance containing Amelia Earhart strapped to a secured gurney moved slowly through the Manhattan traffic, Bellevue's primary research affiliation was with Columbia University. Had she known this bit of trivia, Amelia doubtless would not have cared. Her mind was racing too fast in too many directions to appreciate irony. Had Dr. Margaret Mead been sitting in the ambulance with Amelia perhaps holding her hand and assuring her that an event such as this could only be experienced and appreciated in the fuller context of the drama of the whole of humanity the irony would have been noted and later become the subject of an article or even another book which would sell out shortly after the first publication. Dr. Mead was not in the ambulance and Amelia was far from able to identify irony. In fact, strapped to the gurney, she spoke in a language understood by no one save a handful of people on an almost invisible island in the South Pacific and, not coincidentally, by the world-famous ethnologist and anthropologist Dr. Margaret Mead for whom Amelia had searched in the lobby of the American Museum of Natural History.

Bellevue Hospital has given this country and the world many medical milestones from the first ambulance service to the first maternity ward to the development of polio vaccine to the Nobel Prize winning work of Cournand's and Richards' development of the world's first cardiopulmonary catheterization laboratory. Its name is most closely associated, however, with services to the mentally ill. It was at the doors of the hospital's Emergency Psychiatric Admittance Department that the ambulance stopped. The admission process into a psychiatric unit of a hospital sometimes goes much smoother and quicker than, say, the admission of someone with a broken leg into the medical unit of the same hospital. The unfortunate patient with the broken leg can still speak in a generally coherent manner and can provide basic information such as name, address, birth date, social security number and, of course, payment information. Since little if any of that information is available in most psychiatric emergencies, things speed up a little.

Amelia offered plenty of information to anyone who was close enough to hear. None of the information she presented, however, made much sense. Having abandoned English almost completely in favor of her island dialect, nobody noted even her professed identity. Attendants, in fact, admitted her to Bellevue Hospital as Jane Doe number ninety-three and charted that she appeared to be Caucasian, in relatively good physical health, possibly over seventy years in age, and – though hospital staff could have simply asked the police officer and not bothered to pry open her mouth against her will – in possession of all of her teeth.

They wheeled her, still strapped onto the gurney, directly to the locked unit. Once inside a small room furnished only with a bed bolted to the floor, they released her from the restraints.

"Have a seat on the bed and someone will be right with you. Okay?' a nurse mumbled more to herself than to the new patient.

Then they wheeled away the gurney and the nurse who had promised that someone would be right with her okay left and Amelia, Star of the Sea, sat alone in the empty room with only the bed and her racing thoughts already slowed to the point where when she looked around her at the blank cheerless walls and at the closed door with its small wire reinforced double plexi-glassed safety window and when she listened carefully to the sounds of untold miseries surrounding her and when she looked at the bed bolted to the floor she was able to consider quite clearly and quite slowly that she was in a jam. A good old fashioned nothing fancy jam. Nothing as dangerous as when over the Atlantic on that oh so famous first woman to cross the Atlantic flight her fuel line had started leaking into the cockpit. Now that was a jam but this particular jam was certainly a jam that she had never before encountered. Such was her mind and such was her training that nothing sharpened her senses and cleared her thoughts quicker than a jam requiring immediate and careful attention.

Having something on which to focus was a lucky break for Amelia because she sat alone in that cell-like room for quite some time before a tired-looking, overweight charge nurse opened the door and entered holding a clipboard in one hand and dragging a metal chair behind her with the other. Without speaking or even looking directly at Amelia, the nurse placed the chair in the open doorway, sat on it, and stared at her clipboard as though searching for a guide to inform her of her next activity. Finding no such guide, the nurse finally looked from the clipboard to the woman sitting on the bed. The nurse felt neither alarm about nor compassion for the old woman with the completely white hair and bizarre attire. What the nurse felt had little at all to do with the woman sitting across from her and more to do with fatigue and anger that her raise had not gone through and hunger because she had not been able to take her last meal break and with this new admission would likely miss her next meal break, too, and uncertainty about the pilot program of twelve hour days three days a week work shifts actually working because staff was already completely exhausted.

With all of that to occupy her thoughts and her emotions, the nurse simply sat and stared at Amelia until Amelia herself felt compelled to say something to break the silence and put the unhappy looking nurse at ease.

"How do you do, my dear?" Amelia asked in her best imitation of a sweet little old lady.

The nurse stared blankly at Amelia for a moment and then answered.

"I'm fine. My name is Lucy. How are you?"

Again keeping in mind how she thought any sweet little old lady would behave in a similar situation Amelia replied, "Lucy, I seem to be in the midst of an adventure."

Tired, hungry, obese, angry, defeated Lucy smiled at Amelia and then began to chuckle and then finally throwing caution to the wind leaned back in her chair and laughed the laugh of one who has seen it all and has nothing to lose. Amelia remained in her sitting up straight as a broomstick best little old lady pose primarily because she feared that if she relaxed she would once again find herself strapped to a gurney and transported to some other even more sterile facility. Eventually the nurse who called herself Lucy gained control of her laughter and regrouped for a second before again speaking to Amelia.

"So," Lucy finally observed, "You bit a policeman."

"Is that why I'm here?" Amelia asked. "Am I under arrest?"

"No. You are not under arrest. You have been placed on an involuntary hold and you can be here up to seventy-two hours for assessment and observation. You can wear your own clothes and use the pay telephone to make personal calls."

Amelia blinked several times as though trying to make sense of what Lucy had said. Unable to think of anything else to say or ask, Amelia finally to hear her own voice if nothing more, repeated her question.

"Am I under arrest?"

Lucy studied her papers before answering.

"No. You are not under arrest. You are on an involuntary hold. Now, it says here you were running in circles at the American Museum of Natural History. You were jumping up and down onto and off of some sort of bench. Some guy named Dick something or other said you tried to attack him. You claimed to have an appointment with Dr. Margaret Mead. Oh, yeah, and you claimed you were Amelia Earhart. Then, of course, you bit the policeman."

Lucy stared at Amelia and Amelia stared at Lucy.

Lucy blinked first and said, "You've had a busy day."

"At my age it's good to maintain a full schedule. Keeping busy is, I believe, the key to good health," Amelia said and believed what she said.

Lucy nodded her head and said, "I see," and as she did so frequently during her workday wondered how thin the line between sanity and complete madness could become.

Again the two women studied each other. Amelia, again, broke the silence.

"You know, Lucy, I have not been myself for quite some time. Perhaps the events at the museum of which I have no memory were simply part of this phenomenon."

"Could be," Lucy said, warming to the old woman who reminded her of a character in a movie she had stayed up way too late the night before watching. What was the name of that character, Lucy wondered as she looked more carefully at the old woman across from her. Amanda Wingfield. That was it. Amanda Wingfield in *The Glass Menagerie*. Wow! That was some movie. Of course, this woman was way too old to be or play Amanda and she didn't have a Southern accent. In fact she had some sort of garbled accent that sounded like she'd lived on the moon for a number of years. Who was that actress? She'd been on Broadway doing all sorts of stuff. But Lucy couldn't remember the name of the woman who had played Amanda Wingfield in the movie that had kept her awake until almost four in the morning which left little opportunity for sleep before reporting to work for a seven o'clock in the morning twelve hour shift. Relieved to have at least made the connection between this old woman recently brought in on an involuntary hold and Amanda Wingfield in *The Glass Menagerie*, Lucy felt ready to begin asking her routine I know them by heart intake questions.

"So," Lucy began, "do you know where you are?"

Amelia considered the question and all of her possible responses for a moment then said, "I am nowhere I had planned to be."

"Okay. I get that you hadn't planned on being here but do you know where here is? Do you know the name of this place?"

Again Amelia gave careful consideration to the question before responding, "No. Perhaps you could tell me the name of this place."

"You are in Bellevue Hospital."

"My Lord," was Amelia's shocked and unplanned reply. "This is terrible. No offense to you, Lucy, but this is not a place I would have chosen to spend an afternoon. I've heard of Bellevue. Again, no offense to you, Lucy, but this is a terrible place."

Again Lucy smiled but kept herself from surrendering to the laughter steadily building inside of her.

"Come on," she said, "It's not that bad. I'm here."

Amelia, worried that she had said more than was necessary

about her knowledge and opinion of Bellevue Hospital, decided to say nothing more until she had carefully weighed her options and considered her situation. The fuel, after all, was leaking into the cockpit but the plane was not yet on fire. She decided to speak no more. Silence could on occasion extinguish cockpit fires. Amelia shook her head. Perhaps she was mistaken about that. At any rate, silence seemed a wise choice. Lucy, after studying Amelia for several moments, decided to carry on whether or not Amelia participated in the conversation.

"Okay," she began, "I have to ask you these questions so that we can learn a little about you and figure out what we can do to help you. Okay by you?"

Lacking a response from Amelia, Lucy continued.

"First question. Name? What's your name?"

After studying Lucy for a moment, Amelia decided to speak. After all, there were as yet no fires.

"I believe you said that my name is part of the reason I am currently sitting in this room with you."

"That's part of it, I guess. You were claiming to be Amelia Earhart. Do you have any identification that would prove to me you are, in fact, Amelia Earhart?"

Always a quick study, Amelia believed that she was gaining a feel for this new game.

"Of course I don't. How on earth could I have such identification? Didn't she disappear a hundred years ago or so?"

Pleased with the patient's apparent movement toward stability, Lucy replied, "Yeah. Something like that, I guess."

More than anything Amelia wanted to say you fool, it was forty-one years ago not hundreds do I look that old to you but she checked herself and said instead, "My name is Mrs. Mary Anderson. My passport will prove that to you."

"Okay. That's good. Where's your passport? I'll make a copy of it and we'll have your name and your address."

The question stunned Amelia. Her passport was in her bag along with Margaret's herbs and metal box. The question greater than the location of her passport was the location of her bag. Where on earth was the bag? Had she thrown it at Dick A Research Assistant? Had someone stolen it? Amelia sat very still and very silent and replayed in her head the events in the museum lobby. She saw everything with what she believed to be great clarity. She forced the motion to slow down, studied each movement, and carefully listened to each word and each sound until she saw herself swing her bag back to hit Dick A Research Assistant full force in his smug ersatz academic face and felt the bag pull from her hand and saw it in Elijah's hand and then she remembered seeing him put it over his shoulder as she looked up at him from her tethered place on some sort of wheeled in motion bed.

With a sinking feeling, Amelia said, "My passport is in my bag. My friend has the bag."

"Okay. It's not that important. What's your social security number?"

It is an interesting phenomenon of mental illness that almost everyone experiencing acute psychiatric distress can remember and clearly articulate their social security number. A man at the height of a manic episode who has spoken nonstop for hours with the final word of each sentence in rhyme with the final word of the previous sentence can interrupt that out of control high-speed bullet train of thought to pause and slowly, as to be easily understood, recite his social security number. A woman consumed by delusions and psychotic experiences insisting that the Emperor Hadrian's foot soldiers have kidnapped her and taken her to a secluded castle where she will become the concubine of Hadrian can reclaim reality long enough to provide her social security number.

It did not occur to Lucy that this old woman seemingly so calm and so centered would not with perfect diction and without hesitation provide those nine digits. That did not happen.

Instead, Amelia stared at Lucy and was clearly finding the question to be confounding.

"I beg your pardon?" Amelia finally asked.

"Your social," Lucy replied in a louder voice convinced that the old woman had simply not heard her.

"My social," Amelia repeated and Lucy nodded encouragement.

Amelia allowed her mind to race backwards through years of information and conversations and headlines and finally she smiled and saw relief flood Lucy's face.

"I believe the President once made reference to his new old age pension. G. P. and I were dining with the President and Mrs. Roosevelt and, you know how the President would go on. Once something was in his head, he just could not seem to stop talking about it. As I recall, he said that he was going to call this type of insurance 'social security' or some such. I probably was not paying as much attention as I should have. However, I believe the President said that would benefit the elderly should they become impoverished and also the unemployed and if I'm not mistaken widows and orphans. My memory is possibly blurred on that last point. However, I remember clearly that Mrs. Roosevelt was very supportive of this segment of The New Deal. I hope that answers your question, Lucy."

The relief so recently flooding Lucy's face changed first to disbelief and then to an expression of absolute surrender to the situation. She stared blankly at her clipboard for several long seconds and then finally repeated her question.

"So. What's your social security number?"

Amelia smiled indulgently.

"Dear, I've never needed such charities. Just because Franklin and Eleanor championed that project doesn't mean that I participated."

So it was that the charge nurse admitted Amelia into the acute psychiatric ward of Bellevue Hospital on an involuntary hold as a danger to others because of the symptoms and behaviors of a mental illness. As a Jane Doe with no visible funding source, she did not receive priority attention from the staff. She did not see a psychiatrist or an internist until the next day. Unable to produce documentation identifying her as Mary Anderson of whatever address had been used for the passport and remembering the less than satisfactory outcome when she had revealed her actual identity, Amelia simply refused to answer any question including benign questions such as, "How are you?".

When the seventy-two hours of her involuntary admission ended Amelia attended a hearing the name and purpose of which she did not understand. Someone introduced her to her representative and because neither she nor the representative could produce any evidence of identity or address and because Amelia continued to answer all questions directed to her with silence, her seventy-two hours of involuntary hospitalization was extended to fourteen additional days.

"And then I can be released?" Amelia asked reluctantly breaking her silence.

The hearing attendees looked startled by the sound of her voice. Her representative cleared his throat and looked uncertainly around the room.

"If all goes well," he said, "that would be a reasonable expectation. Discharge is certainly what we all hope for."

"Certainly," Amelia agreed. "What might be the date of that discharge?"

After consulting his calendar, her representative replied, "We can't say exactly. If all goes well perhaps the last week of July or the first week of August."

"1978," Amelia clarified.

The attendees seemed surprised at this sudden and seemingly new orientation.

"That's right," they said in almost perfect unison.

The range of possible discharge dates did not comfort Amelia. In fact, it sent her spiraling toward a panic not experienced in decades. The cockpit was about to catch fire. Normally under such circumstances the only sane thing to do is bail out. Sanity, to Amelia, did not appear to be an option in this place so focused on and so famous for defining and reclaiming and achieving sane behavior and sane thinking. She wanted to jump up and down and scream and run in circles and fling rocks and hug trees and count to five hundred forwards and backwards but she did nothing except thank the hearing attendees for their kindness and patience all the while screaming inside her and thinking her head would fall off her shoulders from the pain and perhaps hoping it would fall off of her shoulders because only its complete removal could possibly reduce the pain she felt not just in her head but throughout her entire being.

Amelia walked back to her room, which she referred to as her cell, accompanied by her representative and by a nurse not Lucy. She wondered, as she had for the past seventy hours or so, about Elijah and her bag. Back in her room, she sat on the bed and continued wondering if she had been a fool to have trusted and cared about him and decided that in her life she had many times acted foolishly but not where Elijah was concerned.

"He will come," she said to the room and looked up to see him standing in the doorway.

"And he did," Elijah said.

As he stepped into the room Amelia stood and they threw their three arms around each other and held and swayed and laughed and felt that they had known each other for years instead of two days and when they each took a step back to look at the other, Amelia couldn't help but notice that Elijah wore a business suit.

"Well, my goodness," she said. "Aren't you the handsome gentleman!"

Elijah smiled and his face seemed to flush. Then, like Lucy before him, he pulled a chair into the room, motioned Amelia to sit on the bed, and then sat on the chair with his back to the open door.

"So. How are we feeling today?" he asked.

His question stunned and confused Amelia.

"I beg your pardon?" she replied with a caution recently and quickly adapted.

"As your psychologist," Elijah continued, "I need to have this chat with you. Shall I close the door so we can speak more privately?"

In that instant Amelia understood so much more than the staff in the locked psychiatric unit of Bellevue Hospital believed her capable.

"Certainly. Privacy would be welcome. Thank you."

When the door was closed, Elijah said, "Sorry I took so long to get here. I tried a couple of times to just come visit but they didn't know your name – actually neither did I until the other day – and, of course, they looked at me like they were going to lock me up, too. Which, by the way, they have done before. As it works out, most people don't even look at the patients here much less remember their faces. At any rate, I had to take some time to figure this out."

Amelia smiled.

"You, too, have been incarcerated in this horrid place?"

"Yeah. Just once. That was enough."

"Did you bite a policeman while claiming to be Amelia Earhart?"

Elijah laughed.

"Nothing that neat. It was just, you know, stuff. They said I was psychotic. They were wrong. I was just seeing some awful stuff I didn't want to see again. It kind of leaked through."

Amelia studied him and then nodded her head.

"Some things are hard to keep out."

"Yeah."

"So you have become my psychologist."

"Come to find out, it's easier to convince people you're a doctor if you're wearing a suit than to convince them you're not going to go berserk if you're dressed like a bum. And you know what else? Not only did no one recognize me from the time I was locked up here, no one recognized me as the bum from the other day. They probably never even saw me. Being invisible has its advantages. Anyway, here I am."

"Here you are."

Elijah was clearly excited by his ruse and continued with his narrative.

"When I told them I was looking for Mrs. Mary Anderson they said that they never heard of you and I didn't want to blow my thing that I'm your psychologist so I told them that sometimes Mary Anderson claims to be Amelia Earhart and they said, 'oh, her.' I brought all of these papers proving that I'm a psychologist and they didn't even bother reading them. They just glanced over them and walked me to your door. That's pretty crazy, don't you think?"

Among Elijah's papers was her passport. She stared at it and dreaded what she might find if she opened it.

"I'm rethinking my definition of crazy," she said. "Where did you get that suit? It must have cost a fortune."

"It's borrowed. I know a guy who works for a mortuary."

Unable to formulate any type of response to that statement, Amelia opened her passport and stared at it as though she had never before seen it which was partially true because she had never gotten past the name of Mary Anderson.

"I appear to have an address," she said.

"I know. 211 Central Park West. Quite ritzy, too. The Beresford. Man. That's famous. I went there and gave the doorman a note letting him know that you're here. How'd you get clear over on Flatbush Avenue that day? I feel really stupid. It never even occurred to me to ask you if I could look at your identification.

I could have had you home a long time ago. Of course, I'd miss being with you but at least I'd have gotten you back home."

Amelia stared uncomprehendingly at him and he could see that he was not making sense.

"Don't you live up on Central Park West? 211 Central Park West? You were practically home the other day. The museum is just down on the next block."

"I have lived on and off in New York City but not for over forty years. I came here at the request of a friend."

Elijah studied the old woman carefully and allowed himself to accept and believe what he was hearing. She watched his mind work and waited silently until finally he spoke.

"You know I got these clothes and faked those papers to help you get home and to your people. When I looked at your passport – and by the way that dried grass and stuff is still in your bag – when I looked at your passport and saw your address I figured that you had wandered away from home and couldn't remember your name or where you lived. I was glad we had found each other because you're – well – I like you. I mean, I really like you. And you play a mean banjo. But I came here to take you home."

"Thank you, Elijah. It would never occur to me to not trust you completely and I profoundly appreciate all that you have done to help me. Yes. I hope to return to my home. However, this is not my home. This city … I never liked it."

Elijah considered her response. He seemed to be carefully measuring his words before he spoke them.

"Your name isn't Mary Anderson, is it?" he finally asked.

Amelia looked directly into his eyes and whispered, "No."

Again Elijah considered her response before speaking.

"The other day in the museum. That was the truth, wasn't it?"

Amelia looked deeper into his eyes and felt the room grow cold. Breaking a vow, breaking a silence of forty years, was not in the agreement and certainly not in her character.

She opened her mouth to speak and then she closed her mouth and then she opened it again and said simply, "Yes."

The rush of air she heard was not divine intervention or retribution but simply the sound of Elijah releasing the breath he had been holding. He smiled.

"Well. We kind of have a different situation here, now, don't we?"

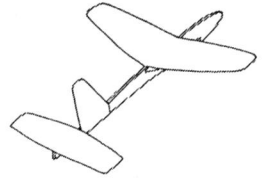

Chapter Twenty-Six

Life on the locked unit of a psychiatric hospital becomes routine. Aside from the furniture bolted to the floor and the locked doors, the locked unit can be pretty much like any other hospital floor except for the frequent codes resulting inevitably in someone's being strapped to a bolted bed, the almost constant wandering of at least one person experiencing mania, and occasional screams. Twice a day staff urged Amelia to attend a group of one sort or another. She sat in on one cognitive therapy group and found it mindless. A well-intentioned social work intern encouraged her to 'journal her feelings'. To not disappoint the graduate student, she accepted a journal. She quickly filled every page with compass headings, routes, and everything she could remember about the Lockheed Vega. She dared not mention the Lockheed Electra for fear she would be the next person on whom staff called a code. When the student asked if she would like to 'process' the feelings in the journal, Amelia told her she could keep it as a souvenir.

"I signed it," she added. "There aren't many of those around."

As the days passed, Amelia yearned for a calendar on which she could mark her progress toward the end of this humiliating incarceration. Lucy spent as much time as possible with this so very different patient. She couldn't fathom why she liked the old woman but even when she wasn't working the jaded charge nurse who believed she had seen everything Bellevue had to offer couldn't get her out of her mind.

To Lucy nothing about Mrs. Mary Anderson seemed even remotely in keeping with life on the locked psychiatric unit.

"She's never combative. She's always polite. I just don't know, Elvis," Lucy said to her cat as they shared a cup of tea in the tiny fourth floor walk up East Village apartment Lucy had first rented while she was still in nursing school. "There's just something about her. It's like she's from another world or another time and doesn't quite know what to make of any of this."

Nurse and cat stared at each other briefly. When Lucy again spoke, the cat left the table to look out the window onto never dark and never dull First Avenue.

"No one seems to know her except her psychologist. And I gotta tell you, Elvis, that Dr. Copeland seems like an okay guy but he's sure not like any psychologist I ever met. You know how smug and precious all of them are? Elvis, pay attention. This is interesting stuff."

The cat returned to the table to drink more tea and at least pretend to listen.

"Well, this Copeland guy seems real down to earth. And he seems interested in what I have to say about his client. Man, he could teach his colleagues a thing or two. Maybe I could line up a few sessions with him. Sometimes I feel just like Mary Anderson must feel – like I just don't belong here. Next time he comes on the unit, I think I'll ask for his card. Whatta you think?"

Indeed, the man claiming to be the psychologist of Mrs. Mary Anderson, so recently called Jane Doe, visited every day. Sometimes Dr. Copeland spent the entire afternoon either in the room with the door closed or simply sitting with his client in the day room. To Lucy they seemed content to sit in silence. She marveled that the psychologist could spend so much time with his client and she yearned for such caring attention.

"Aren't you supposed to be on the Promenade?" Amelia once asked Elijah.

"Family comes first," was his only response.

"Yes," she said without hesitation.

Elijah eventually managed to arrange a case consultation with Amelia's attending psychiatrist, the charge nurse, and the social worker. The consultation was scheduled for two in the afternoon. They sat in a room on the locked unit normally used for group therapy. No artwork adorned the drab walls. In places the paint peeled away to reveal layers of older drab colors. The door to the room was open. Amelia had not been invited to attend. She stayed in her room with that door open.

"As you know, we extended the hold by fourteen days," the attending psychiatrist began the meeting. "Those fourteen days are up today. However, Mrs. Anderson continues to exhibit what appears to be long-standing delusions and has not yet achieved any type of success in restructuring some of those erroneous beliefs. But then, I'm sure you are aware of these symptoms, Dr. Copeland. Additionally, we are concerned that she refuses to take any type of medication. We hesitated to request a hearing to allow us to administer enforced medication. We were hoping collaterals could be located. Obviously we appreciate your participation in her care. We were hoping you might have persuaded her to become compliant with at least a minimal medication regimen."

Elijah looked at each member of the treatment team, cleared his throat, and said, "Taking medications is against the religion of Mrs. Anderson. She is a very religious person."

"She hasn't participated in one group," the social worker interrupted as though eager to begin healing the wound Amelia's lack of group attendance had inflicted upon her own sense of well-being.

"She doesn't like crowds," Elijah countered.

Elijah looked at the charge nurse and his expression invited her to also itemize the ways in which their patient had failed them.

Lucy wanted with all of her heart to say, "For God's sake. She's just confused. She doesn't belong here." She couldn't say what she felt, though, because the thought of losing her job terrified Lucy more than any of her other almost consuming fears. And everyone knew that disagreeing with the treating psychiatrist was what they all called a CLM – a Career Limiting Move. Lucy paused as though to again consult a clipboard but finding none in her hands she finally spoke.

"She's sweet. She's been cooperative. She does seem out of touch with this time and place, though. Meds would really help and…"

The social worker, always eager to show her disdain of Lucy, interrupted.

"We appreciate finally having an address for her, Dr. Copeland. We would feel more comfortable if we knew more about her living situation. Is there someone in the home to watch out for her?"

Elijah looked from the psychiatrist to the charge nurse to the social worker and – hoping to buy himself some time to keep from making a bad situation worse – directed his response to Lucy.

"Well, you know, of course, that there are issues of confidentiality and…"

The social worker, who seemed to Elijah to be genetically predisposed to rudeness and anger, interrupted him.

"We're not asking you to disclose what the two of you talk about in therapy. All we need to know is whether or not there is a responsible person in the home."

While the social worker spoke, Lucy looked at Elijah and rolled her eyes. The social worker, oblivious to the silent communication between Lucy and Elijah, continued.

"In the on-going presence of her set and fixated delusions, her refusal to take medications, and the assaultive behavior she exhibited prior to admission, I'm suggesting that she be referred to the Public Guardian's office to be placed on a conservatorship."

"To what fixations are you referring?" Elijah asked.

"At the time of admission she strongly identified with Amelia Earhart to the extent that she stated the belief that she was Amelia Earhart. She can provide no background history. She has not been cooperative. I fear this fixated belief system will significantly impair her ability to adequately function in her environment."

"She hasn't claimed to be Amelia Earhart since her admission," Lucy was no longer able to hide her irritation.

Even the psychiatrist looked uncomfortable and shifted in his chair.

"I believe," he began and cleared his throat before continuing, "that properly supervised and supported, her delusions would fade even without medication."

"You know," Elijah said, "it's okay that sometimes she pretends she's someone she's not. We all do that a little bit. I'll help her sort that out again. She had a trauma which I can't discuss and it kind of set her reeling. I mean, look at her. I know you get a lot of folks in here who think they're some famous person or other. But look at where she lives. Look at me. She's got a therapist. I'm her psychologist. We spend a lot of time together. Don't you think this is different?"

"They're all different," the morally outraged social worker replied. "If you can produce someone who will be in the home with her, I'm willing to consider discharge. Otherwise, I'm going to insist on a hearing to extend the hold for an additional twenty-one days. It's for her safety."

The sound of moaning and pacing could be heard from Amelia's room. Lucy looked sharply at the social worker.

"Maybe you should have kept your voice down a little," she said.

The social worker glared back at Lucy.

"There is no time. I am running out of time," came the voice from Amelia's room.

"See what I mean," the social worker practically gloated. "She lacks sufficient impulse control to even tolerate what she hears from eavesdropping on this conversation. She is far from stable."

The combination of Amelia's moaning and pacing and the social worker's increasingly loud voice and the usual noise of the unit – ringing telephones and typewriters and patient and staff conversations – hid the first sounds of the approach. No one on the unit had heard the doors unlock when they entered and no one heard their footsteps countered by the rap of the stick. As they came nearer, however, the steady whap of the stick grew loud enough to alert everyone on the unit that a presence was among them. Typewriters stopped in mid word. Telephone conversations ended. Discussions became first hushed and then abruptly finished. All faces turned to the hallway down which walked a tall man in a business suit and a short, elderly, frail looking woman wearing a red cape and accenting each step she took with a rap on the floor with the chief's stick she held firmly in her right hand. Her left arm was wrapped through the right arm of the man with whom she walked. They walked slowly. If each step was an agony for the white haired woman, the strength with which her stick hit the floor in counter rhythm to her steps told a different story. The woman's eyes, through thick glasses, blazed like lava about to begin its slow path of downhill destruction.

The blazing eyes first bore into Elijah. Elijah stood to face such an intensity as he had never before encountered. The psychiatrist, the social worker, and Lucy also rose. Only when all stood before her did the woman – eyes still burning into Elijah – speak in a voice of unhesitating authority.

"Dr. Copeland? Elijah Copeland? Thank you for your note. I am truly grateful. Now, where is…"

The sentence was not finished.

"You are here," Amelia no more than whispered from the doorway of her room and yet her voice seemed to grow until the three words she spoke filled the locked psychiatric unit of Bellevue Hospital and broke the locked doors open and snapped the bars off of the windows.

Amelia stepped from her room. The two women looked at each other across oceans and islands of time and longing and despair and hope and rage and forgiveness and regret into eyes full of gentle sadness and limitless passion. Amelia took another step closer to the woman whose frailty seemed to those standing in stunned silence to transform into towering strength with each step taken by the woman now known to the hospital ward as Mrs. Mary Anderson.

Pausing after each step as though waiting for the floor to collapse under the combined weight of their presence, Amelia moved toward the other woman. Neither looked away from the other – not even when only inches separated them. Finally Amelia with a trembling hand gently touched the other woman's face. The other woman – as though participating in a familiar ritual – did not move. She could not, however, keep her lips from betraying her otherwise fortress like presence with the slightest hint of a smile. After a moment, Amelia slowly backed away from the other woman and then bowed to her, then slowly returned to her, touched her face, slowly backed away from her, bowed to her, slowly backed away from her until she had repeated the routine five times to stand once again near the door of her room on the locked psychiatric unit of New York's famous Bellevue Hospital.

Satisfied that the routine had ended, the woman wearing a red cape and holding a chief's stick at last spoke.

"Yes. I am here," she said.

Only then did the two women more than walk more than

move more than glide – they as though pushed and propelled by an unseen unnamed energy – became in each other's arms. No one noticed that Amelia closed the gap between them first and no one noticed that she almost completely supported the other woman and no one noticed their tears flowing down separate cheeks and merging in what little space existed between them. They clung to each other until even that felt to each like too great a distance so they each took a step away to again stare into eyes for too long seen only in memory's vision. And then they laughed. They laughed until they wept and then, exhausted, fell again into open arms yearning for just such an embrace.

Perhaps from some need to safeguard whatever privacy might be squeezed from a hospital unit for this most different reunion or perhaps for no reason at all, the man in the suit turned to Elijah.

"Ah, Dr. Copeland. It's so good to finally meet you. I'm Daniel Sullivan, corporate counsel for Bellevue."

As the two men shook hands, the two women stepped apart. Only then did the frail woman again speak.

"Mary Anderson. How many times have I told you to stop telling people you're Amelia Earhart? Let's go home, now. Dr. Copeland, won't you accompany us? Your patient will doubtless require some special time."

With that the ill woman extended her arm toward Amelia and Amelia, as only old friends or lovers can do, immediately slid her arm to lock with that of the woman for whom she had waited and searched. Immediately and automatically Amelia moved close enough to invisibly support the other. Together they turned to begin a slow in step walk out of the ward and the hospital. For several feet the only sound in the unit was the chief's stick rapping the floor.

Elijah moved to the other side of Amelia and thought he heard, just before the doors closed behind them, the social worker start to say, "But in my opinion…"

Then he thought he heard Daniel Sullivan interrupt with, "This patient has already been discharged. The papers are complete. Mrs. Mary Anderson has been discharged into the care of Dr. Margaret Mead."

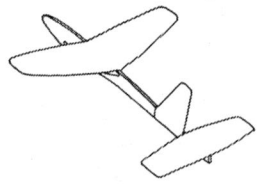

Chapter Twenty-Seven

Immediately outside the locked unit, the dying woman collapsed into her waiting wheelchair. While Elijah stood beside them like a bewildered sentinel, Amelia kneeled on the floor to lay her head on Margaret's chest. She heard strained, ragged breathing and the steady, strong pounding of a heart too stubborn to miss even a single beat. She felt a hand stroke her hair. The hand and the touch were so familiar it seemed to Amelia she had never been without them. The voice so strong moments before on the locked unit now sounded frail and bent.

"The car is in front," she said as both Amelia and Elijah strained to hear.

Elijah pushed the wheelchair and Amelia, carrying the chief's stick, walked beside them, keeping a constant hand on the sagging shoulder of the slumped woman.

There was no need for conversation as the Town Car made its way back across and uptown toward the American Museum of Natural History and beyond. The two women simply sat together in the backseat. The chief's stick lay across their laps and each held it as though by holding it they held each other. Elijah, trying in some coherent fashion to wrap his mind around the events of the day, sat in the front seat only occasionally glancing at the uniformed driver and blinking back tears of wonder. Once when he dared glance into the back seat, he noticed with a certain amount of pleasure that Amelia was again wearing her leather flying cap.

"She's feeling like herself again," he thought and felt grateful for the thought.

The Town Car stopped in front of The Beresford and the frail woman spoke again.

"Give us a moment."

With those four words Amelia knew that the soul of this woman was not diminished by illness or approaching death. Asking for favors was not her habit. Giving directives was an everyday form of communication. A tremor went through her body and she felt a distance begin between them far greater and far more terrifying than the distance between this never sleeping city and their very own paradise somewhere in the South Pacific.

With those four words, Amelia also knew that the next words would not necessarily be positive or pleasant and in her mind she thought, "Here we go again."

When they were alone in the car, Margaret shifted to face Amelia.

"What on earth took you so long? I sent you the ticket and the money and the passport almost a year ago and now after all of this time I have to pull strings and orchestrate your release from a locked psychiatric facility because you were assaulting people in my museum and claiming to be Amelia Earhart. I believed you would leave Nani immediately. I expected you here months ago. My precious darling you have always been so completely unpredictable. One minute you're sad. The next you're happy. One minute you are on the ground and the next you are flying into the clouds. I so love you and I have always accepted you for all the glory that is you. But this most recent escapade is beyond even what I might have expected."

What Amelia wanted to say was, "First of all, I am Amelia Earhart, or have you forgotten? Have the years of keeping me hidden on one of your islands led you to believe that you had no involvement in those events? I have gone hungry and I have slept in wood chips and I have done everything except move mountains to get here because you asked me to come. Never once did I say to you 'come to me' because I knew you would never have done such a thing unless your schedule permitted it. But you say come to me and I come. Why? Because I love you and because we made an arrangement which only I have honored. And now you dare challenge the length of time it took me to make this impossible journey."

In her mind Amelia saw herself jumping out of the Town Car, slamming the door, grasping Elijah's hand, and returning to Brooklyn to live out her days playing the banjo on the Promenade and sleeping in a greenhouse in the Brooklyn Botanic Garden. Amelia, though, did not leap out of the Town Car nor did she give voice to her thoughts.

Instead, she lowered her head and said, "I'm sorry. I should have gotten here sooner. You are absolutely correct. I suppose things were more complicated than either of us anticipated."

In response to those words, the dying woman leaned forward and kissed Amelia on the forehead.

"I love you," Amelia whispered.

"Oh, my darling. And I, you. You are here and that is what matters."

For several moments they sat with only their foreheads touching. Finally Amelia pulled her head back and reached to open the car door. Margaret stopped her with a hand on her arm.

"There is something else," she began.

Amelia's hand left the door to stroke Margaret's face. Margaret took her hand and held it in both of hers.

"There is a potential complication and you must know of it before we leave this car."

Amelia felt her stomach lurch upward as though attempting to flee her body through her throat. She tasted terror forming in her mouth and knew that the gas leaking into the cockpit had finally ignited. Soon the cockpit would be in flames. She had begun this flight without a parachute and had certainly not acquired one along the way. As her mind itemized choices her hand left Margaret's to reach again for the door. As she prepared to open the door she concluded that she had only two choices. Either ride the burning plane all the way down or leap to fly planeless as long as possible. Either choice ultimately left her dead in the water. Before she could actually open the door, Margaret pulled her hand back into hers.

"Oh, there you go again," she teased. "Getting ready to run off before you even hear what I'm about to say. Your impulsiveness has not diminished with your age. I am somehow strangely pleased and comforted by that. I suppose, though, if you were your former impulsive self you would have gotten here much sooner. However, we've already covered that topic – at least for the time being. Apparently we all slow a bit with age."

Amelia took a deep breath. She was finding it difficult to breathe in the burning cockpit and hoped to get out of the crashing plane as soon as possible.

"What is the complication?" she asked.

"For some time I have lived with a *companion* of sorts."

Amelia stared through the thick glasses into the eyes of Margaret Mead. Her silence filled the Town Car.

"We began collaborating on a number of projects in, I believe, 1940. She is quite a brilliant anthropologist and I found our collaborations to be particularly satisfying. She has served as my research assistant for the past several years. And, of course, you and I were ... well ... you know ... not geographically close."

The plane was completely engulfed in flames. The cabin felt so hot that Amelia's face was immediately drenched with sweat. She could barely see because of the unbearable heat and the dancing flames. She yearned for the ocean's cold water.

"In 1955 I decided to rent the bottom two floors of her home on Waverly Place. I had been back from the South Pacific, and you, my dear, for no more than a year or so and I truly always planned on returning forever to be with you. The living arrangement seemed a good idea at the time. Gradually the distinctions between her top two floors and my bottom two blurred. Eventually we moved here to The Beresford. There is only one place, though, that I've ever truly considered home."

Margaret paused to smile at Amelia and to trace her fingers across her lips. Her breathing seemed to grow more difficult but Amelia in her flaming plane plummeting toward the ocean was not able to assist in any way. She was already preparing for impact. There was no time left to bail out with or without a parachute. More missed opportunities to add to the steadily growing list.

"And your new friend," Amelia said through the flames, "is waiting for you inside?"

Only a truly great pilot could have such a conversation while wrestling an airplane engulfed in flames. There was no point in looking at her instruments. They no longer made sense just as whatever rationale Margaret presented made no sense. All information was wrong and useless.

"I'm flying by the seat of my pants, here," Amelia said through gritted teeth and clenched jaw.

"I know, dear," Margaret soothed. "I'm right here with you."

While Margaret stroked her face, Amelia forced herself to concentrate on the airplane and the flames and the rapidly approaching ocean.

"I've mentioned before," Margaret continued as though she did not see the water racing toward them, "that I expected you to be here sooner and so, since I believe in the inherent societal value of monogamy, I ended the relationship quite some time ago. There were other reasons, but the overriding reason was that I wanted to be with you. My 'new friend' as you call her moved to Vermont."

They did not crash into the ocean. At the last moment, the

very last possible moment, Amelia was able to dip the airplane's nose to gain just enough airspeed to pull the plane parallel to the water. Now if she could only figure out a way to extinguish the fire they could possibly get back to Nani.

"However, you did not arrive."

"My God, woman," Amelia wanted to shout, "be quiet so I can think."

"I never doubted your intention," Margaret continued despite the fact that Amelia silently screamed for silence, "but, my darling, you have never been too terribly reliable. Time passed and my strength steadily faded. I convinced myself you would not come. Not more than a week ago I asked her to come back. I needed help."

Not even the most brilliant pilot could keep a burning airplane airborne with only a few feet of space between it and the ocean. Amelia's airplane hit the water hard and fast. Glass broke and shards sliced her face. She felt the cuts and the salt water's sting. The cockpit quickly filled with water. She looked around for Margaret and then remembered that this was a solo flight. Margaret had bailed out long ago and floated safely home under the canopy of her always-available parachute.

"Solo. Always was and always will be," she said to which Margaret could not reply.

Amelia welcomed the cold water and opened her mouth to fill her lungs with its deadening relief. She tried to breathe in the ocean's comfort but could suck in nothing – not air, not water, not fire. Her eyes stung from the saltwater. The only movement of which she was capable was to lower her head into Margaret's lap and when she did that she found herself taking in deep breaths of air rich with the scent of this woman who could so easily fling the burning plane into the ocean and just as easily reach into the still flaming waters to lift Amelia out of the wreckage to safety.

"Oh, there, there," Margaret whispered and removed the leather flying cap to stroke Amelia's hair. "You poor thing. I never meant to hurt you. Never. Not once did I mean to hurt you. Now sit up."

Amelia sat up and again looked into those eyes and at that face and knew that all over again she would ride the plane into the ocean and live a life separate from the rest of the world just to gaze if only for moments separated by years and thousands of miles into that face and feel that touch and hear that voice and breathe in such love. Margaret wiped the tears from Amelia's streaked face.

"My goodness you're a mess," she said and they both laughed so hard that Margaret began to cough and coughed a racking cough for several moments and when the coughing ended she collapsed back into the seat of the Town Car and Amelia wiped sweat from her face and fanned her with her flying cap.

"Well," Margaret continued when she had rested enough to speak again, "this body of mine is not going to last as long as I had hoped. But we are together. Let's go deal with my complication, shall we? She's a good woman. However, she does tend to, shall we say, protect me. Perhaps your Dr. Copeland can confuse the situation so much that she won't notice us."

"Doubtless, Margaret, you've told your friend our entire story? Every little detail, I would imagine." Amelia said and smiled.

"Doubtless. That's an interesting word, isn't it my darling," came Margaret's smiling reply.

Amelia considered for a moment more then said, "It is an interesting word, Margaret. Even more interesting is why, if your friend has returned to resume living with you, we are entering the home you by your own admission share with another. Or is it possible that, in your vast and awesome vocabulary, the word *awkward* does not exist?"

"As we both know from personal experience, Amelia, anything is possible."

Margaret then motioned Amelia to open the car door. Before they got out of the car, Margaret reached toward Amelia, pulled her flying cap back onto her head and touched a finger to her nose. Amelia's head was throbbing and she had long before lost track of her emotions. She had experienced so many while sitting in the backseat of the Town Car that all she currently felt was utter fatigue. She wished desperately that she were back on her island in her hut in her bed sleeping soundly as the ocean breeze gently propelled the tiny airplane hanging from its cord on circular journeys above her.

The driver left after determining that Elijah would push Margaret in her wheelchair. Once again Amelia carried the chief's stick and walked beside and once again the two women held hands and did not feel the need to speak. They had reclaimed their natural rhythm and were riding their own roller coaster of heart melting gentle warmth interrupted at irregular but eventually predictable minor moments of death-defying and death-inviting rage and recrimination and remorse and at last again the heart melting gentle warmth that so defined who they were to each other.

"Rhoda, we have guests for dinner," Margaret announced to the woman, considerably younger than herself, who opened the door.

The dinner guests received an icy stare that left their ears so frostbitten they could barely hear, "You've overdone it. You're exhausted."

Without looking at their guests, Dr. Rhoda Metraux pushed the wheelchair in which Dr. Margaret Mead sat into the living room of their Beresford home. Amelia and Elijah were left standing outside the open door. Despite the chill wind that held them captive in the doorway, they clearly heard Margaret's voice.

"We have dinner guests."

"Fine," came the answer.

Thus Amelia and Elijah entered the home of Dr. Margaret Mead. Sketchy introductions presented Mrs. Mary Anderson and Dr. Elijah Copeland to Dr. Rhoda Metraux as journalists researching current conditions in Samoa and other South Pacific islands. Amelia decided to not mention the fact that she needed no research on the topic since she had only recently arrived from forty uninterrupted years living on an island in the South Pacific and currently wished she had never left said island. Margaret introduced Dr. Rhoda Metraux to Amelia and Elijah only as her colleague and did not notice or else successfully ignored both women looking at her with expressions of pain and betrayal.

Despite the fact that he charmed his host with his knowledge of sociology and anthropology and especially of her writings, Elijah would remember that evening as one of the most uncomfortable of his life. Neither Amelia nor Margaret was able to eat for entirely different reasons. Margaret could not eat because much of her intestinal tract was being consumed by cancer. Amelia could not eat because much of her being was consumed by the joy, rage, sadness and loneliness she felt in the presence of this woman. The other woman attempted to coax food into Margaret's mouth and either pretended Amelia and Elijah were not at the table or actually forgot about them, even though Margaret maintained uninterrupted eye contact with Amelia and actively engaged in conversation with Elijah. By the end of the meal that neither she nor Amelia ate, however, Margaret was clearly exhausted.

"I'm afraid I must go to bed, my dears," she said and folded her unused napkin back onto the table. "When Rhoda has finished helping me prepare for bed, Mary, would you come in and spend a moment with me?"

Amelia looked across the table with steely eyes that said, "How dare you not use my real name. How dare you not claim me."

"Of course, Dr. Mead," she replied.

Sitting beside her on the bed, Amelia saw how weak and frail Margaret had become and her heart ached until it broke. Whatever rage she had felt at the dinner table melted. Of course, that had always been the case with whatever rage Amelia felt toward Margaret. She stroked Margaret's head and played with the never orderly strands of hair, pulling them away from her face only to watch them fall back over her forehead. She smiled and it seemed that she had done nothing for the past forty years except sit and look into this face and stroke this forehead and arrange this unmanageable hair.

Finally rested sufficient to speak, Margaret said, "Amelia, my darling..."

"Don't you mean Mary my darling?" Amelia interrupted.

"Please, Amelia. Not now. I'm too tired. Perhaps tomorrow we can pursue that topic. At the same time I started paying for open airline tickets, I rented an apartment in The Alden so we could have a place of our own. It's been waiting for us all of these months. At this point, I suppose it's just waiting for you. I've no idea where you've been keeping yourself aside from Bellevue or even how long you've been here. You can tell me all about your travels later. For now though, you have a home. I'll take care of all your expenses. The key to our apartment is in the night stand. Obviously if your psychologist or journalist friend needs to stay with you, so be it."

"Oh, Margaret, you so love to organize my life, don't you?"

"Well, darling, it seems someone has to. Don't you agree?"

As both women smiled, Amelia saw Margaret sink further into her pillows and felt her heart begin to break all over again.

"I have been living in Brooklyn since my arrival. I don't remember how long that has been. Obviously matters became confused. For now, though, I prefer to go home with Elijah."

"You'll come again tomorrow, though?" Margaret whispered.

"Will your *colleague* let me in?"

"By then I will have created a convincing scenario to satisfy whatever questions she might have."

"In addition to my journalistic research?"

"Please, Amelia, not now."

"That I was discharged from Bellevue into your care isn't sufficiently convincing?"

"You just never know when to stop, do you, my love?"

They smiled at each other and for a moment felt again the waves of pleasure in which they so long ago each day swam.

And then, "Good night, my darling."

And then, "Good night, my love."

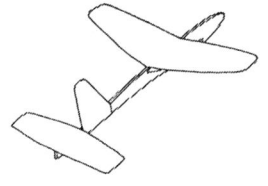

CHAPTER TWENTY-EIGHT

Elijah and Amelia left The Beresford to return to Brooklyn and the greenhouse in the Botanic Garden. For Amelia it did feel almost like home. She slept well and awoke at dawn.

During the night Elijah returned the business suit to his friend at the mortuary. Amelia awoke to see him sitting cross-legged back in his 'street clothes' writing in a spiral bound notebook. She sat up and stretched and marveled as she did many mornings that a body so advanced in years could continue being so lithe. Her stretches complete, she turned onto her back and did sit-ups until her abdominals felt like they were about to cramp and then she turned onto her stomach and did push ups and when she finally stopped she felt more fit than at any time since leaving Nani. Elijah stopped his writing and smiled at her.

"Well, good morning, Mama," he said.

She studied him a moment.

"Are you writing your memoirs at such a young age?" and motioned with her head to his notebook.

"Nah. I'm just trying to keep track of what's been going on during the past few days. I feel kind of confused sometimes."

Amelia nodded her head in agreement, then stood and stretched some more.

"Life can sometimes be quite confusing," she finally agreed.

"So I'm taking notes."

"So you can turn the notes into music?"

"Yeah. I guess that's how it works."

"Don't you think this story is bigger than one song? At least make a musical out of it."

"Then a musical it is."

"Would there be dancing in your musical?"

"What's a musical without dancing?"

"I'm not a very good dancer. Margaret has never even tried except when she participated in tribal dances. Of course, by the time this is performed on Broadway she will…"

Amelia could not finish her sentence. Elijah did not ask for completion. As soon as they left the greenhouse to walk toward the Promenade they began salvaging edible trash from garbage cans and dumpsters. While sorting through one dumpster, Amelia found a chipped, broken piece of façade that had fallen off an old building. Stamped on the back was the imprint of a long ago defunct Flatbush Avenue foundry. She thought the piece resembled the face of a Polynesian god and put it in her bag for Margaret. At the Promenade she and Elijah and the musicians ate their breakfast and Amelia remarked that fresh garbage tasted much better than the food served at Bellevue Hospital.

"I'll bet the company here is better, too," Jack said.

Amelia agreed and added that at Bellevue you never knew who you were going to meet.

"I had the pleasure of meeting three different Messiahs," she said and they laughed.

"Of course," she continued, "I myself claimed to be Amelia Earhart. There were already too many Messiahs. At least I followed suit and chose a being not bound by gravity."

They laughed until silence settled between them. After several moments, Nick picked up his bongos, walked to the railing and, gazing down at the traffic on the Brooklyn Queens Expressway, beat a slow and somber rhythm. The other musicians joined him. Solemn drumbeats gave way to the music of the street band. Amelia listened to several songs then stood.

"I've got to go to her," she said.

"I'll go with you."

"You don't need to, even though, of course, I do like being with you," Amelia said as they walked to the train.

"I'll just hang with that driver and the doorman. We hit it off yesterday. They're cool. Besides, you never know when you're gonna need your personal psychologist."

"Most of the time, I would imagine. You know, today you are not dressed like the famous Dr. Copeland."

"It's casual day."

The doorman expected them and greeted Elijah with a variety of handshakes which Amelia wished Margaret could see because she would have something fascinating to say about the social phenomena of greeting. Margaret's companion admitted Amelia into the apartment and escorted her to an office, which, if Amelia's memory was correct, was a duplicate in miniature of the famously cluttered office in a turret of the American Museum of Natural History. The room was a tangle of artifacts – masks and pottery and woven wall hangings and pieces of driftwood. A table served as a desk and it was stacked high with books and papers. An electric typewriter sat in the middle of the table and in front of the table sat Margaret Mead. A pillow helped support her. Her chief's stick leaned against the desk within arm's reach. When Amelia entered the room, Margaret looked over her glasses and smiled.

"Close the door," she said with a greeting that would have been the same for whoever walked into the sacred office space of this dying world treasure.

Amelia closed the door and awaited further instructions. Margaret motioned to a chair near the desk. Before Amelia sat in it, Margaret motioned for her to pull the chair closer to her.

"I expected you earlier," she said in a soft but firm professorial voice.

Amelia looked at Margaret for a moment, then took a deep breath and with heart pounding and palms clammy said, "You know, Margaret, our visits might be far more pleasant if you did not begin each one with a scolding."

The icon challenged by no one considered Amelia's words and her face softened.

"You have a valid point, my darling."

Amelia, having braced herself for yet another fatal crash into the ocean's cold waters, felt first shock and then euphoria to find herself floating gently and safely and peacefully into the lush landscape of a love so different as to be uncharted and unnamed. So complete was her euphoria that she felt giddy and slightly out of control and suddenly fearless.

"Margaret, if I may be so bold, I would like to say something else."

The softness vanished from Mead's face and she lowered her head to stare again at Amelia over her glasses.

"Before I begin, do you actually see better when you look over your glasses? I've been wanting to ask you that for years."

The famous scowl immediately gave way to the famous smile and then Margaret laughed and then Amelia laughed and without either woman looking four hands clasped together and held tightly until the laughter exhausted them both.

Then, never one to avoid a direct question, Margaret Mead replied, "Of course not. But you must admit the look does give me an impressive façade."

"Oh, speaking of façade," Amelia said and pulled her gift from the woven bag.

Margaret took it and examined it with the scholar's eye. She turned it in her hands and smelt it and felt its weight.

"This is very reminiscent of a tribe I once visited. It's wonderful."

Seemingly lost in scholarly thought, she pulled a book toward her, opened it and searched through it, her eyes dancing with interest and determination. Finally she tapped her finger on a page and closed the book.

She turned her attention back to Amelia and Amelia saw the dancing eyes and the mouth struggling to remain pensive.

"This is a classic example, I believe," Margaret began, "Of the Fugittaboutits. As you doubtless know, they are indigenous to the lesser of the five boroughs – an insignificant cluster of buildings called Brooklyn and primarily the part of Brooklyn called Flatbush Avenue. I shall write my next best seller about this people. I shall first, however, travel extensively through the area and remain for an extended period of time in hiding with a world famous but believed to be tragically missing aviatrix. Then I shall return to Manhattan for a brief visit during which I shall discover that I am with child and be forced to remain in Manhattan and the world because raising a child while in hiding somewhere in Brooklyn is not, I believe, optimal parenting. However," and her face again softened as her eyes filled with tears, "I shall so deeply wound the woman I love that I shall spend the rest of my life wishing I had done differently. I will visit her sometimes for extended periods of hiding but always with subterfuge so the world will not suspect. And I will know that those visits can never repair the deep wound I have inflicted upon her. I shall send menial and pointless gifts to remind her of my love and of the difficulties of life. And, yes, I will enter into other relationships because even in this huge metropolis life is lonely and I am weak and in need of comfort. You being who you are doubtless will seek no such comfort. The friendship and warmth of a man so strong he would cut off his own leg will suffice for you. I am very different. I could not do what you did and for that I beg your forgiveness."

Amelia stood and gathered the dying woman into her arms and held her and stroked her hair and whispered again and again and again, "I forgive you. I love you. I forgive you."

When Amelia returned to her chair, Margaret said, "And I forgive you, too."

Amelia's determination to say one more thing returned with greater intensity than she had previously felt. She looked at Margaret and mentally measured her words before she spoke.

"First of all, Margaret, I don't need your forgiveness because I have done nothing to harm you."

"Then I forgive you for all that you didn't do."

Too exasperated to carry the conversation further, Amelia sighed and said, "All right, Margaret. This is the other thing I wanted to say. You accuse me of dawdling and that's just not true. I came as quickly as possible."

Amelia had gone over these words many times in her mind. Having said them, she felt suddenly drained. She slumped back in her chair. The two women sat in silence. Somewhere in the room a clock marked time's passage with its steady and unremitting ticking. Outside the room, on the street below, car horns honked and sirens announced danger and possible rescue. The light coming into the bedroom through the open window dimmed as the day moved toward evening.

Finally Margaret spoke.

"Again, I ask forgiveness. True forgiveness. I have been ungracious and, yes, unloving. I'm sorry.

Amelia's eyes filled with tears. Through those tears Margaret seemed so frail and so small Amelia feared she might drown in a single drop.

"I won't leave you. We will ride this out together," Amelia softly said and Margaret nodded her head.

"Thank you, my love," Margaret replied and fell into a deep sleep.

Amelia did not leave the room while Margaret slept. She listened to the labored breathing and saw her wince in her sleep from time to time. As the room grew dark with evening, Margaret awoke and stared at Amelia before finally becoming oriented to her present realities.

"You're here," she finally said and smiled a gentle, dreamy smile previously observed by Amelia only at the first light of dawn as they began the process of untangling limbs and bodies from a night's sleep spent as one.

"Where else would I be?" Amelia informed rather than asked.

"Indeed," came the whispered reply.

They sat in silence for several more moments before Margaret struggled and finally with Amelia's help sat up straighter.

"Rhoda will bring me my dinner soon. There's something you should know."

Again Amelia's mind began racing with possibilities and again she wished she had brought along a parachute. She felt her muscles tense and she felt her heart pound and she felt her knuckles tighten on the arms of the chair in which she sat. Margaret's voice interrupted Amelia's involuntary ride it down or jump without a parachute but get away from this as soon as possible response.

"Why do you so often look at me like I'm about to inflict a mortal wound?"

Amelia could think of no response to this question and so said nothing. Margaret looked at her and her eyes once more filled with tears.

"I see," she said.

Another, heavier silence settled between them. Margaret raised her hand and Amelia took it as though together they might withstand silence's weight.

"I suppose, then, my next words will only wound further. I have this situation. Rhoda is a good woman. Sometimes choices are made for the sake of simplicity instead of integrity. I understand that. I hope you do, too."

Amelia stiffened.

"I need, I want, you by my side throughout this ... current challenge. I needed a fiction to safeguard your presence. Without consulting you, I have woven a reality. It involves a bit of subterfuge but, then, we are accustomed to that, aren't we?"

Margaret paused to rest and breathe as deeply as possible. Amelia looked at her face and saw the beginnings of deep lines of pain. She knew that whatever preposterous scenario this woman proposed, she would become a full and unhesitating participant. Margaret took a deep, difficult breath.

"I have recently taken an interest in the paranormal and psychic phenomena."

Having no idea if that statement reflected reality or the upcoming fantasy, Amelia said nothing.

"It's nothing unusual for a person in my condition to seek alternative forms of treatment. I have begun that search and you have arrived."

Amelia sat and waited for Margaret to tell her more. The minutes passed and nothing more was said. Apparently Margaret, Amelia decided, felt her few words had explained everything.

"Well, that is typical behavior," she said to herself.

Aloud, she said to Margaret, "I'm not altogether certain I understand you."

Margaret's next smile was generally reserved for children or students unable to understand the intricacies and complexities of her thought processes. She nodded her head as though accepting Amelia's similar inability to comprehend.

"You are Sister Mere de Corazon from the jungles of Mexico. You possess healing powers which will, if not save my life, certainly prolong it for several years. In that woven bag of yours are herbs and amulets with which you will do, well, things mysterious and exotic. You must speak with an accent and occasionally you and I will speak in the language indigenous to Nani. Since no one will understand us, they will assume we are speaking the language of your Mexican jungle."

Amelia stared at Margaret for a long moment before speaking.

"I thought I was a journalist."

Margaret's blank look concerned Amelia almost as much as

did her gasps of pain. Finally Margaret's expression registered understanding.

"That was yesterday. Today you are sister Mere de Corazon."

After another long moment Amelia nodded her head and asked, "This will keep me at your side?"

"I believe so. Yes."

Amelia stood, walked to the bedroom window, stared across Central Park West into the trees of Central Park and briefly wondered how far she could fly if she simply jumped out of the window. Then her desire to flee was replaced with a rage so intense it terrified her. She whirled from the window, strode back to Margaret's desk, and looked again at the Fugittaboutit façade. To Amelia it seemed to broadcast waves of power.

After a moment, Amelia slowly backed away from the facade and then bowed to it, then slowly returned to it only to slowly back away from it, bow to it, and then slowly back away from it until she had repeated the routine five times to stand once again at the desk and the chair in which Margaret sat observing this all too familiar behavior.

In a calm and steely voice Amelia finally said, "I've never been to Mexico. Why don't you just tell the truth about us? Did you ever once think of doing that?"

Margaret returned Amelia's gaze and did not blink.

"Telling the truth did occur to me. In our simple truth would you be the fictional Mrs. Mary Anderson recently released from the locked psychiatric unit of Bellevue Hospital for claiming to be Amelia Earhart or would you be the long presumed dead Amelia Earhart claiming to be Mrs. Mary Anderson? Let's not pretend we could go down either path without encountering many challenging repercussions ranging from embarrassment to incarceration. I chose subterfuge for a number of reasons but primarily because at this point in my journey toward the end of my life I don't have strength for confrontation."

"Except with me."

"There is always strength for life's essentials."

Amelia, totally against her will, smiled.

"I won't speak with an accent."

"Oh, my dear," Margaret, smiling, said, "you already do. Forty years spent speaking another language necessarily impacts the manner in which you speak the language of your birth."

To which Amelia replied in the Polynesian dialect spoken and understood only by those who lived their entire lives on a small, unknown to the world, island in the South Pacific and by two other people who now faced each other in this room filled with artifacts and death and life, "The honor of forty years rests lightly on my shoulders."

Battling fatigue and pain, Margaret softly spoke a traditional response to such a statement saying, "Upon your shoulders rests my life."

Margaret then pushed a package across her desk toward Amelia.

"I've taken the liberty of organizing your costume. I've added shirts and slacks and whatever essentials I thought you might need along with some money so you can buy what I've forgotten. We will attract less attention if you come and go as my guest and not as the person I love more than life itself. Our apartment in The Alden is just across Eighty-second Street. I hope you'll change your mind and stay there. It's so close we'll practically smell each other. I put the key in the envelope with the money."

Amelia stared at the package for some time before saying, "I prefer staying in Brooklyn."

"Even now we must live on separate islands," Margaret sighed and felt the words choke her.

Amelia stroked Margaret's face and softly said, "We'll see. Maybe I'll at least take luxurious baths at The Alden."

"Perhaps I'll join you," Margaret said and sobbing grasped Amelia's hand. "I'm sorry. I'm doing the best I can."

"I know," Amelia replied. "You always do your best."

"We've gone too far and too long with this deception to end it now," Margaret said. "There is no time left to untangle our threads of deceit. It's all too complicated and dangerous. I suppose from the get go we knew there would never be any turning back. You were the expert on points of no return. I suppose I'm an expert now, too."

"You should have stayed on Nani. We could have been together all of these years."

"I know."

Amelia stared blankly at Margaret for a moment before opening the package. After another moment, she held several items up between them: Beaded necklaces. A feathered headdress. Scarves. What appeared to be a large tooth with a hole drilled in it. Three bones.

"These are lovely and certainly in keeping with how people dress in Mexican jungles. I'm pleased to notice that you're not asking me to go bare breasted," Amelia laughed as the items fell back into the box.

"Lovely as the sight would be, I believe some decorum must remain. Besides, I don't easily share what I love."

The two women stared at each other as truth settled over them like a welcome quilt on a chilly evening.

"Neither do I," Amelia replied.

They both heard a gentle tap on the door, which was immediately opened by the woman who for years had shared a home with and been the companion of Dr. Margaret Mead. The three women stared at each other. Finally Amelia closed the package, stood and reached into her woven bag. She took out the leaves dry and powdery. She removed an ancient pottery bowl from a shelf and carefully placed into it all that was left of the island vegetation carried halfway around the world. She brushed her hands together to deposit every possible crumb into the bowl. She raised the bowl above her head, then slowly lowered it to her face and breathed in the scent of the island. She held the bowl to Margaret's face and she, too, smelled its contents. Amelia held the bowl between them and the two women stared across it each into the eyes of the other and in their minds they lay in the island's heavy growth and in their minds they felt the joy of their entwined bodies and in their minds they grew old together never separated by more than the beat of a heart or the touch of a hand.

Amelia set the bowl on the desk in front of Margaret, who watched her every move with more than her customary scholar's intensity. Again Amelia reached into the bag and produced the tin box given to her so many miles away. She placed it on the desk next to the bowl.

"It is said," Amelia began and then stopped herself to speak in a different language, "And so that which was hidden is returned."

Margaret reached an unsteady hand to her desk and picked up the box. She studied it a moment and then held it to her breast before returning her gaze to Sister Mere de Corazon.

"For all this and more, I thank you," she said in the language of their island.

"Tomorrow, as always," Sister Mere de Corazon said, "brings with it strength for hope and renewal and healing."

She then picked up the package, threw her woven bag over her shoulder, turned and walked out of the office and out of the apartment.

She did not hear Rhoda Metraux say to Margaret Mead, "You don't need to play this charade for me. I won't leave you again."

Nor did Amelia hear Margaret Mead reply to Rhoda Metraux, "I know. I'm not doing it for you. I'm doing it for the world."

When the elevator doors opened and Amelia stepped into the lobby of The Beresford, Elijah stood as though his wait had only been for a moment. Together they returned to their own hidden island in Brooklyn.

When Sister Mere de Corazon returned the next day she

wore a beaded shawl over her leather jacket and a tie-dyed scarf around her flying cap. A bone was knotted into the scarf. She brought with her incense, a chime, three pebbles, and her assistant in all matters psychic, a man who very much resembled the psychologist Dr. Elijah Copeland but who was, according to the healer from the jungles of Mexico, Quetzalcoatl, constant companion of Sister Mere de Corazon. Quetzalcoatl wore a shirt recently sheared of its sleeves, ragged denim shorts and a feathered headdress. What appeared to be a large tooth hung from a scarf tied around the stump of what had once been his arm. Introductions took place again in the cluttered office in the presence of both Dr. Mead and her companion, Dr. Metraux, who more than once rolled her eyes toward the ceiling. Margaret listened carefully to Sister Mere's introduction and explanation of her assistant and after a thoughtful moment replied, "Of course. Quetzalcoatl. How fitting. The god of universal rebirth. Sister Mere, you have chosen your assistant well."

Elijah stepped toward Dr. Mead, glanced at Rhoda, and then turned his attention back to the dying woman.

"I believe that, even more important than being the god of rebirth, it should be noted that in some traditions Quetzalcoatl is best known for bringing culture and chocolate to the world."

"Ah, how true," Margaret smiled. "And what is one without the other. You are well named."

"My parents were wise people."

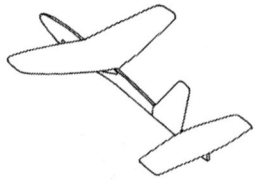

CHAPTER TWENTY-NINE

Despite consuming pain and diminishing strength, Dr. Margaret Mead maintained throughout August, 1978, a rigorous work schedule. Shortly after the arrival of Sister Mere de Corazon and Quetzalcoatl, Dr. Mead spoke at the One Hundred Year Celebration of the Literary & Scientific Circle of the Chautauqua Institution in upstate New York. Those who attended the celebration would remember how thin she had become and how she sometimes seemed exhausted. Several commented that fatigue couldn't possibly be surprising considering the unremitting schedule Dr. Mead had maintained throughout her life. Because she was frequently in the company of "characters" as her more conservative devotees called them, no one who attended the event ever mentioned the presence of the healer from the jungles of Mexico nor of the healer's assistant.

Later that same month Dr. Mead flew to Portland, Oregon, to speak at a conference of the American Correctional Association. Attendees remarked that Dr. Mead – always of the quick and famous temper – seemed even shorter tempered than ever. By the end of her brief trip she could not walk through the airport to her departure gate. Airport staff believed that they saw a one armed man pushing her in a wheelchair. Staff could not remember whether or not Dr. Mead and the one armed man were accompanied by anyone else. What was remembered, however, is that Dr. Mead flew back to New York first class because the severity of her physical pain necessitated such an embarrassing extravagance. They remember this because when she was awake Dr. Mead spoke at length about socioeconomic inequities needing to be corrected forever.

"And here I am," a stewardess quoted her as saying, "a participant in those very inequities."

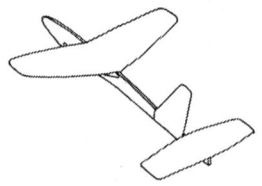

Chapter Thirty

Throughout the month of September, Sister Mere de Corazon, Quetzalcoatl constant companion and assistant of Sister Mere de Corazon, and world famous anthropologist and ethnologist Dr. Margaret Mead settled into a public routine of incantations, incense burnings, herb wavings, pebble examinations, and scarf wrappings.

"At what point," Amelia once asked, "do you want me to disembowel a bird?"

"We at least owe the world a good story," came Margaret's whispered reply before yet another swarm of guests entered her office.

"I thought we'd already given it one," Amelia whispered back as the door opened and she began blowing incense smoke in front of Margaret's face which caused the steadily failing woman to laugh until tears rolled down her cheeks and coughs overcame her.

Since guests – under normal circumstances – had rarely known what to expect when visiting her, none questioned Dr. Mead's current "accomplices" as she called them nor her current behavior, which seemed often more like that of a love-struck adolescent than of a dying icon.

Public moments were many. Times when Margaret and Amelia were actually alone together were few. Often Quetzalcoatl sat outside the door of either the bedroom or the office protecting, as he put it, their "connections with invisible energy forces." While seldom interfering with or interrupting Dr. Mead's sessions with Sister Mere, Rhoda Metraux made no attempt to hide her disapproval and her resentment. Mainly, however, she simply avoided her companion and the companions of the companion.

Twice Sister Mere walked with Margaret to the Museum of Natural History. They walked slowly because for both women each step was an agony. Together they stood at the foot of the steps looking up at the massive doors. Once they were able to walk to the corner of Seventy-seventh Street and Columbus Avenue to stare up at what had been for over fifty years the office of Dr. Margaret Mead.

"It looks so empty," Margaret finally said.

"It is empty," Amelia replied.

"This was bound to happen."

"I suppose."

"I just didn't think it would be this soon."

"I know."

That walk back to The Beresford from the museum was their last. Never again did Margaret Mead stand at the back entrance to her office and never again did she stand at the main entrance to the museum. While physically she might have managed a few more trips, emotionally she could not. When they walked they crossed Central Park West into the park. Sometimes they sat on a bench across the street from the museum. Other times they sat on benches from which the museum could not be seen.

"I wish I had come sooner," Amelia once said as they sat together in the September sun.

"I know," was Margaret's strained reply.

The sun warmed her shoulders a moment longer before Margaret spoke again.

"I wish I had stayed on Nani."

"I know," was Amelia's strained reply.

Toward the end of September the walks in the park became too much for Margaret and she consented to Quetzalcoatl's pushing her in the wheelchair. Elijah the one-armed man had to constantly struggle to keep the wheelchair going in a straight line instead of constantly veering in the direction of his missing arm. A guy named Quetzalcoatl, he would later observe, would have not encountered such a struggle. Finally wheel-chaired trips into the park became impossible.

The visits between Sister Mere de Corazon and the dying Margaret Mead changed to frequently involve nothing more than the two women lying in bed together or sitting in the office so close to each other that the skin on each face rejoiced from the breath of the other as they spoke in low tones.

"Do you remember the time," Margaret once asked, "you took Eleanor for that joy ride?"

"I do, indeed. I think she was terrified."

"The plane had no cockpit."

"Of course it had a cockpit. It just wasn't enclosed. It was a de Havilland Moth."

"Of course. A Gypsy Moth. She never told me that she was frightened."

"Of course she wouldn't. I don't think her screams in the air were of joy, though."

"I thought the President was going to kill you when the two of you returned to the White House."

"I could outrun him."

"That's not kind."

"But true."

Often their laughter could be heard and felt through the walls of the apartment in The Beresford. Never again, though, did anger or recrimination or blame seep through the cracks in the walls or under the space at the bottom of the door. Their times together contained no room for anything except loving gentleness and quiet words of their hearts. Margaret's efficient and devoted companion, despite her disapproval and avoidance of Sister Mere de Corazon, maintained a strict schedule for all other visitors but placed no restrictions on those of Sister Mere and Quetzalcoatl. Occasionally visitors were turned away rather than interrupt the increasingly sacred sessions between the two women guarded by their odd sentinel. More than once Amelia wondered at the absurdity of their charade and the stern companion's seeming acceptance of the reality of the healer.

"Surely she is not that gullible," Amelia once rhetorically stated to Margaret.

"I can't imagine she is," was Margaret's reply through teeth increasingly clenched in pain.

As the month of September passed, the condition of Margaret Mead became visibly worse, her strength shockingly diminished, and her pain horrifyingly greater. Any pretense at ritual or healing or psychic phenomena disappeared once the door to either the office or the bedroom was closed. Often the public pretense, too, blurred and visitors left feeling not duped, certainly, but definitely bewildered.

Despite the public denial of the severity of her condition, together in either the bedroom or less and less frequently in the office, both Margaret and Amelia, when they looked at each other, knew their time together had begun to be measured in moments and not in possibilities.

They never stopped touching and holding and comforting and caressing each other. They smiled at old jokes and they laughed at the best of those jokes even though laughter ultimately reduced Margaret into episodes of racking coughing or screaming agony. They found, in the middle of the unimaginable pain and sorrow, new secrets to smile over and to sometimes laugh about and always to hold to their hearts as they watched themselves grow closer with the shadow of the ultimate separation looming larger above them.

"I should have been braver," Margaret once whispered and stared wild-eyed with pain into the eyes of Amelia.

"Oh, my darling, you are so very brave," came Amelia's whispered response.

"Not now," came Margaret's stronger voice. "Then."

"Oh, yes. Then. I suppose back then the world needed you more than I."

A silence broken by Margaret's rattled breathing and then, "How long ago was back then?"

Amelia smiled and stroked Margaret's hand and forced herself to step around the trap laid with no awareness and no intention.

"My dear Margaret," Amelia cautiously began, "You so love a good fight, don't you? Let's not squander our moments."

"I'm only curious," came Margaret's gauntlet.

Amelia nodded her head, picked up the gauntlet, studied it for a moment then replied, "I suppose that back then was as recent as several months ago."

With those words Amelia gently replaced the gauntlet in Margaret's lap and Margaret smiled a weak smile of appreciation.

"Thank you for not talking to me with that distant politeness reserved for the dying. Only my body is disintegrating. I still think and feel with unimpaired vigor and I so enjoy repartee. I do love you, Amelia. You know that, don't you?"

"I have never doubted your love, Margaret."

"Only the wisdom of my choices have you doubted?" but the gauntlet remained in Margaret's lap because Margaret screamed as pain further invaded a body already consumed and defined by nothing save pain.

Finally able to speak again, Margaret said, "I would like to think that the world really did need me more than you did. Lately I suspect that I believed I needed the world more than I needed you. I now know I was mistaken."

Then she laid her head on the pillow and slept.

Awake again, Margaret said, "So many years apart. So many regrets. And all of it my fault."

"It was our arrangement. We were equal partners. We still are."

Margaret looked deep into Amelia's eyes and smiled.

"Indeed we are that. Equal in every respect of the word save choice. I chose to become a visitor to the island and you were essentially stuck there."

"We're all stuck somewhere, aren't we?"

"Ah, the existential challenge of life. I suppose we are stuck. Otherwise I would certainly vacate this body and enter another."

Living by the side of a gravely ill loved one assumes a unique rhythm and logic guided by moments of serenity broken by moans of agony and smiles of memory and unfathomable terror and metered touches and stolen laughter and screams of pain. Conversations ramble, and silences comfort and alarm. Every moment becomes precious and passes too quickly. Touches meant to linger for an eternity last only a second. Days and nights lack distinction.

In early October this at home logical rhythm ended when Margaret hemorrhaged. At first tiny specks of blood appeared on her face and her hands but soon blood oozed from her nose and her mouth. Amelia, unaware of the existence of any type of emergency response system, screamed for Elijah who, without hesitation, ran for Rhoda who without hesitation dialed 911 and then both she and Elijah raced into the bedroom where already, in the few seconds since Amelia's scream, Margaret lay in a pool of her own blood.

The ambulance left The Beresford with sirens screaming and with a man – who to concerned and curious bystanders looked like some sort of hippie witch doctor – riding along in the front seat.

As the ambulance sped away from The Beresford toward

New York Hospital Amelia and Rhoda stood together staring at the place where they had last seen the woman they both loved. Finally, able to think of nothing to say or do, Amelia sat cross-legged down on the sidewalk as though there she intended to wait for Margaret's return. The other woman looked around and then, apparently unable to think of any meaningful activity, sat down on the sidewalk next to Amelia. The doorman stared out at them and pedestrians walked around them. They sat without speaking or even looking at each other for perhaps a half hour.

Finally the younger of the two women stood and said, "Let's go upstairs and straighten up a little. Then we'll go to the hospital."

Amelia, without uncrossing her legs, stood in one motion and followed the other woman back into The Beresford where they cleaned the bedroom of paramedic detritus, remade the bed with fresh sheets, and straightened the constant clutter on the bedside table. Neither woman spoke. When finished, Sister Mere de Corazon reached into her bag, took out several pebbles and ceremoniously scattered them, with a rhythmic waving of her arms, onto the clean quilts. The younger woman watched her and when she spoke, Sister Mere's heart stopped its beating and her blood froze in her veins.

"Amelia," the other woman said, "save some stones for the hospital. Sister Mere de Corazon will need them and all of her magic there."

The other woman correctly read the expression on Amelia's face as one of terror and continued, "You know, I am a controlling bitch but I'm not stupid. Nor will I keep the woman I love from being with the woman she loves."

Another long moment of silence passed with little change of expression on Amelia's face.

The other woman continued, "We all have secrets, Amelia. I have no intention of betraying either yours or Margaret's."

Only then did Amelia's face begin to relax. She reached for the stones on the bed but was stopped by Rhoda.

"Let's leave them there. Perhaps their power will bring her home. We will take this, however."

Rhoda placed the façade picked up from the street by Amelia and placed first on the desk and then at the bedside of Dr. Margaret Mead into her own bag.

During the first days of her hospitalization, Margaret often appeared unaware of her surroundings and of the people surrounding her. Occasionally she appeared to not recognize friends and family. Always, though, she knew by name the mysterious healer from the jungles of Mexico. During those first days, her conversations with Sister Mere de Corazon were whispered and, others would later observe, seemingly urgent. During those moments, neither woman appeared aware of any other person in the room. Whenever Sister Mere would step away from the bed or out of the room, Margaret even when only courting consciousness, searched and waited for her return. Despite pain and confusion and overwhelming despair, neither woman forgot their subterfuge. Had anyone ever overheard them, that person might have thought that the two women spoke from an unchanging script.

"What are you doing here?" Margaret, for example, would ask when the faith healer from the Mexican jungles returned to sit on the bed beside her.

"The usual faith healer routines," Amelia, for example, would whisper as she kissed first Margaret's cheek and then her mouth.

"Sister Mere de Corazon," Margaret would sometimes whisper in reply when their lips no longer touched. "You've got some nerve. Don't you know I'm unavailable?"

Amelia would want to say that you never were available but instead always said, "That's all right. Neither am I. I'm with you."

"Forever?"

As she would pull away from Margaret, Sister Mere would say aloud, "I am here, Dr. Mead. I will not leave you."

When she would look around the room, Amelia would notice as though for the first time that it was crowded with people she did not know. She would always immediately retreat to a far corner and allow herself to collapse into a chair as though exhausted by a healing ritual, which appeared to involve breathing life-giving breath directly into the mouth of Dr. Mead.

Sometimes the suite was packed with research assistants or friends or relatives or colleagues. During those times Rhoda and Sister Mere and Quetzalcoatl allowed themselves to fade into the further reaches of the rooms or they waited in the halls. Once in awhile, but not often because the distance felt unbearable, they waited in the lobby or on benches in the hospital garden. Sometimes Sister Mere and Quetzalcoatl waited and Rhoda stayed in the room and sometimes Rhoda waited and Sister Mere stayed in the room. They became a team of comfort and support.

Once Dick A Research Assistant arrived carrying stacks of books and papers, which he placed in a chair near the bed. Before leaving he glanced around the room allowing his eyes to rest first on Elijah and then on Amelia. His face became a Picasso-like depiction of alarm and confusion and rejection of reality as he backed out of the room without speaking.

Margaret, whose mental capacity and sensory awareness had returned, remarked, "He always was an odd fellow."

For the most part, however, Rhoda maintained a strict visitation schedule and allowed only carefully selected people to step into the hospital suite. Once admitted, she carefully monitored the length of the stay and did not hesitate to end the visits of even the two Nobel Prize winners who at different times on different days dropped by to offer words of encouragement.

Despite the pain and through the pain medications, Margaret insisted on doing some work during each day. She reviewed papers and made notes and even began preparing a lecture on the world crisis of starving children in Africa to be delivered to the United Nations in February of the following year. She discussed it at length with Rhoda and Amelia but the person she found to be most helpful on the subject of childhood hunger was

Elijah. She eagerly became his mentor and even when she made no sense at all because of pain and pain medication, Elijah listened intently to her every word.

Once during a rare and short break from hospital routine, Amelia would relinquish reason to a moment of uncertainty and ask Elijah, "Are you really from Mexico?"

To which Elijah would smile and reply, "Sometimes its hard to remember who we really are, isn't it?"

Then with his only arm he would draw Amelia to his chest and she would weep and he would pat her head and stroke her back and remind her that he was neither Dr. Copeland nor Quetzalcoatl, constant companion and assistant of Sister Mere de Corazon, except when circumstances required such identities.

"We become whoever we need to be. The trick is to remember who we really are," he would tell her still stroking her back.

And she would raise her head and look into his eyes and ask, "Do you know who I really am?"

And he would reply, "Yes. I know who you are."

And he would kiss her on the top of her head and she would again lay her head on his chest.

Then they would walk back into the hospital she to the rooms to sit by the bed and he to stand outside the door of Margaret Mead whose condition, after transfusions and medications, had stabilized into one of constant pain and diminishing days.

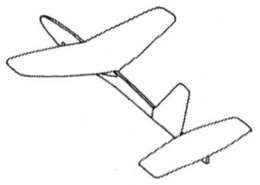

CHAPTER THIRTY-ONE

In all of their sick bed conversations nothing was too sacred for discussion. Discussions ranged from the profound to the mundane to fill the silences because silence at a death bed can all too easily be filled by death itself. So anything is better than dreaded silence. Yet neither Amelia nor Elijah nor Margaret ever mentioned the incidents at Bellevue Hospital.

At Bellevue Hospital no one mentioned them either because – aside from a national treasure banging a chief's stick on the floor as she walked down the hall and a patient being released into the care of said national treasure – the events that day were hardly remarkable to any of the staff working shifts at Bellevue's famed psychiatric unit.

No one there gave that day a second thought. No one, that is, except Lucy, the Charge Nurse, who couldn't seem to get the old woman and her flying cap out of her head. She had, as she had stated during the team conference, taken a liking to her. Lucy didn't share many of her thoughts with her colleagues at the hospital. For the most part they seemed to her a bunch of unimaginative clock punchers who didn't particularly like where they worked or who they worked with. So no one on the unit knew that Lucy couldn't get the events of that day out of her head just as no one knew that at the end of almost every inhumanely long shift she found herself in Sheridan Square at a bar called The Duchess. Certainly no one at Bellevue knew about this because if they knew about this they would also know, if they knew such things, that The Duchess was a bar which welcomed women who loved women and Lucy felt in constant need of someplace where she was welcomed. At the end of every shift for the past eleven years Lucy sat at the bar at The Duchess wishing her life were different.

Predictably, Lucy was on that one evening in mid-October, sitting at the bar staring blankly over her scotch at the television screen upon which appeared a news reporter standing outside New York Hospital. He was providing an update on the condition of Dr. Margaret Mead, icon of the American Museum of Natural History and Columbia University. Apparently Dr. Mead was improving and receiving visitors and preparing lectures from her hospital bed. The reporter switched to footage taken earlier in the day. The screen showed three unidentified people entering the main doors of the hospital. The voice of the reporter, apparently hoping that this footage would prove his statement that Dr. Mead was well enough to receive visitors, told the audience that these three people entering the hospital were going to visit the steadily improving Margaret Mead.

Two women and one man walked quickly with eyes fixed on the hospital's door. Everything about them communicated to the reporter that they wanted nothing to do with him. The entire footage lasted no more than ten seconds. In those few seconds Lucy saw a tall, one armed, black man walking between two women. She could not see the woman on his left. The woman on his right, though, wore a knee-length leather coat and something on her head that appeared to Lucy to be a leather flying cap.

As the hit song *Electric Boogie* filled the bar and shook the walls, Lucy took a gulping swallow of her Johnny Walker Red that gagged her and sent her into a coughing episode during which she staggered – still holding her half full glass of scotch – from her bar stool and onto the dance floor where she found herself briefly participating in an electric slide line dance before staggering to the far corner of the room and collapsing into a chair. Her vision blurred from the coughing and the scotch and from tears streaming down her face. Sitting in the chair recovering from sensory overload in all departments of her being, Lucy realized that during all of the years she had frequented this particular establishment she had never once danced or even sat on this side of the dance floor. It was during that moment of realization that she looked at the wall to her right.

"Holy fucking shit," she said aloud and felt immediately self-conscious because Lucy was not prone to public obscenities.

She immediately looked around to see if anyone had overheard her. No one had. The music was loud and even if anyone had, 'Holy fucking shit' was not sufficiently vulgar to alarm even a first time visitor to The Duchess. Satisfied that her dignity and privacy remained intact, Lucy gazed again at the framed photograph of a young, smooth skinned, faintly smiling woman standing next to an airplane. The airplane's propeller seemed to almost rest on the woman's shoulder. The young woman in the photograph wore a knee length leather coat and, on her head, a leather flying cap. Lucy stared at the photograph on the wall for a long time before she smiled a knowing smile of shared secrecy and, feeling stronger and more whole than she had felt in her entire life, finished her drink in one swallow.

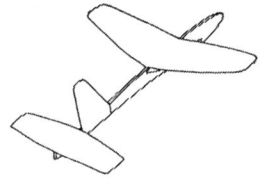

CHAPTER THIRTY-TWO

On October 15, Rhoda entered the hospital room, walked directly to Margaret, and placed a New York Yankees cap on her head and then walked directly to Amelia and placed a similar cap on her head.

"It's the seventh inning stretch. No one is going to enter this room until the game is over," Rhoda said as she pulled her own cap down on her head, turned on the room's television, which until that moment had not been used, and positioned herself in front of the set.

"From an historic perspective," Amelia said, "I'm a well documented Brooklyn fan."

Rhoda turned to face Amelia but Margaret spoke first.

"Oh, my dear, there is no more Brooklyn. The Dodgers left long ago. Brooklyn moved to Los Angeles. Circumstances proclaim that you root for the Yankees."

"Of all the adjustments I have endured since my return to what you laughingly call civilization, this is the most offensive," said Amelia as she adjusted her Yankees cap and settled in next to Margaret on the narrow bed.

The three women watched the Yankees beat the Dodgers in Yankee Stadium twelve to two in the fifth game of the World Series. For the length of a baseball game the pain and terror and desolation filling the soul and the body of each woman was diminished by the normalcy of baseball.

Soon October's autumn fled, chased by November's chill. The street musicians moved from the Promenade to subway stops under the direction of their one armed conductor who they saw only occasionally late some nights in a greenhouse that never knew winter's cold. All other moments of the days and the nights Elijah remained close to Amelia, who never left the hospital suite. Her presence with Margaret was constant.

On one occasion, hospital staff would remember, some sort of street band made its way into the suite. The band's music soothed not only the hospital's most famous patient but, as it drifted through the halls and up and down the stairways, eased at least for the length of a song the misery of all who lay within the walls of New York Hospital. The last song the band played before returning to the subways was *Pennies From Heaven*. If a dying woman and a healer from the jungles of Mexico could dance while lying absolutely still next to each other in a hospital bed, then the light fantastic was definitely tripped during that song. When the song ended, Margaret felt as exhausted as though they had actually danced. Amelia assured her they had.

Always, when colleagues or family or friends or complete strangers entered the room under the strict rules of Rhoda, Amelia reassumed the guise of Sister Mere de Corazon and muttered incantations from a corner or distributed pebbles gathered from the hospital's garden onto the bed or bedside tables or waved feathers above the feet of the dying woman. During those times Dr. Mead would characteristically launch into an explanation of the power of ancient healing rituals and of the curative nature especially of shamans from the jungles of Mexico. During several of these visits Quetzalcoatl constant companion and assistant of Sister Mere de Corazon would enter the room to stare intently at the rituals performed and would often remark on the clear and positive impact they had on Dr. Mead, who would smile in agreement and wave a weak but approving hand toward the mystical healer.

When not acting out the part of Sister Mere de Corazon, Amelia sat by Margaret's bedside reading whatever passages from whatever books Margaret requested. Other times they lay together on the bed and still other times Amelia sat beside the bed stroking Margaret's hand and softly singing an old and favorite song. Other times she sat with hands in her lap saying nothing because even the breath of a voice increased the level of pain threefold.

It was apparent to all that not even the strongest pain medications could ease the agony experienced unremittingly by Margaret. It was also apparent to all that Margaret refused to acknowledge the extent of her pain and the extent of carnage wreaked on her body by the cancer's steady march. Conversations interrupted by screams or moans were quickly resumed as though the interruption had been caused by nothing more significant than a sneeze.

The conversations between Margaret and Amelia became increasingly succinct until finally they seemed to be in a code known only by these two women who had lived their lives in undecipherable style.

Lying side by side on the bed staring at the ceiling and imagining stars instead of acoustic flecks they said things like, "Remember that time on the roof?"

"At Columbia?"

"Of course."

"Of course."

Not once did Amelia succumb to the absurdity of suggesting sleep or rest to a person desperately clinging to the far edge of life. Aside from her awareness that such a suggestion would have been insulting to this woman who so passionately wanted life's every moment, she also knew that such a suggestion would have resulted in Margaret's using her last precious strength to verbally beat Amelia to death before she, herself, died.

So they filled their every moment together with life and ignored the specter of death's unrelenting attempts to get past the vigils of Elijah and Rhoda and enter the room to claim Margaret as its own.

"I don't want to leave you," Margaret said.

"So many years we could have spent together," Margaret said.

"Islands are wonderful places to raise children," Margaret said.

Eventually the words and the sentences and the regrets and the delights and the life reviews and the renewed vows of love began to merge into single, uninterrupted thoughts punctuated only by moans or weakening screams or smiles of heartbreaking sadness and expressions of uninterrupted and unending love.

"Tin box. Oroiti. Waves. Hidden. Ariki. Reclaimed. Two keys. Never forgot. Find the key. Home. Found. You. RM knows. One for me. One for you. Us. Ours. Apart never more."

Later Margaret seemed to acquire a different type of energy. She spoke in complete thoughts and carefully constructed sentences.

"There will be other lives and other opportunities, you know. This I believe. I shall make different, better choices. This I now know. Please forgive me."

Amelia held Margaret in her arms and forgave her.

"I would do it all over again for just this moment," Amelia soothed.

To which Margaret replied, "Let's choose a different moment. This moment I am dying. Let's choose a moment of youth and health and promise and potential."

"But this moment is different," Amelia said. "It's the only moment we have."

"This time around," Margaret whispered. "Next time will be different."

"Yes," my darling," Amelia half whispered and half crooned. "Next time will be different."

"There will be a next time. I know that there will be a next time."

"Yes, my love. There will be a next time and it will be different."

"We will never be apart."

"We will never be apart."

The tears of Amelia Earhart streaked the face of Margaret Mead and the tears of Margaret Mead streaked the face of Amelia Earhart as they held each other closer than the fact of the human body had ever before allowed.

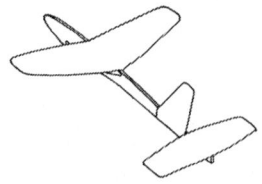

Chapter Thirty-Three

On November 15, 1978, Dr. Margaret Mead died.

In the room at the time of her death was her companion of many years, Rhoda Metraux, a few family members, and a few colleagues. In the shadows of the room were the mysterious Sister Mere de Corazon and her assistant. Even though the healer, whose constant presence in the suite had become so ordinary as to be unnoticed by the many visitors, never emerged from the far corner of the room, it seemed to those gathered next to the deathbed that Margaret's eyes never left those of Sister Mere de Corazon. So intense and obvious was the connection between the two women that it almost seemed to those gathered as though they were embracing. Later those gathered would report that the shaman from the jungles of Mexico actually held Margaret's ravaged body as her breath became increasingly shallow and increasingly infrequent. Margaret did not move and she did not speak during those last moments.

Finally an awesome silence filled the room. It took several seconds for those gathered to realize that the silence was death. Dr. Margaret Mead had breathed her last. The weight of this breathless silence bore down on the room and upon those in the room and seemed capable of crushing chests and denying breath to those still living. The weight permeated every corner of the room.

When death's weight reached finally the corner occupied by Sister Mere de Corazon and Quetzalcoatl her constant companion and assistant, Amelia screamed the scream of one whose still beating heart has been torn from her chest and held in front of her eyes for examination. The room became as cold as any New York day can become. A roar as though from an off the track out of control locomotive shook the room and rattled the windows and sent sailing books and papers off of a bedside table onto the floor. A wind of major hurricane strength swept through the suite of rooms and flew open the door so hard that it would later be discovered to have cracked the hallway wall. Still screaming, Amelia ran through the door carrying with her a woven bag from a South Pacific island and in it the willing and rejoicing spirit of Dr. Margaret Mead.

Quetzalcoatl, the constant companion and assistant of Sister Mere de Corazon, walked immediately and quietly and noticed by no one out of the still open door to follow Amelia down the hall and out of the hospital. Only when Sister Mere de Corazon and Quetzalcoatl and Elijah and Amelia and the spirit of the gratefully liberated Margaret Mead had left the room did the door swing closed with a gentle but firm and final snap. The books and papers remained scattered on the floor as a reminder and as proof of the astonishing events surrounding the death of Dr. Margaret Mead. Of all the people gathered in the room, only Rhoda Metraux, the long time companion of Dr. Mead, noticed that the Flatbush Avenue façade brought to the room to comfort and heal and, if necessary, transport, was no longer on the bedside table nor was it, she would later realize, anywhere in the suite of rooms once occupied by the dying Dr. Margaret Mead.

Amelia stumbled more than she walked. Her glazed eyes barely noticed the cars in front of which she stepped. Frequently Elijah stopped her or pulled her out of harm's way. Despite her stumbling and her inability to distinguish safe from unsafe crossings, Amelia did not deviate from her journey due south down

First Avenue. When they walked past Bellevue Hospital, Amelia did not display any memory or recognition. When they reached the Brooklyn Bridge they walked across the East River and into Brooklyn. Once across the bridge Amelia hesitated and Elijah pointed in a set direction and, her stumbling having turned into a stride, they walked directly onto the Brooklyn Promenade and only there did Amelia allow herself to wrap her arms around a huge tree and, holding it, sink onto the grass to moan and weep and finally to strike her fists onto the ground over and over again until even the ground seemed to flinch from her sorrow.

When Amelia eventually began to feel the strength and the wisdom of the tree enter her being, she stopped beating the ground. She looked at her grass stained hand and then at her skinned knuckles. She released her hand from its clenched fist and smoothed the grass over as though apologizing. She stroked the tree's rough bark. She stood, turned her back to the tree and leaned the full weight of her body against it. She felt the tree's energy enter her spine and travel up and down and throughout her entire being. She turned to face the tree and stepped to it as though they were lovers never separated by time or by miles or by death. She again wrapped both arms around the tree and held tightly to all she had lost until she was ready to let go. With that releasing she thought of her island and of her people and of Ariki who called himself Oroiti. Of all the losses of this day, this loss alone shook her body with uncontrollable despair. A chilly, almost wintry breeze came toward her carrying with it ocean and harbor scents. She turned and lifted her head toward the water. As she looked past the Statue of Liberty she saw the lady smile and motion her to join her in the cold waters.

"Not now," Amelia said aloud. "Maybe later."

Elijah did not ask Amelia to whom she spoke. He simply stood by her and watched her journey through more pain than life should ever, in his opinion, inflict on one person.

Shunning the invitation from the Statue of Liberty, Amelia's gaze continued under the bridge, through the Narrows and out to sea. She turned and kissed the tree and backed away from it only to return to it and hug it and kiss it and back away from it until she had completed a cycle of five repetitions. Slightly calmed by this ritual, Amelia turned finally to walk to the railing of the Promenade as though moving just that far nearer the ocean would allow her a better view of the tiny speck of land she so desperately yearned to see. After several more minutes, Amelia bent her head until it rested on the railing and her shoulders shook from the violence of her weeping.

Elijah did not speak nor did he reach out to touch her. His best comfort was to stand in silence beside her. Eventually, as is the way with broken hearts, Amelia's sobbing slowed and then stopped. Both she and Elijah knew there would be more but for now she had no strength left for despair. Consuming numbness would have to do. Consuming numbness and a headache so severe Amelia could no longer see.

"I've gone blind," she said in a voice so matter of fact that she might have been announcing a change in the price of milk.

"Okay," Elijah answered in a voice so calm that he might have been acknowledging that aforementioned change in the price of milk.

He made his remaining arm available to her and she, practiced in the reverse of this particular routine, slipped her arm through his. Together and in step Elijah and Amelia returned to Flatbush Avenue and Prospect Park where the musicians were just beginning dinner.

"Smells good," Elijah said and guided Amelia to a bench at the table.

The musicians knew by the faces of Elijah and Amelia that the vigil had ended. They placed food in front of Amelia, who sat with eyes closed. No one spoke. There were no words for occasions such as this and everyone at this banquet of vagabonds knew that when there were no words none should be offered.

When it was obvious Amelia would not touch her food, Elijah distributed it among the musicians.

Amelia did not open her eyes until they arrived at the greenhouse. When she did open her eyes her vision had returned and her head no longer hurt.

"My sight has returned," she said in that same matter of fact voice with which she had announced her blindness.

The first thing on which she focused was Elijah bent with despair. She walked to him and placed a hand on his shoulder. When his despair did not diminish, she sat beside him and held him to her breast while he wept.

Amelia that night visited, it seemed to Elijah and the musicians, each plant in the greenhouse. She spoke to plants. She stroked plants. She kissed fronds and she made cooing noises to the ficus. The woven bag never left her shoulder. Even when she finally laid down to finally rest and fall into a deep sleep she held the bag close to her breast as though she were embracing it and all that was in it.

The next morning, Amelia rose seeming refreshed. She and Elijah resumed their journey along Flatbush Avenue as though it had never been interrupted. She was surprised to see that the musicians accompanied them as they gathered breakfast from dumpsters and trash cans and even more surprised when, instead of going to the Promenade, they returned to Prospect Park and ate breakfast at the same bench where they routinely ate dinner.

After breakfast Elijah distributed subway tokens and the band made its way into the underworld of subway tunnels to play on moving trains and at stops. Throughout the day, Amelia frequently played the banjo and sang old and familiar songs though never *Pennies From Heaven*. All of the band members agreed, at the end of the day when the money was counted, that Amelia and her banjo definitely brought in the "bigger bucks".

"Well," she remarked, "who wouldn't pay to see a heartbroken old lady play banjo on the subway."

She had never asked before and didn't know why she chose that moment to do so but over pizza dinner in the park, Amelia asked and learned that Elijah put most of their earnings into a savings account.

"One day," he said, "we can say goodbye to the greenhouse."

Amelia's eyes filled with tears and her soul felt a new weight. To leave the greenhouse would be, for her, to leave the last remnant of her island so far away.

"I'd rather stay in the gardens," she quietly whispered and added, "If I have a say."

"Everyone has a say," Elijah said. "But one of these days the groundskeeper I know will leave and we'll get caught. Or they'll just fix the fence. Either way, this can't be a long-term thing. One day we'll start making real money and my songs will start selling and we'll buy a house or at least rent an apartment. You just wait and see. Then you can have yourself a real bed. Your own room, too."

He reached out and squeezed her hand to tell her that he and the musicians would always care for her.

"We're family," he said.

"I have lost Nani," Amelia said to herself.

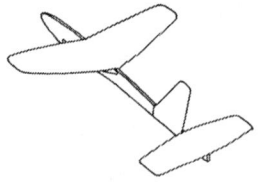

CHAPTER THIRTY-FOUR

Dr. Rhoda Metraux had neither a homeless composer nor a famous psychologist nor an assistant to a shaman from a Mexican jungle to comfort her and walk her home. Eventually those gathered around the deathbed, holding each other for comfort and for strength, left the suite of rooms. Rhoda was left to at last be alone with the woman she, too, had loved. Staring at the container that had once held such a spirit as Margaret Mead's, Rhoda knew that everything that made the woman she loved who she was had departed with another.

Eventually the body of Dr. Margaret Mead was removed. Eventually hospital staff began to strip the bed and eventually Rhoda gathered all of the personal possessions dear to her and walked from the room having been assured that the remaining books and papers and artifacts would be delivered to The Beresford by noon the next day.

On her way out of the room, Rhoda reached for the chief's stick that had been leaning against the wall near the bed. It had not been touched for weeks. When she wrapped her fingers around the wood, Rhoda would later remark, she felt a pulsating warmth.

With unflinching attention to detail, Dr. Rhoda Metraux would still later organize a delegation to return that chief's stick to Manus Island in northern Papua, New Guinea. She would not accompany that delegation because she feared she might follow the scent of the woman for whom she mourned and search each of the twenty or thirty thousand islands in the South Pacific until she found a tiny speck of land on which to spend the rest of her days sitting on the shore weeping.

In The Beresford apartment Rhoda occupied herself with wandering through their home and feeling the emptiness of rooms once so full of life. She sat at the sacred desk of Dr. Margaret Mead and dared to touch papers and books. She stared around her at masks and baskets and bowls. Her eyes fell finally on a tin box on the desk next to a bowl. She picked up the box and felt its weight. She replaced the box on the desk and stared at it and considered its possibilities and hers.

For over one week the tin box remained untouched and perhaps forgotten on the desk of Dr. Margaret Mead. Finally on Thanksgiving Day, November 23, Dr. Metraux again sat at the still cluttered desk. Again her hands touched the papers and the books until they finally settled, again, on the tin box. Again she held it in her hands.

The instructions had been clear. However, when a world figure dies the grief, it seems, belongs more to the world than to the individuals who knew and loved and cared for and fought with and laughed with the person claimed by the world as its own. Or at least it certainly seemed that way to Rhoda sitting at the desk of the woman who had never quite been hers. How simple it would have been to have thrown that box into the trash. How simple and how uncharacteristic of the woman who held it that would have been because the instructions had been clear.

"Make sure it gets to her. Don't just give it to her. Make certain that she understands. Help her. Please. Promise me."

"You cannot control me from the grave," Rhoda said to the empty office and to the memory of the voice and to the acceptance that, yes, she would be controlled from the grave especially in this one remaining matter.

On the morning of Thanksgiving Day, 1978, Dr. Rhoda Metraux put on her winter coat, put the tin box in the pocket, picked up her purse and left The Beresford to hail a taxi and search for Amelia Earhart.

"I have gone completely insane," she said to herself as she settled into the back seat.

In response to the driver's "Where to?" Rhoda laughed and marveled that she was in a cab looking for the long lost and presumed dead aviatrix Amelia Earhart who just happened to be, as it turned out, the love of her recently deceased lover's life.

"I have absolutely no idea," came her reply.

"Ya gotta go somewhere," the not unkind driver observed.

His observation, to Rhoda, seemed a reasonable summary of life.

"I suppose that's true," she said.

Passing motorists rolled down their windows to curse at the cab and honked their horns as though cursing and honking would move the cab out of their way. Still Rhoda sat in the back seat. Finally she gave the driver five dollars and got out.

"Thank you so much for your time," she said.

As the driver pulled back into traffic to move south down Central Park West, he glanced into his rearview mirror to see Dr. Rhoda Metraux walk down the stairs of the Museum of Natural History subway stop.

For several minutes Rhoda stood near the turnstile. She had no tokens. She had not ridden the trains in years. People pushed by her and still she stood looking beyond the turnstile to the stairs leading eventually to the tracks. She heard trains arrive and she heard them depart. Finally she turned and walked back up onto the sidewalk in front of The Beresford. The first cab for which she signaled stopped.

Once in the back seat, Rhoda said without hesitation, "170 Joralemon Street, Brooklyn Heights."

The cab left Rhoda standing in front of a fortress of a building. Two flags hung from second story poles. One flag was the red, white, and blue flag of the United States. The other flag was red with the word *Packer* in white letters. An icy wind whipped both flags back and forth. Rhoda looked from the flags to the arched doorway.

She read aloud the words etched in the curved glass window above the doors.

"Packer Collegiate Institute."

She looked from the words to the column of windows to her right and allowed her gaze to travel to the top and the building's turreted, multi-windowed office. Her body shook possibly from the cold as she remembered another turreted office in another fortress of a building a lifetime away from this school of her youth. Unable to fathom the reason for her arrival at this place, Dr. Rhoda Metraux turned to sit on the steps of her old school and weep.

Far too practical to allow such indulgences to go unchecked for more than a moment, Rhoda stood, wiped her face, and turned toward the sea. She walked two blocks down Joralemon Street to Hicks Street, turned right to walk two more blocks to Montague Street then turned left to walk two more blocks. Six blocks she knew as well as the cracks in the sidewalk between The Beresford and The American Museum of Natural History.

As she walked she remembered the sounds and the smells of these streets and wondered what had become of the years. Lost in thought, she soon found herself standing at the railing of the Brooklyn Heights Promenade gazing across the waters to the Statue of Liberty remembering a time when the glory of New York City had seemed far away and impossible to grasp. The concrete pavers at her feet were slick with ice and the top bar of the steel railing burned her fingers with cold. Rhoda put her hands in her coat pockets. With her right hand she felt the round, tin box. She looked across the East River to Manhattan Island and vowed to fulfill her final obligation to Dr. Margaret Mead because Dr. Rhoda Metraux was not a person to break a promise.

"None of the rest matters," she said to the Statue, "if our commitments mean nothing."

The Lady seemed to nod her head in agreement.

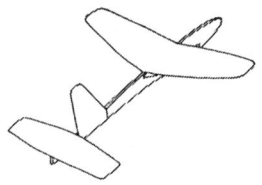

CHAPTER THIRTY-FIVE

The New York City subway system is one of the oldest modern public transportation systems in the world. Unlike other subways, New York's system never closes. Tracks cover almost a thousand miles and trains stop at almost five hundred stations making it possible to live a constantly in motion life rarely seeing the light of day all for the price of a single token.

Rhoda did not intend to spend the rest of her life riding the trains searching for a street band, its one-armed leader, and his elderly female companion. However, she could think of no other way of locating Amelia Earhart than to look for Elijah Copeland and his musicians and she could think of no other place to look for them than on the trains and platforms.

She rode from Brooklyn to Queens and from Queens to Midtown Manhattan and from Midtown Manhattan to The Bronx and from The Bronx to Harlem and from Harlem to Battery Park and from Battery Park to Greenwich Village and from The Village back to Brooklyn to begin the circle once more.

She rode the Broadway Local and the Jamaica Express. She rode the Seventh Avenue Express and the Eighth Avenue Local. She rode the Myrtle Avenue Local and she rode the Broadway Express. She got off trains to stand on platforms. She walked from platforms upstairs to stare across the turnstiles at bored attendants in glass booths. She descended stairs to stand again on platforms to once again board just one more train. She chased snatches of song and hollow drum beats because always some one person or some group of people made music on the trains and on the platforms hoping that just enough money would be dropped in the hat or the can or the open guitar case to buy food or drink for just one more day. Not one beat of one drum led her to Amelia Earhart. She began to think she had been the one in Bellevue claiming to be someone she wasn't.

Thanksgiving Day turned into Thanksgiving Night and Thanksgiving Night turned into the Day After Thanksgiving without her having marked time's passage. Sometimes she sat alone in empty cars. Sometimes she stood on crowded platforms. Sometimes the sounds of people and trains and life assaulted her senses. Other times the only sound she heard on a deserted platform was the constant drip of water that always threatened to break through the tunnel walls.

"One drop at a time," she said aloud, "is all it takes to wear us down to nothing."

Then she shook despair and fatigue from her head to once again board yet another train to go someplace as pointless as the next or the last all for the price of a single token.

When finally Dr. Rhoda Metraux admitted that once again she had failed the woman she had spent so much of her life trying to please, the train stopped and she walked through the sliding doors onto one more desolate platform. As she gathered her coat and her defeat around her chilled-to-the-bone body, she read the name of the stop and realized that she was home. She climbed the steps out of the American Museum of Natural History subway stop to step into the bitter cold of this Day After Thanksgiving Day.

As she stood on the sidewalk in front of The Beresford, Rhoda blinked her eyes and believed that the bright sun played tricks with her vision.

"Too many hours spent in the dark," she said to no one and to the world.

She shook her head to clear her vision and still the apparition remained. On the steps of the American Museum of Natural History, a street band of six people were playing *Pennies From Heaven*. A woman wearing a leather coat and what appeared to be a flying cap played the banjo. Next to her, sentinel-like, stood a one armed man.

Rhoda looked from the Museum to her home and back to the Museum and wondered if she had the strength to walk one more block. She thought of the turreted museum office with its huge cluttered desk and walls of books and artifacts and of her own hidden in a corner out of sight desk in that same office suite and forced herself to one more time walk south on Central Park West.

As she approached the musicians their music stopped and Rhoda wished she had remained hidden just long enough to hear the rest of the song. She had no strength left with which to climb the steps. Elijah and Amelia walked down them to her. In silence the three stood. Finally Rhoda took the tin box out of her pocket.

"Here," was all her strength allowed her to say.

She pressed the tin into Amelia's hand.

Amelia stared at it and pressed it back into Rhoda's hand saying, "I brought this for her. It belongs to her."

"She wanted you to have it," said Rhoda pressing the box back into Amelia's hand. "I promised her I would give it to you."

Elijah took the tin box and, putting it into his pocket, said, "Let's go someplace a little warmer."

Together Dr. Rhoda Metraux, Elijah Copeland, five street musicians, and Amelia Earhart walked back to The Beresford to escape the day's barren cold.

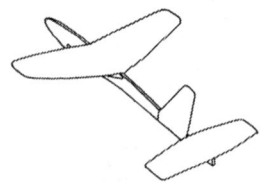

Chapter Thirty-Six

The safe deposit box vaulted in the basement of the Chase Manhattan bank was assigned jointly and separately and equally to Dr. Margaret Mead and Mrs. Mary Anderson both residing in the city of New York, New York. The chilly basement felt warmer than the cold New York day.

Rhoda Metraux walked into the guarded area as though she had been there many times before. She showed Amelia where she should sign her name as Mrs. Mary Anderson and reminded her to prove her identity with her passport. The bank clerk motioned Mary to follow her. Rhoda did not move.

"Mary," Rhoda began and repeated the name louder to make sure of Amelia's focus. "Mary, you need to go inside alone. Whatever has been stored in the box is between the two of you. Dr. Copeland and I shall remain here."

Amelia fought panic as Rhoda and Elijah walked the few steps to a bench and sat down. She even took a step forward to follow them but was stopped by Rhoda's steady gaze.

"You can do this, Mary."

So Amelia did. She followed the clerk through the wide steel frame of the vault and down rows of locked slots. When they finally stopped in front of, according to the clerk, the right row, the clerk reached high to insert a key into one of the two locks.

Amelia, as though she had been engaging in just such activities for the past forty years, handed the clerk the key she held in her hand.

The key had been wrapped in layers and layers of cloth almost a half century before and placed in a tin box and hidden on an island far enough away to forget if only Amelia could forget about it because forgetting was better and more bearable than living with the knowledge that she would never again feel the nourishing breeze of that island in her face.

The bank clerk turned both keys in their locks, opened the door, and motioned to Amelia to withdraw the actual box from the slot. Amelia reached up and withdrew the box. She followed the clerk into a small room and sat down in the indicated chair. As she put the box on the table in front of her, she heard the clerk close the door to leave her in the small room staring at the closed safe deposit box.

For several minutes Amelia did nothing except stare at the box. Finally, she opened it. On top of whatever was inside the box was a sealed envelope. Instead of an address, in handwriting hauntingly familiar to Amelia were the words *Open This Before Looking Further.*

Amelia opened the envelope and unfolded the single sheet of paper.

My dearest, darling Amelia,

Frankly, I always thought I would outlive you and spend my remaining days wondering and regretting. However, since you have opened this box and are reading this letter, my body clearly has relinquished its hold on life and my spirit is traveling, I know, with you.

Please, please know that I cherished every moment we spent together. I never laughed harder or loved more deeply with any other person. You have been my constant in a world which so often seemed to be swirling around me.

Throughout the years I made choices that, I know, wounded you.

I wish I could blame you for something but we both know such accusations would be absurd. You are the most perfect person I have ever met. You did nothing except love me, wait for me, and be your own unique and wonderful self.

Please don't be angry with me anymore. If I could do everything all over, somewhere and somehow I would find the courage to be with you.

If you are reading this letter, you came to me when I most needed you. The journey from Nani to Manhattan could not have been easy. If I didn't make it crystal clear to you how much your coming meant to me, please forgive me. Again and again and again I ask your forgiveness.

I assume that my last moments did not contain my clearest thoughts and because of that I can't imagine I said even half of all of the loving and grateful things on my mind.

I hope I died well.

With you by my side I know that at least I died well loved.

And now to practical matters.

Everything in this box belongs to you to do with as you please. You deserve so much more and, again, I so hope we were given the time and had the courage to go over all of that before my death.

In spite of how events unfolded, my life has been the richer because of your love. I would so like to know that I added positive elements to your life, too. Now our journey is changed but never ended.

My undying love,
Margaret

P.S. Dearest, some last advice from the grave. Tell no one about the contents of this box. Please tend to these words. This is not a time to follow those wonderful and unpredictable instincts of yours which have so endeared you to me all of these years. This is crucial. Our secret must remain ours. It is not for the world to know. Please. Tell no one.

Again, all my love.
MM

Amelia reread the letter five times before folding it and putting it back into the envelope. She then removed a small folded shopping bag from the safe deposit box and saw beneath it bound packets of currency. She looked around her to make sure she was still alone in the room and then began removing the stacks from the box.

Beneath the packets of money was another envelope bearing a hand written directive - To Dr. Margaret Mead and Miss Amelia Mary Earhart. In the upper left hand corner of the envelope was the Great Seal of the President of the United States. Amelia's hands trembled. She lowered her head until her forehead touched and steadied the envelope.

"Eleanor," she whispered, "what have you done?"

When her hands and her heart steadied, Amelia opened the envelope and withdrew a single sheet of parchment. It, too, bore the Great Seal of the President of the United States. Under the presidential seal, numbers and words did barrel rolls and loops and spins before Amelia's eyes until finally they flew steadily and directly into every fiber of her being. Among coordinates of longitude and latitude Amelia clearly understood that an island in the South Pacific decades before claimed through some forgotten and pointless transaction as American soil along with hundreds of other unnamed and essentially invisible rocks in the waters had been by order of the President of the United States of America deeded in perpetuity to Dr. Margaret Mead, Miss Amelia Mary Earhart (aka Mrs. Mary Anderson) and/or their designees. The document, dated June 1, 1935, was signed by Franklin Delano Roosevelt, President, United States of America.

When finally she remembered to breathe, Amelia could not. The small room spun around her. She grasped the table and then the chair desperately trying to steady herself and stop the room's spinning. At last the spinning slowed enough for her to gasp for and obtain breath. Her heartbeat returned to normal. The perspiration on the backs of her hands evaporated as she placed the packets of money in the bag. Finally she placed the letter in its envelope in the bag. And last, she placed the deed again in its envelope in the bag. She closed the now empty box and stepped out of the small room.

With efficiency and focus that took her completely by surprise and reminded her of the young woman she used to be, Amelia summoned the bank clerk and together they returned the box to its slot and turned their keys back into locked position and each reclaimed their original and proper key and then Amelia walked out of the vault area holding her woven bag to her chest with one hand and her shopping bag to her chest with her other hand.

At her approach, Rhoda and Elijah stood. Neither person reached for the shopping bag. They walked out of the basement and out of the bank onto the street in silence. When the cold bit their faces, Amelia didn't flinch and watched with detached curiosity as Rhoda pulled her scarf over her face.

"May I buy you a cup of tea?" Rhoda shouted above the noise of the wind and the traffic.

Amelia looked at Elijah and Elijah shrugged his shoulders and the three walked quickly into a coffee shop not noted for its ambience or its teas but which was warm and quiet. Sitting at a table near the window, the three drank their tea in silence. Rhoda did not ask about the contents of the box. Since they were far beyond small talk they had nothing to say. Each, however, seemed to acknowledge the need for such a gathering.

At last Rhoda spoke.

"I don't know why I'm sharing this with you. I hardly think Margaret would approve."

Neither Amelia nor Elijah replied.

"I left her."

Rhoda looked at Amelia but could read nothing from her blank face. Amelia felt secure in the pilot's seat. The skies were calm. The plane was steady.

"I knew she was desperately ill and needed me. Still, I moved out."

Amelia looked ahead into clear skies.

"She wouldn't stop talking about wanting to return to the South Pacific. She became obsessed with plans. Nothing I could say or do could distract her. She lost all interest in everything that was us. This went on for weeks. It was endless. She planned on being – actually being – in the South Pacific by the end of this year. Her pain and her health – nothing mattered to her. I knew that I also no longer mattered to her. So I moved out."

Tears rolled down Rhoda's face as she spoke.

"Then she asked me to come back. So I did. I felt you should know."

Amelia eased back on the throttle, pulled the stick toward her, and said simply, "Thank you, Rhoda."

As she spoke those words, Amelia made a perfect landing into her chair across the table from Dr. Rhoda Metraux. The two women smiled across an ocean neither cared to cross.

Finally Rhoda, after paying for their tea, stood. Amelia and Elijah also stood. Together they walked out of the coffee shop and back into December's greeting.

"I'd like to give you some money," Rhoda said. "Margaret would never forgive me if I at least didn't make sure you had food and shelter."

She produced a roll of bills from her pocket, which she extended to Amelia. Amelia smiled.

"You are a generous woman, Rhoda," she said. "However, I can't accept your gift. I have everything I need here with me."

Elijah beamed and placed his hand on Amelia's shoulder.

"Good bye, then," Rhoda finally said.

"Yes. Good bye," came the reply from both Amelia and Elijah.

With no more words exchanged, Rhoda stepped to the curb to hail a taxi as Amelia and Elijah walked south into the approaching storm. There seemed also no words for Amelia and Elijah as they made their way across the bridge and into Brooklyn. The shopping bag seemed to Amelia to grow heavier with each step she took and with each step she took the silent distance between her and Elijah grew also.

It was far too cold to eat in Prospect Park and so dinner was late and eaten in the greenhouse. Amelia had no appetite and Elijah and the musicians looked at her with concern as she picked at her food. Claiming exhaustion, she lay down in her usual place and, holding her two bags tightly to her chest, closed her eyes. But she did not sleep. She listened to Elijah and the musicians talk in voices hushed because they didn't want to awaken her.

They spoke of the weather and the cold. They spoke of music old and new, composed by Elijah and composed by others, performed by others and performed by them. They spoke of loves lost and loves sought. Their conversation was gentle and spoken by souls without malice.

Their dreams contained no greed. They dreamed of a permanent address and magazine subscriptions and bills to pay and hot showers and bed linen. They dreamed of summer gardens and they dreamed of snow shovels with which to clear the walkway of a home they knew they might never own. And, yes, they dreamed of concert tours and adoring fans and fame and gold records but most of all on that cold night they dreamed of clean sheets and patchwork quilts.

Amelia lay on her bed of redwood chips and her closed eyes only slowed but did not stop the tears from escaping through her lashes and onto her face. Soon the redwood felt damp beneath her.

Morning did not bring sunlight but more darkness and Amelia remembered yet another thing about New York which she loathed. Winter had officially arrived. There were no ticker tape parades in open convertibles to welcome it home but, nevertheless, it had returned. To Amelia her soul felt as dark and as cold and as bereft as did the day. She stood stiffly and looked down on the still sleeping musicians. The stump of Elijah's missing arm seemed ragged and sore and sad. She struggled to imagine this man shoveling snow on the walkway to his own house. She knew, though, that he would find a way to do that and more. She also knew that one day soon they would fail to wake with the dawn and when that day came their trespassing would be discovered and they would be arrested. She could not imagine these gentle souls surviving in prison any more than she could imagine herself enduring another New York winter.

So she took a deep breath and said aloud, "Rise and shine, my friends. Today holds miracles for us all."

As the band stirred into consciousness she emptied the contents of the shopping bag save the letter from Margaret and the deed to Nani onto the floor among them. While they stared through sleep filled eyes, Amelia said, "Let's go find home."

There was no grabbing and stuffing of bundles of money even though the musicians had to leave the greenhouse as quickly as possible. In something resembling an orderly fashion, Elijah returned the packets of bills to the shopping bag and helped the others gather their things to – as they did each morning – leave no trace of their nightly visits behind them. When the band left the greenhouse and the Botanic Garden the only person to look back was Amelia, but she was not saying goodbye to the Brooklyn Botanic Garden. She was simply remembering and reminding herself of another place.

The brownstone at the end of Pierrepont Street had been on the market for some time. Real estate transactions take time and escrows must be honored. However, under the circumstances of cash, the realtor they enlisted suspected things would move along quickly. Indeed they did. Escrow closed three weeks after Elijah and Amelia and the musicians made their offer. Amelia insisted that the home be placed in Elijah's name and Elijah insisted that it be placed in each of their names including that of Mary Anderson. Amelia stopped trying to convince him to do otherwise.

"You have a home now," Elijah would comment to Amelia.

To which Amelia would reply, "I've never been without a home. However, now you have a place to create beautiful music. I shall look forward to singing it and dancing to it some New Year's Eve."

"As long as I can have that dance," Elijah beamed.

Amelia only smiled. Together she and Elijah walked into the brownstone's backyard, opened a gate, and stepped onto the Brooklyn Promenade.

"It's good to be close to work," he said.

"Indeed," she replied.

Through the falling snow Amelia walked across the pavers. Elijah watched her from their home. She leaned on the railing and looked out at the Statue of Liberty who seemed cold and aloof and no longer inviting. That evening as they sat on the floor of their completely empty brownstone eating baked chicken from a neighborhood take out, Amelia looked directly into Elijah's eyes and when she did so he nodded his head. Then she spoke.

"As you doubtless know," she said, "I came to this city for a purpose. Years ago I made an agreement with a woman for whom I would have died. I have honored to the letter that agreement. I shall miss her every moment of every day of my life. I shall carry her spirit with me always."

Amelia paused to look at the other musicians – Nick and Lyle and Bud and Jack and Bob – and then she looked back at Elijah.

"You have made it possible for me to honor that agreement. For that I am grateful. You also reminded me that adventure can be found on the ground as well as in the sky."

Elijah and the musicians continued looking at her and not at each other. Because of this Amelia saw Elijah's eyes fill with tears which quickly, to her, became waves coming to Nani's beach at high tide. She could already see a hut on a mountain and in the hut a small airplane suspended from the ceiling by a string forever circling its world.

"I must return to my home. I have been in this place long enough. I shall carry each of you in my heart – and in my entire being."

With that she bent to kiss Elijah on the forehead. He stood and they held each other in an embrace of sorrow and of parting. The next day Elijah researched all the airlines flying from John F. Kennedy Airport to Sydney, Australia, and from Sydney, Australia, to Port Moresby, New Guinea. He purchased one-way tickets for Mrs. Mary Anderson on Pan American Airways because she said that even though their fares were slightly more expensive she had a fondness for the airline. From Port Moresby Elijah arranged passage on a chartered ship to take Amelia around the tip of New Guinea to a small town called Wau. He could make no further arrangements. He did not know her final destination and she did not tell him. Lyle placed two envelopes, one bearing the Great Seal of the President of the United States, and several bundles of currency into a cloth bag and sewed the bag into the bottom of the woven Dracaena bag, which had never left Amelia's side or breast. Elijah had put the rest of the money – which Amelia insisted he keep – in their savings account.

"You take the banjo," Jack said on the night before her departure.

"You are too kind," she replied and rubbed her hand over the shiny wooden neck of the banjo.

"However," she continued at last, "I have a banjo in my home – in my other home. One should always have a banjo in every home. What I would like to take back, however, is an extra set of banjo strings. At one time I preferred Martin strings. I have no idea if they are still available."

Amelia left – wearing her leather jacket and her flying cap – in a taxi at noon the next day. Standing on their freshly shoveled walkway, the musicians waved to her as the cab pulled away. Elijah blew her a kiss which she caught and held to her heart. Later when she would look into her bag, she would find five sets of Martin Strings for the tenor banjo and she would hold them to her lips and she would finally allow herself to weep for everything in her life that had been lost to her. All of this weeping she would do while sitting in her leather first class seat on the Pan American Airways DC-10 Jet.

"Elijah," she would have said to him had he been seated next to her, "you are too extravagant."

Then she would remember another first class seat on a flight from Portland to New York because Margaret was in too much pain to endure any other type of seating. She would remember the frail hand that held hers throughout the entire flight. Then she would hold her woven bag to her breast and force herself to not scream in agony. Later, sipping one of a series of Manhattan cocktails in a conscious, final farewell to the life she had years ago abandoned, Amelia would look out of her window at the Kansas prairie below and remember the smell of the summer wind as she flew over those same fields so many years before in another very different airplane in another very different life. Later she would again look out of her window at the Pacific Ocean seeming so deceptively close that she felt she could almost step out of the plane into its waters. Then she would remember the feel of those waters as she swam out of another very different airplane to claim a very different life for herself and, yes, for the woman who never became a full time resident of the life they had both planned so carefully.

After the down payment on the house in Brooklyn had been made, Amelia and Elijah had counted the remaining money and, not believing their first count, they had counted it again.

"All I need," she had said to Elijah, "is enough to take me home. And then enough to buy whatever Ariki requires. And maybe a little for some presents now and then."

"No round trip tickets for you?" Elijah had asked even though he had known the answer.

"A person can only travel in one direction at a time," Amelia had said as she pressed her lips to Elijah's forehead.

"I know your address," she added. "I can always send for you."

"And I'll come," he said and touched her nose with the tip of his finger.

"Then we have an arrangement."

"Yes. We have an arrangement."

The flight from Sydney to Port Moresby was not first class because the plane was not large enough for classes. Amelia did not care. She sat with straight back and unblinking eyes and dared the pilot to fall behind schedule. The pilot was apparently not a man who accepted a dare and the plane landed on time. Amelia Earhart had returned to the South Pacific. She took a cab from the airport to the harbor and without difficulty located the ship on which her passage around New Guinea's tip to Wau was reserved. Once the ship docked at Wau, she knew, the careful scheduling of Elijah would end. From there she would have to find her own way home.

"When I leave this island I shall do so without fanfare and flash bulbs. I shall leave quietly without subterfuge."

The passage around New Guinea's tip took longer than she expected. She paced the deck watching the year come to an end. Finally she walked down the gangplank and onto the dock of the small harbor in the small town of Wau on the other side of New Guinea's long finger-like tip. She turned to stare north at the waters of the South Pacific.

In Wau's docks Amelia walked from boat to boat attempting to seek passage to an island at least a two-day journey from where she stood. Her quest was complicated by the fact that she refused to state the name of the island to which she sought passage. Eventually she saw a man dressed in white standing in the bow of his boat looking down at the passersby and waving not to them but to her.

"Hello, there," he shouted. "You ready to go back?"

Amelia stared at the man in white for several seconds before stepping aboard the boat.

"Hori," she said. "Tiller of the soil."

"Yes. Star of the Sea. Your journey of honor is now complete?"

"Soon. Yes. Soon."

"Good."

"Do I owe you any money from our last sailing?" she asked.

"No. But I need to remind you that this is not a sailboat. This boat has an engine. We do not sail. Perhaps you don't remember."

"My mistake. Forgive me," she said and sat down on the same bench she had occupied so many months before when her world became large once again.

"Again you have no luggage?" Hori asked.

"Still only my bag," she replied and shifted the frayed woven dracaena fronds from her shoulder to her lap.

Hori again stood in front of her. A silence fell between them. Eventually he cleared his throat and spoke.

"There is an awkwardness here that must be remedied," he said in a formal tone.

Amelia looked up at his face. "I beg your pardon?" she said in English and, realizing that he had not understood, repeated her question in their common language.

"Forgive me for speaking these words but there is the issue of the fee for your passage."

Amelia's face again turned red. "Forgive me," she said. "Apparently I have become one of those people who travels much and learns nothing."

"I seriously doubt that to be the case," Hori replied.

Amelia withdrew one hundred dollars from her bag and Hori took the money from her.

When they left Wau they retraced their original course. Amelia tracked their progress by the night sky. She did not sleep but lay outside looking up and into the heavens. With each beat of her heart she felt closer to her return and closer to reclaiming a life that had turned out much different from the one she had planned so many years before.

When the boat docked at the end of the journey, Amelia stepped onto an island whose name she had either never known or had forgotten. She was at first shocked and then comforted when she realized that she didn't care.

"You have to know where you are before you can go someplace else," she turned back to Hori and said. "The only place I'm going is home."

"You are here," came a voice from behind her.

She turned away from Hori and his boat to look into the ancient, ageless eyes of Kahil who had brought her to this place in the makeshift boat she had helped build decades before from the scraps of an airplane once flown by engines never intended for water. Amelia walked down the pier and climbed aboard that very same boat powered by the only engine salvaged from that long ago flight.

"When did you arrive at this place," Amelia asked Kahil, happy to speak again the language of her island.

"Early in the month you occasionally call July or late in the month you occasionally call June. The time of your arrival to this place is the time of our arrival."

"Six months ago," Amelia said to herself in the language they did not understand.

As the engine that had once helped power a twin engine airplane roared into life, Amelia marveled at what a fine machinery a piece of saltwater-salvaged junk could become if novice mechanics spent six straight months doing nothing except fine-tuning it to perfection. She stared through the crystal clear waters to the boat's keel.

"NR16020," she said aloud as she read through memory's waters the tail number that once identified a very famous and for decades presumed missing Lockheed Electra.

Then Amelia Earhart laughed because she knew all things the heart desired were ultimately possible.

The boat quickly gained speed and within minutes was nothing more to that island and its people and Hori than a speck on an endless horizon. Soon it was not even that. The water was rougher and the wind stronger than all aboard the boat had anticipated and thus their journey home took longer. By the time the engine was cut to glide the boat to the rough wooden dock the sun was setting on the next to the last day of the month of December of the year 1978. The next day would be the eve of the new year. The islanders would celebrate and rejoice for many reasons this year more than ever.

When the boat had stopped and Afi as quickly as the fire of his name had jumped out to tie the mooring rope to a post, Amelia stood up and stepped from the boat onto the dock. As she stood so, too, did the old man once called Ariki but who, after cutting off his own leg, changed his name to Oroiti. Under his arm he held a makeshift crutch. Behind him stood Kaula.

Her woven bag still hanging from her shoulder, Amelia ran the length of the rough, planked dock onto Nani's moist, warm sands. She stopped inches from the face of Oroiti to see at their feet – half buried as though it had been on that shore since the island's birth – a chipped, broken piece of façade bearing the stamped imprint of a long ago defunct Flatbush Avenue factory. Looking from the façade into his eyes, Amelia took off her flying cap and fell into the old man's open arms. As they embraced they felt a gentleness leave the woven bag and encircle them and hold them until the sand felt solid and certain beneath their three legs.

Only then did the Mother Chief expand her embrace to hold the entire island to her breast. As Amelia and Oroiti turned toward the mountain and the hut, almost but not quite hidden by lush foliage, life sang and life rejoiced.

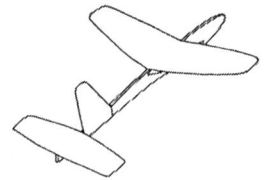

ABOUT THE AUTHOR

Mary Walker Baron is a clinical social worker. *Contrary Creek*, her first novel, which she wrote in partnership with her brother Tom Walker, continues to receive high praise. Although she has never lived on an island in the South Pacific, Mary has proven to herself on more than one occasion that any landing you can walk away from is – if not perfect – at least good enough.

Visit her at http://MaryWalkerBaron.com

Learn more about her novels at http://ButThisIsDifferent.com *and* http://contrarycreeknovel.com